The Day We Left

caroline bond

CORVUS

Published in paperback in Great Britain in 2023 by Corvus, an imprint of
Atlantic Books Ltd.

10 9 8 7 6 5 4 3 2 1

A CIP catalogue record for this book is available from the British Library.

Paperback ISBN: 978 1 83895 409 3
E-book ISBN: 978 1 83895 411 6

Printed and bound by CPI (UK) Ltd, Croydon CR0 4YY

Corvus
An imprint of Atlantic Books Ltd
Ormond House
26–27 Boswell Street
London
WC1N 3JZ

www.atlantic-books.co.uk

The Day We Left

Caroline Bond was born in Scarborough and studied English Literature at Oxford University. She has worked as a cleaner, a receptionist, a kitchen designer, a market researcher, a company director and a victim support volunteer. She has an MA in Creative Writing. Caroline lives in Leeds with her husband and one of her three children... the other two having grown up and escaped.

*This book is dedicated to the many decent men in my life;
Chris, Alex, Joe, Joseph, David, Isaac and my
lovely, much missed dad, Pete Bond.*

PART ONE

Chapter 1

Lizzie started awake.

The clock on her bedside table insisted it was 7.26 a.m. She stretched out her hand. The duvet on Ian's side of the bed was thrown back, the sheet cold. Could she have slept through the alarm? Or had it not gone off? Why hadn't he woken her?

Click. 7.27 a.m.

She scrambled out of bed and shrugged on her dressing gown. She had time and ground to make up.

She made it down to the kitchen by 7.28 a.m.

At 7.32 a.m. she found herself on her hands and knees on the kitchen floor.

By 7.38 a.m. Ian's packed lunch was made and neatly wrapped in foil.

He kissed her goodbye at the door at 7.42 a.m.

Between 7.45 a.m. and 8.02 a.m. she tidied the kitchen, washed her face, brushed her teeth and got dressed.

She rang in sick at 8.03 a.m. Sean, her department head, made sympathetic noises, but she could tell he wasn't pleased. She'd already taken quite a lot of time off to attend her prenatal appointments.

For the next eighty-four minutes she sat on the edge of the bed and watched the minutes click by on the traitorous alarm clock.

She left the house at 9.27 a.m.

That was the seemingly mundane timeline of the cold, bright May morning that changed Lizzie and Ian's lives, irrevocably.

Chapter 2

LIZZIE WENT the back route to her friend Heather's house. When she pushed against the garden gate it didn't open. It had been a wet spring and the wood was swollen and uncooperative. For a moment she stood in the chilly sunshine, defeated, then she rallied and used her by-now considerable body weight to get it to budge. It was an ungainly entry, but thankfully, at 9.30 a.m. on a midweek morning, there was no one around to witness it.

Heather's back garden was well tended – the raised beds were full of heavy-headed tulips and lots of frothy white flowers that Lizzie didn't know the name of. The flagged path was puddled with the previous night's rain. It soaked into her slippers, staining the edges black. She took the three steps up to the back door carefully, her fear of falling acute. She knocked and waited, but not for long. She was relieved; she'd left the house without a coat and it was cold. The door opened. But it wasn't Heather; it was Mick, her husband. That threw her. She stuttered out a 'Hi'.

'Hello, love. Are you looking for Heather?'

'Yes.'

'She's off visiting her sister in Gateshead.'

'Oh.' Lizzie's mind went blank. No other options presented themselves. There was a pause. She didn't move; she couldn't face going home.

Mick seemed equally at a loss. After a couple of seconds he said, 'You're welcome to come in, if you want to. I was about to stop for a brew.' He opened the door wider. Lizzie stepped into the kitchen, grateful his politeness had outweighed his shyness.

Heather was the one who did the talking in their marriage. Mick was friendly enough, he smiled and waved when he saw Lizzie across the street, and he would always offer to carry her bags if he saw her walking home from the shops, but that was the extent of their interaction. She got the impression he was a man's man. This reputation was reinforced by the pair of pliers and the dismantled light fitting that currently lay on the worktop.

He saw her looking. 'The strip light under the cupboard has been flickering. It's been driving Heather mad. Steam from the kettle getting into it, most like.' He stopped talking, aware that she had little interest. 'Do you want a tea? A coffee?'

'Tea, please.'

'Go through.'

She left him to it.

The lounge was very familiar to Lizzie. She and Heather had spent a lot of time in it over the past three years, even more so recently. Despite the age gap, they got on. They knew each other well enough to be comfortable in each other's company, but not so well that there was any great pressure to share anything really personal. They chatted rather than talked, normally about the trials and tribulations of work – Heather was a doctor's receptionist and Lizzie a teaching assistant in a primary school – and about the best dramas on TV. In recent months Heather had volunteered some pregnancy and parenting advice, although never too much, she was not the sort to impose her opinions. Mundane as their interactions were, Lizzie was grateful for them. She knew she was always welcome in Heather's home.

She lowered herself onto the sofa and listened to Mick pottering about in the kitchen, took a moment to settle.

Heather and Mick's house was a mirror image of Lizzie and Ian's in terms of size and layout, but it was very different in feel and decoration. It bore the patina of the many years they'd lived there. Heather and Mick were the street's second longest-serving residents; only Margaret, who lived at number eight, pre-dated them. The room Lizzie was currently sitting in was busy with stuff. There was an array of framed family photographs on the windowsill – they had three children, all in their twenties – a TV cabinet stuffed full of DVDs and a number of paperbacks scattered around the room. Heather was an avid reader, novels mainly, all different types, although she had a penchant for historical fiction and doomed young queens. Lizzie had quite a few of

Heather's 'recommended reads' at home. She'd started a number of them, but had got no further than the first few chapters; her concentration wasn't what it used to be. Heather never quizzed Lizzie about her 'literary loans', she simply kept offering more, as if the next paperback might hold the key.

'Sugar?' Mick shouted.

She didn't usually take it. 'Yes. Please. One.' She still felt queasy.

'Right you are.'

Was Mick putting off coming through to sit with her? Perhaps. She had no idea what they were going to talk about. The ache in her back deepened and the pain in her knees and hands throbbed. She tilted her head back and closed her eyes, grateful for the peace. The sound of a mug being put on the table brought her back into the room. Mick took the chair by the window. He kept hold of his own drink. He had big hands, short, clean nails, a simple wedding band. Workman's hands. 'So, how are you doing, love?'

She roused herself. 'Me? I'm okay. Just a bit tired.'

'Understandable.' He took a mouthful of his tea. 'And how's Ian?'

'He's fine.' Ian and Mick sometimes spoke, about what she didn't know. A shared interest in electronics? Sport? Ian never said. 'His firm has picked up a new contract refitting a lot of council offices – DHSS, I think – so he's working all over the place at the moment, but at least it's guaranteed work.'

Mick nodded. 'I did a few years on the rigs when me and Heather were first married. It paid for the deposit on this place, but I knocked it on the head when she fell pregnant with Claire.'

It was Lizzie's turn to nod, Mick's to take another gulp of tea.

'Expensive things, kids. In more ways than one.' There couldn't be much left in his mug. 'But worth it.' He had a nice smile. She should let him get on; this was uncomfortable for both of them.

It happened as she shifted position and attempted to stand up. Instinctively she sat back down. Mick continued to smile at her. She felt shivery. The pain in her lower back tightened and threaded deeper inside her.

'Are you sure you're okay, love? You've gone very pale.'

How to tell him? 'I'm so sorry, Mick, but I think I might have wet myself.' She looked down at the circle of darkness that was spreading around her.

Mick's expression shifted from smiling discomfort to smiling concern. 'Oh. Right.' He put down his mug. 'Well, that's not a problem.' He stood up, then sat down again, pushed his mug further away in preparation for action.

'That or my waters have broken.' Surely she should know the difference? Fear overtook the shame. 'Mick, I'm not due for another nine weeks.'

'Okay.' He paused. 'Well, it's probably best we get you to the hospital. Get things checked out. Just to be on the safe side.'

She knew he was right, but she couldn't make herself stand up. It was as if her belly was full of bones. Her stomach muscles, which she'd thought had stretched to the point of no return, were rigid. 'Mick, I think something's wrong.'

He came over and sat beside her. 'I'm sure it'll be fine. Heather's been saying how you've being doing all the right things... been for all your check-ups and whatnot. Eaten your greens.' It was a weak attempt at levity. He switched tack. 'From what little I can remember, you can have these false alarms. Heather went in at least twice with our Steve before the real event. Braxton Hicks, they're called.' He seemed pleased to have been able to recall the medical term.

Lizzie wanted to believe him, but the cushion beneath her was soaking and her belly was rock-hard. That wasn't normal, not at this stage of a pregnancy. Her body was rebelling.

Mick touched her hand. 'What we're going to do' – she loved him for taking charge – 'is you're going stay put and I'm going to get my car keys. I'll open up the car and get us ready to roll. Have you packed a bag?' He tapped the top of her hand lightly, summoning her attention. 'For the hospital? I can go and fetch it from your house, if you want me to.' He gestured at the keys in her hand.

She passed them to him. He was talking to her as if she was a child. In her current state of panic she didn't mind. But as he stood up, a glimmer of common sense reasserted itself. There was no point him trailing over to her house – she hadn't packed a bag. 'No.'

She wasn't ready for this. The cot was still in its box in the nursery. True, she had bought some baby clothes and there was a steriliser on the side in the kitchen, but there were no bottles as yet. And she only had one pack of muslins. Heather had bought them for her, told her you needed loads in the first few months, for mopping up. She'd been planning on buying more, she really had, but she hadn't got round to it. She'd been too busy with work and the house and Ian. The panic gathered momentum. If she couldn't even manage the basics, what chance had she of being a good mother?

Mick smiled. 'Hey. It's all right. Ian can always bring your bits to the hospital later, if you need to stay in. You just sit tight. Try and stay calm. I'll be back in a minute. Two, tops.'

She tracked his movements: to the kitchen to collect his car keys, into the hall, out of the front door. She heard the car beep, a door opening, the engine firing up, his footsteps again. There was a brief pause then he was back in the room – as good as his word.

'Do you need a hand?' Without waiting for a reply, he offered her his.

She didn't want to move from the damp safety of her perch. 'I'm sorry... about your sofa.'

'Lizzie, look at me.' She did. It helped. 'It's going to be okay. Come on. Up you get.'

She took his hands. The skin on his palms was rough

and calloused, but his hold was steady. Everything about him was reassuring.

He tugged her to her feet. 'That's it. Off we go.'

She made the mistake of glancing down.

There was blood on the cushion. A large patch of it. Black against the green. Neither of them commented on it.

He propelled her out of the house.

As Lizzie lowered herself awkwardly into the car, he shielded her head with his hand like she'd seen police officers do with criminals on TV. He pulled the seatbelt around her belly with care and respect. One click and she was in. He climbed in beside her. 'Comfortable?' She nodded. A lie. 'What about Ian?' he asked. She didn't know what to say, what was for the best, so she said nothing. Mick persisted. 'Do you want me to call him?'

'Not yet.' Contacting Ian was tantamount to admitting the worst was happening. 'I don't want to worry him.'

'If you're sure. Okay. Well, let's get you to the hospital.'

He released the handbrake gently and they set off.

Chapter 3

SHE WOULD NEVER forget that drive.

Her memory of the distress and panic faded to an indistinct, ugly smear with time, but not her recall of Mick's valiant and sustained efforts to distract her. Because the man who never said more than was strictly necessary never stopped talking the whole way to the hospital.

He talked as they made their way along the familiar roads and sat at the seemingly innumerable red lights and at the traffic-clogged junctions. He talked as they pulled into the hospital grounds and crossed the car park, at a snail's pace. He talked as they shuffled through the revolving entrance doors and when they stepped out of the lift into the unnervingly quiet corridor.

And what he talked about – as Lizzie held her breath and her distended belly – was the joy of being a parent.

He told her how overwhelming he had found holding his daughters, then his son, for the first time, and what respect he had for the strength of women, having seen three births at close quarters. He spoke about how having children had cemented his and Heather's marriage, turning it into something unbreakable. And, most of all, he talked about the happiness his children had brought him. How hearing your child laugh was one of the best sounds in the world. How you loved them instinctively, but how you had to learn to trust them and let them be. And he described how life became far more complicated, but at the same time far simpler, once you had a child, because once you became a parent you knew, without a shadow of a doubt, what really mattered.

And he didn't stop talking until he handed her over into the care of the nurses on the maternity ward.

By that point, panicking and in pain as she was, Lizzie knew why Heather loved Mick and what a good husband was.

Chapter 4

WAKING FROM THE ANAESTHESIA was a messy business.

Lizzie was violently sick, twice. She rolled around inside her sticky sheets and made things worse. Hands gripped her and someone tried to speak to her, and although she could hear their voice, she couldn't make out what they were saying. Nothing made sense. Confused and disorientated, she closed her eyes, wanting nothing more than to go back to sleep, but they insisted on cleaning her up. She didn't cooperate. That didn't stop them. They were rough with her, yanking and pulling. But awful as it was, it was worth it, because when they'd finished she was dry and not cold anymore. Indeed, as the heat trapped between the sheets rose, so did her consciousness.

She was in hospital.

Mick had brought her in.

There had been an ugly black stain on Heather's nice green sofa.

Blood.

And pain.

Now there was nothing, only a strange numbness.

She opened her eyes, blinked at the ferocity of the overhead light, forced herself to keep her eyelids raised. She lay still, signalling that she was compliant, sane, back to normal. This was not about her anymore. A face appeared above her: a nurse in pink scrubs. The nurse flashed a smile. That was surely a good sign. 'Well, hello. Back in the land of the living at last, I see. Nice to meet you, Elizabeth. Is that what people call you? Or do you prefer Beth?'

'Lizzie.' It came out as a bit of a croak.

'Well, Lizzie. We've had some fun and games with you, but nothing we haven't seen before. How are you feeling now?' The nurse didn't wait for an answer. 'Don't worry about the lack of feeling, that'll come back soon enough. Do you want me to prop you up a little bit?'

'Yes, please.'

The nurse set about raising the bed and repositioning Lizzie on the incline. 'There, that's better; you can see what you're doing now.'

It was true, Lizzie could, or at least she could see where she was. She was in a curtained-off area. She sensed there were people in the other bays, though she couldn't see them.

'You're in Recovery. As soon as we're happy with your stats, we'll get you transferred onto the postnatal ward.'

Postnatal. She was no longer pregnant. She had given birth. She had no recollection of it. 'And my babies?'

'They're up in the NICU. Being well looked after.'

'Both of them?'

The nurse stopped fussing with the equipment. 'Yes, both of them. Low birth weight, but holding their own.' She held up her hand. 'Before you ask, I'm afraid I don't know anymore than that, but rest assured they're in the best possible place. Someone will, no doubt, come and tell you all what's been happening, soon, but for now you're the priority.' Lizzie closed her eyes. 'Hey, now. No drifting off, or I'll have to keep you here even longer. And you don't want that, do you?'

'No.'

'Right,' the nurse became brisk again, 'let's have another look at your oxygen levels, now you're nice and calm.'

Lizzie let the nurse work, but as she lay passive and immobile on the bed she felt a pressure building inside her. She wanted someone – and the only person she had nearby for the time being was this woman – to acknowledge that she'd given birth. That she was a mother.

'They're boys, my babies. Twin boys.'

The nurse didn't look up. 'That's nice.'

Chapter 5

LIZZIE HAD TO WAIT another two hours before anyone came to speak to her, by which time the whole thing had taken on an unreal, nightmarish edge.

All the other women on the ward had cribs beside their beds and bundles of tightly wrapped babies. She saw them as they wheeled her in, before they briskly drew the curtains around her bed. They kept the curtains drawn after they'd settled her and left her *to rest* – as if that were possible. A woman without a child was, understandably, something to be kept hidden on a postnatal ward.

The other thing that marked Lizzie out was her lack of a partner. There was still no sign of Ian. Lizzie didn't understand it. Leicester was a long drive, but she'd been in the hospital since late morning and it was gone 5 p.m. now. When she asked, yet again, if anyone knew where he was, one of the nurses took pity on her and lent her a phone.

Her call went to voicemail. The message she left sounded desperate because she was.

The doctor, when she eventually came, was sympathetic, but it was precisely her kindness that threatened to undo Lizzie's tenuous leash on her emotions. After quickly checking Lizzie over and making reassuring comments, the doctor took a seat. She explained that Lizzie's placenta had ruptured and it was this that had caused the bleeding. 'Unfortunately it was a full separation, which meant there was nothing we could do to stop it. Your babies' oxygen supply was failing and, as a consequence, they were in danger. Hence the need to perform an emergency Caesarean. Given their gestational period, your babies are, obviously, very small. The main concern is their breathing. Lung function is always a problem with prem babies and, of course, there's their vulnerability to infection. We'll also have to monitor all other areas of their development, including their cognitive function.'

'What do they weigh?' Lizzie was afraid to hear the answer.

The doctor checked her notes. 'Three pounds fourteen ounces and two pounds seven ounces.'

Lizzie couldn't image what a baby weighing less than three pounds would look like. Her brain spun with fear at the disparity in their size, and the impact it might have on their chances of survival.

The doctor smiled, an attempt at reassurance after so much bad news. 'We are recognised as a centre of excellence for neonatal care.'

That might help, but her fear wouldn't. Lizzie knew she had to get it under control. 'When can I see them?'

'Whenever you feel up to it.'

'Now?'

'Of course. I'll speak to one of the nurses and we'll get someone to take you up to the NICU. I have to warn you, it can be a little overwhelming at first – lots of complicated-looking machines – but the staff will explain everything to you. Ask anything, as many times as you want. The days of keeping parents at arm's length are, thankfully, over. You and your husband will have an integral role to play in the care of the twins. Regular early parental contact helps hugely with outcomes.' She stood. 'I'll swing by to see you again tomorrow, examine your wound again, check you're doing okay.'

Her beep went off, she glanced at it, then slipped it back in her pocket.

'Your sons will have their own specialist paediatric team assigned to them now, but I'll keep an eye on them as well. Oh, and a word of advice: you must pace yourself. A C-section isn't a small operation. We gave you a blood transfusion and so, fingers crossed, that should reduce your risk of becoming anaemic, but you've been through the mill and caring for prem babies is a long haul. You'll be no use to them if you're not feeling strong yourself.'

Lizzie nodded, although she wasn't really agreeing. The doctor was wrong. Now was precisely the time to start putting her twins first, but she could only do that if she was with them. 'You'll ask – about me going to see them.'

'Yes. I promise.' The doctor disappeared through the gap in the curtains, her mind on the next patient.

Chapter 6

THE NEONATAL INTENSIVE CARE UNIT was the place no parent wanted to be, but her boys were here, and therefore so was Lizzie.

As the ward sister helped her on with a disposable apron and gloves, she explained the hygiene protocols. Lizzie tried to concentrate on what the nurse was saying, but it was difficult. Certain words ballooned and obliterated everything else: *susceptible*, *compromised*, *vulnerable*; above all... *vulnerable*. Then, without any warning, they were on the move into a big white room. It was surprisingly busy, filled with medical staff, silent parents and lots of blinking, bleeping technology.

For a second or two Lizzie felt a wave of pure, unadulterated panic wash through her. The urge to flee was overwhelming; she simply wasn't strong enough to cope with this. But running away wasn't an option – her boys needed her. She made herself focus on the nurse's voice. This was going to be a steep learning curve, and Lizzie simply had to cling on as best she could. And after a few seconds and some deep breaths, it became apparent that the seeming chaos did have a certain logic. The nurses and the machines were clustered into hubs, and at the heart of each hub there was an incubator, inside which lay a tiny, skeleton-like creature.

The harsh reality was that any of these nearly-children could be Lizzie's sons.

She scanned the room and saw Ian – her brain was picking up speed, returning to a more normal functioning pace – which meant that the incubator he was leaning over, his blue-gloved hand through the hatch, must contain one of her babies. It was time to face reality, head-on.

At her approach, Ian looked up.

So much had happened since they had last been together.

They had become a family. Albeit a very fragile one.

His face looked different. It seemed softer, less defined somehow. Shock could do that to a person, she supposed, shake the certainty out of them. This man, unlike her normally self-assured partner, looked frightened – which made absolute sense, in the circumstances.

'Oh, Lizzie. Thank God. At last.' Even his voice had changed. He carefully withdrew his hand from the incubator and studied her, searching for... what? Reassurance? Understanding? Forgiveness?

The nurse pushed Lizzie into the gap between the incubators, reached down and flipped the brakes on her wheelchair. 'I'll leave you to meet your sons, but I promise I'll be back soon, then we can have a proper talk about where we're at.' She walked away to assist with another tiny, struggling baby.

Ian reached out for Lizzie. The wheelchair was a major hindrance, but, undeterred, he crouched at her feet and wrapped his arms around her. He held her tight, his forehead pressed against hers. His voice was gentle, fractured. 'I'm so sorry I wasn't there. I'll never forgive myself.'

He clung onto her and she felt his desperation, understood it, but in that moment she had nothing to give. She waited for him to release her. She needed to see her boys. Still he held onto her, his face filling her vision, his voice pleading.

'When Heather rang and told me Mick had taken you to the hospital, well, I was beside myself. Jesus, it was awful imagining what you were going through... on your own. I drove like a mad man, but I was too late, they'd already put you to sleep by the time I got here.' He swallowed, the emotion obviously still bitter in his throat. 'Everyone was rushing about. You could tell they were worried. They sat me up at the top, out of the way. It was so frightening seeing you out cold like that. Really frightening. It all happened so quickly. When they lifted them out, first one, then the other, I could hardly bear to look. But, Lizzie,' his eyes filled, 'it was amazing. One minute they were inside you, and the next they were out.'

She was thrown. 'So you were there for the birth?'

'Yes. Just.'

'Oh.' Drained and distraught as she was, she felt a flash of jealousy. Ian had seen their babies born. He'd been at their side ever since, while she'd been alone, frightened and in pain. He'd chosen them over her. That was a shock. His devotion to her was the one aspect of their relationship she'd always been certain of. She dug deep into her reserves of selflessness. Perhaps it was a good sign. It was the right choice. Good parents put the needs of their children above everything – and everyone – else.

'Ian, please, let me see them.'

'Oh Christ, sorry, yes.' Finally he let her go. He stood up and moved out of the way.

She released the brakes and edged the wheelchair slowly forward, terrified of bumping any of the equipment. When she was level with the incubators she finally looked at her sons.

Their little bodies were starkly different.

As she'd feared, twin two – as he'd been labelled at every appointment over the preceding six months – was unbelievably tiny, a scrap of humanity. His frail body was barely visible beneath all the tubes, splints and bandages. He looked as if he was being held together by the brown tape that encased him. It surprised Lizzie to see his little legs waving in the air. Such a clear sign of life seemed incongruous, in the face of so much evidence to the contrary. She glanced in the other cot. Even to her untrained eyes, it was obvious that twin one was stronger. He was noticeably bigger, more fully formed.

He was also on a ventilator, but inside his incubator there seemed to be more baby and less machinery.

'They're so small.' Lizzie spoke in a whisper, foolishly fearful of disturbing them.

'I know,' Ian touched her shoulder, trying to soften the blow, 'but there's a little girl over there who was only two pounds four ounces when she was born, and she's doing okay.'

This was what they must do now: hang onto such slender shreds of hope. Lizzie put her hand through the aperture in the side of the incubator and nervously touched her first-born child's blue-veined belly with her fingertips, saying the gentlest 'hello'. She repeated the greeting with the second-born child. Finally she had touched her sons. Surely that made them hers.

After a little while Helen, the nurse who'd introduced her to the ward, came back and for Lizzie's benefit – Ian already knew all this stuff – explained the various machines that were keeping the boys breathing and hydrated and fed. She deftly but subtly acknowledged that twin two was the greatest cause for concern and, although she was calm and reassuring, she made no promises. She stressed that, with prem babies, every hour they got through was a milestone. 'It's the slow accumulation of hours that turn into days, and of days that turn into weeks, that gives them the time they need to catch up.' The gentle wisdom of her words would have been beautiful if it hadn't been so terrifying. Explanation over, Helen set to work – cleaning and adjusting the boys' breathing tubes. Lizzie had to look away. Listening to the procedure was tough, lessened only by the light patter of conversation Helen kept up as she worked.

'Right, that's you all done. Time to get your brother sorted now.'

Lizzie heard the crash of a bin lid, the snap of new gloves, the crackle of Helen's plastic apron, then the awful sound of the suction tube again. She didn't breathe out until Helen announced that *little man two was all sorted as well.*

With Helen gone, Lizzie and Ian took up their positions in the space between the incubators, facing each other. There was so much to talk about, but they said very little. It was Ian who eventually broke the trance. 'We can't keep calling them "little man one and two".'

He was right, they needed to have their own identities. And naming them might help to anchor them. Or so Lizzie hoped. It had to be a good first step. 'No, we can't.'

Ian peered down at their sons, seeking inspiration. 'Well, we had narrowed it down, hadn't we?' She nodded. 'I reckon this one is Oliver,' he indicated the stronger baby, 'and this one's Joseph?'

They were the names Lizzie had chosen when she'd imagined holding her healthy baby boys in her arms, delivered by a planned, safe, routine C-section at thirty-eight weeks. Did Oliver and Joseph suit these desperate, struggling bundles of thin skin, delicate bone and laboured breath? She didn't know, but she nodded her assent and for the first time since they'd parted that morning, a lifetime ago, Ian smiled – his full-throttle, heart-lifting, joy-filled, oh-so-familiar smile.

'Well, I think they're fine names.' He crouched down beside twin one's cot and, in a voice that sounded much more like his old self, spoke to his son. 'Hello, Oliver. It's good to finally meet you. We know you're a bit busy getting better at the minute, that's fine, but we want you to know that we're here for you, your mum and me, and we can't wait to give you a proper cuddle.' He kissed his gloved fingertips and pressed them against the Perspex side of the incubator. Having welcomed his first-born to the world, Ian swivelled around so that he was level with twin two and repeated the process.

In the face of his simple happiness, Lizzie began to cry.

Chapter 7

IT WAS AMAZING how quickly they adapted to the new routine.

Lizzie spent nearly every waking hour with the twins, watching and waiting and, for the first time in her adult life, silently praying. With the help of the nurses and Trish – the no-nonsense, had four kids and a *'glad to see the back of him' bastard-of-a-husband* ward cleaner – she started to gain some confidence in caring for her sons. Being able to change their tiny nappies and wash their bird-like limbs helped her to slowly feel like a real mother. And although neither of the boys could feed normally yet, she kept expressing milk – *for later*. All of it was difficult, all of it was stressful and frightening, but she persevered as she'd never done before. She had to, because the doctor's words on the day they were born had lodged in her soul. This was down to her. She had to do her best, if they were going to survive.

Ian came in every evening after work, then they sat together with their boys. They had agreed, after the first fraught forty-eight hours, that he would keep working, while he could. They needed the money and, Lizzie reasoned, if he put in the hours now, it would mean he would be able to take more time off when she and the twins finally came home. With reluctance, he'd agreed. They were a tag team now. This was a shared vigil. But they assumed different roles.

Ian was the positive one, relentless in his belief that it was all going to be okay. He talked to all the nurses and doctors and to the myriad of specialists who visited the ward, asking endless questions – within days he was au fait with the technology and most of the medical terminology. He went into overdrive socially as well. He got to know the other parents quickly and easily. Lizzie watched him sharing this most difficult and frightening of times with them as if it was all perfectly normal and natural. Even in this context, his charm worked to his advantage.

Then there was his role as chronicler of what they were going through. His need to record every milestone was compulsive. He took photos of everything: their translucent feet, their tape-smothered faces, their distended bellies, their tiny, claw-like hands, the nurses at work, the machines with their incessant, essential flashing displays. Day and night, minute by minute, it all had to be captured. Or at least that's how it felt to Lizzie. No moment was too personal or too stressful.

Lizzie knew why he was doing it. It was his way of saying, *These are my sons, I am their father, I was there from the beginning, I was there for them every step on the road to recovery* – even when he wasn't. She watched him, marvelling at his energy and intimidated by his optimism about their future.

In comparison, she felt weak and uncertain.

But then, as everyone kept reminding her, she was still recovering from the trauma of the birth.

Ian was very sensitive to how *fragile* she was. Never before had he been so solicitous, so mindful of how she was feeling, physically and mentally. There seemed no limit, despite his own tiredness, to his capacity to care. When he arrived on the ward every evening he always urged Lizzie to go and get some rest while she could, repeating the advice of the doctors – that she must take care of herself. She always refused. She couldn't bear the thought of them being together without her. She only left the ward when he did, heading back to her own bed along the dark, deserted hospital corridors. And even then she often sneaked back in the early hours of the morning. She couldn't sleep, not without the twins near her. She had failed to protect them in the womb; she needed to do better now.

The nurses chided her, but gently, insisting that she came away from their bedside every now and again to drink the tea and eat the toast made for her. They had obviously seen the strength of maternal love before and knew not to underestimate it, even in Lizzie.

The good news, during the first week, was that neither of the twins picked up any infections. Oliver was, they repeatedly reassured her, doing well, his lungs coping better with each day that passed, his weight slowly but steadily increasing. His development was on-track. By contrast, Joseph was still a major cause for concern; his blood pressure and oxygen levels kept dipping dramatically and, to Lizzie at least, inexplicably. Each time the team had to intervene to get him back on an even keel, she felt the hole that had been ripped open in her soul by his birth gape even wider. Watching them work on him, all those hands on his small body, was agony – each time he pulled through was an exhausting relief.

Through it all, Helen was their rock. She was calm, supportive, experienced, professional and, above all, kind. She was still capable of imagining what it was like for them, as novice parents. She kept repeating that all the boys needed was time, that Lizzie and Ian must be patient, especially with Joseph, who was *a little superstar* for *bouncing back* after each *sticky patch.*

The best of times was when they allowed Lizzie to hold her boys. With all the lines and the tubes, it took two nurses to arrange, but when the unit was calm and they could spare the time, they helped Lizzie get the twins out of their incubators, taking it in strict rotation. It was in those rare moments, with either Oliver or Joseph resting lightly – oh so lightly – against her breast, tucked safe inside her top, that she felt anything close to happiness. Holding them near helped her believe that they might, if they were really lucky, all get out of this alive.

Whether she deserved such luck she wasn't sure.

The nurses kept reassuring her. They said that guilt was common among mothers of prem babies, but misplaced – a waste of energy and emotion. 'Look around,' they said, 'pregnancies don't always go to plan. There's nothing you could have done differently. It's just the way it is.'

Lizzie listened to their reassurances, but she couldn't bring herself to accept them.

Chapter 8

THOSE EARLY, EXHAUSTING, blurry days spent shuttling between her largely unslept-in bed on the postnatal ward and the NICU were lonely for Lizzie.

Only immediate family were allowed on the unit in order to limit, as much as possible, the risk of infection, and no one came into the hospital to visit her. Although that was at her own request. Lizzie reasoned that it was pointless. She spent all her waking hours with the boys – there wasn't the time for visitors. Added to which, she simply didn't have enough energy to deal with other people's distress while there was so much going on.

Her friends and work colleagues said they understood and promised to visit her *as soon as things settled down*. Instead they texted – a lot. She appreciated their support, but it was an added pressure. It required her to put on a brave front in her replies, when in reality she was struggling to accommodate any emotion other than terror. After a while she stopped responding to their many messages and barely looked at her phone. It was rude, but it helped. The other benefit of unhooking from the outside world was that it reduced her exposure to her mother.

Her mum had, understandably, been deeply upset when Lizzie had called to break the news of the boys' premature arrival and to request that she put on hold her plans to travel down from Greenock – at least for a little while. It was the first time in years that she'd heard her mother get upset. Lizzie had nearly weakened and let her come, but then Carol had started talking about how God's plan wasn't always clear, and Lizzie had decided that, if prayer worked, it could operate just as well from a distance.

And perhaps He did work in mysterious ways, even for non-believers, because both of the twins made it safely to the end of the second week. They were still seven weeks shy of full term, but they were both holding their own. Indeed, the prognosis for Oliver was now looking positive; as for Joseph, well, as Helen kept reassuring them, Joseph was a fighter.

With both of the boys making progress, albeit at very different rates, Lizzie felt she could finally breathe out, a little, and with more oxygen and space in her brain, she started thinking about the realities of life outside the hospital.

She knew that if she was going to cope, she was going to have to ask for help, so she asked the person she trusted most.

Chapter 9

THEY MET IN THE CAFÉ on the ground floor of the hospital, amidst the smells of milky coffee and grilled cheese – ordinary life in full swing on a sunny Saturday morning. It was a shock to Lizzie. She felt like a prisoner emerging after a long sentence, blinking at the volume and the intensity of it all. Could it really only be little more than a fortnight since she'd sat on Heather's sofa trying to ignore the searing pain in her back, unaware that the twins were already in serious trouble?

'You're a sight for sore eyes.' Heather kissed her cheek. She smelt of fresh air. Lizzie had forgotten how good that smelt. The kiss was a small, but welcome benediction. 'This must all be so stressful for you?'

Lizzie shook her head. 'Don't go being all kind and sympathetic.'

Heather slipped off her jacket and sat down. 'I'm so sorry I wasn't there when it all kicked off.'

'Don't be silly. Mick looked after me. Royally.'

'So I gather.' Heather smiled, pride mixed with some amusement. 'Bless him, you gave him quite a fright. It wasn't quite what he'd had planned for his day off.'

'No. I know. Did he ever get your kitchen light working?'

'Yes. Though he took his sweet time about it.'

Lizzie tried to sustain the banter. 'I'm sorry for disrupting his day... and for the mess. Has your sofa recovered?'

Heather laughed. 'Don't worry about that. It's had worse things spilled on it over the years.'

It was the first time since the birth that Lizzie had been able to find anything remotely funny in what had happened. The memory of the mundane reality of fixed kitchen lights and comfy sofas and Mick and Heather's cluttered but cosy house was very welcome. It was a glimpse of what was normal, and possible.

Heather went to get them a drink. When she returned her tone became more serious. 'It's all quite brutal, isn't it? This whole... giving-birth process.' Lizzie nodded. 'How are you feeling, in yourself?'

'I'm doing fine. They've got the anaemia under control and I'm much more mobile now, which helps.'

'How long will you be staying in?' Heather must have noticed something shift in Lizzie's demeanour, because she hurried on, 'I just wondered how it works, with the twins needing to stay here and you being well enough to be discharged.'

'Nothing's decided yet.' But the clock was ticking. Lizzie didn't want to think about having to go home – leaving the boys behind. It didn't seem feasible. But that was precisely what she was going to have to do in a few days' time. She couldn't stay indefinitely on the postnatal ward.

'Right.' Heather paused, always careful of causing upset. 'And how are the boys doing? Really?'

'Better with every day that passes. Oliver is doing really well. Which is good, obviously. Joseph isn't out of the woods yet. He's still very small and there are some concerns about his development, longer term, because of the oxygen deficit he endured.' Heather covered her distress at this news well, but not completely. Lizzie endeavoured to reassure her. 'But he's making progress, in his own slow but steady way. I'm sorry you can't come up and see them.'

'That's fine. Best to keep them safe, rather than having everyone and his wife trooping through the ward, bringing all their germs with them. I'll be seeing them soon enough. I'm glad things are a little easier. We've been so worried, about all of you.' She paused. 'Whatever we can do to help, just let us know.'

Lizzie noticed how Heather often expressed herself in the plural – the testament of a good marriage?

As if psychic, Heather's next question was, 'And how's Ian doing? Has he got over the shock yet? He was beside himself when I rang to tell him Mick had taken you in. I've never heard him sound like that before. He was in no fit state to drive, really. I gather he made to the hospital in time for the birth.'

'He did.'

'Well, that's something. I see him sometimes, returning late at night.'

'Yes, he's been coming in every day after work. Staying for as long as he can. He's been amazing.' It was true. Ian had been, since the boys had been born.

'That's good.'

They fell silent.

Heather's next question was hesitant. 'Have they established why you went into labour so early?'

Lizzie's gaze went to the lace of froth around the edge of her coffee cup. The pattern was delicate, intricate. 'My placenta ruptured.'

'Do they know what caused it?'

'No. They don't know for sure. It can happen with twins.'

Heather didn't push for any further explanation. She turned her attention to the bag on her lap. 'I brought you some bits and pieces I thought you might need. A few home comforts.' She passed over a cotton tote bag. It had a cartoon hedgehog printed on it.

Lizzie looked inside. There was a pack of nice biscuits, a small box of chocolate gingers, her favourites, and a paperback, because Heather would never give up on trying to turn her into a reader. There was even a mini bottle of champagne – to celebrate the boys' arrival.

She felt a rush of affection. 'Thank you.'

'I'm not sure what the hospital policy is on alcohol but, you know, tradition and all that. I gather Ian has already suggested that he and Mick go out for a pint to wet the babies' heads… when things are more settled. Oh, and I nearly forgot, your keys are in there. You must have left them behind in the panic.'

Lizzie slid her hand inside the tote bag and felt around for her house keys. She gripped them. The teeth dug into her palm. They represented the home that she and the boys would return to. She held them out to Heather. 'Can I ask you to hang onto them for me?' Heather looked slightly perplexed, but nodded. 'I've a favour to ask.'

Chapter 10

THE SENSE OF CALM Heather had bestowed on Lizzie evaporated the minute she pushed through the swing doors onto the unit.

An alarm was going off. Its persistent beeping pierced the air, a shrill reminder that stability was tenuous on the NICU – you took it for granted at your peril. And she had taken it for granted. She had sat and drunk coffee and laughed with Heather as if things were fine, as if they were safe.

It was not fine.

They were not safe. The huddle of nurses around Joseph's incubator testified to that.

She caught Ian's eye. He was standing, rigid, to one side of the cluster of busy bodies, his arms crossed tightly across his chest. She could see the tension in his hands, his fingers digging into the flesh of his upper arms. He was literally holding himself together. Lizzie didn't go any further into the room. She couldn't. The noise of the alarm held her back. Was this the sound she would forever associate with her child dying?

The nurses moved swiftly, quietly and efficiently. They were an experienced team. They knew what they were doing, but they weren't miracle-workers. The beeping seemed to speed up and grow louder, leaving no space to breathe or think or hope.

Then, suddenly, it stopped – leaving in its wake the reverberations of panic. The choreography around the incubator changed, softened, became less staccato. 'It's okay,' one of the nurses said, 'it was a false alarm.' Lizzie desperately wanted to believe her. 'Joseph's stats are stable. That's not what triggered the alarm. One of the plugs seems to have been knocked loose.'

Relief, a drench of cold water, made Lizzie shiver. There was a beat and the nurses began to disperse.

Then...'What the fuck!' from Ian.

The sound of his anger, coming so soon after the fear, was shocking. No one shouted or swore on the NICU. It was an unspoken code, a mutual pact agreed upon to protect raw nerves and exhausted souls. Ian moved, rapidly.

Lizzie was confused for a second, then she realised where, or rather who, he was heading towards. Trish. Lizzie hadn't seen her, standing against the back wall, a cloth in her hand.

'You stupid cow!' Ian had found his target. 'How fucking careless can you be? Where do you think you are? You're not slopping out in some pub. This is an intensive-care ward, you slack, useless waste of space.'

He turned to the assembled staff. 'I want her' – he jabbed his finger at Trish – 'off this ward. Now.'

In a smooth, decisive movement, one of the nurses stepped in front of Trish. Suddenly everyone was talking, filling the vacuum left by the silenced alarm. Trish started apologising, Ian carried on shouting, and the nurses repeated their assurances that *Joseph was fine*. It was chaos – an alien and dangerous concept on the NICU. The other parents watched in horror.

Ian's raised voice was enough to unlock Lizzie.

But instead of going to check on her son, she went to soothe her partner.

She didn't touch him. She knew, from experience, that when Ian was this upset the only way to get through was with stillness. She stepped in front of him, leaving enough space for the panic he was experiencing to radiate off him. Trying to dampen his emotions when he was in such a heightened state never worked; his stress had to be allowed to race, peak and then subside. Hence she said nothing. She let him vent, but stood her ground, in his eyeline: a physical barrier, protecting Trish, and him.

After a few more seconds of ranting, Ian finally looked at her. He stopped shouting. His chest was heaving, his breathing rattly. Lizzie took a slow, deep breath, then another and another, and on the fifth inhale he matched her. Although it was clear he was still wrestling to get himself under control, he began, tentatively, to follow her lead.

The energy dropped out of the situation. Lizzie

felt weak with relief, but she kept breathing steadily, evenly, slowly. Only when she was convinced that Ian was calm and rational did she step away and go to Joseph.

As the conversation began about what was going to be put in place to prevent such an incident ever happening again, Lizzie saw Trish slip quietly away. It was for the best.

Half an hour later, with order restored, Ian mollified and the boys sleeping peacefully in their incubators, Lizzie excused herself. She needed a moment. She went into the Ladies, chose the end cubicle, shot the bolt, lowered the lid and sat down. Only then did she cry – sharp, throat-ripping tears. It was a release that brought little comfort. She allowed herself precisely one minute, then she stopped. She grabbed a wad of toilet paper and scrubbed away the evidence of her breakdown. Her bout of self-pity had left her face feeling tight and thin. She pressed her palms against her cheeks, pushing her mask back in place.

When she emerged from the cubicle she found Trish waiting for her, leaning against the sinks, coat on, her work-reddened hands clasped in front of her. She must have heard Lizzie's outburst, but she made no comment. Lizzie was grateful.

'I'm so sorry. I must have knocked it – the plug.'

'It's okay.'

'It isn't.'

'It was an accident. No harm done.'

'I feel awful.'

'I know you do.' Lizzie did. Trish was hard-faced, but she was not hard-hearted.

'I'd offer you a fag, but I don't smoke anymore and I'm guessing you never have.' Lizzie shook her head. 'Or drink?'

'Not really.'

Trish tutted. 'You're going need at least one vice... to keep you sane. It's essential when you've got kids,' she left a pause, 'and a bloke – like that.' Trish held Lizzie's gaze. 'I suggest gin.'

Lizzie summoned a smile. 'Mother's ruin.' Trish looked puzzled. 'That's what it used to be called.'

'Really? Bet it was a man who called it that.'

They both smiled. Lizzie started to feel a little better. 'I promise I'll buy a bottle when I get out of here.'

'You do that!'

Lizzie's worry about the incident resurfaced. 'You'll be all right, won't you?' She hated the thought of Trish getting into trouble for her own sake, but she was even more anxious that Trish might be moved off the NICU. Lizzie had grown to rely on her school-of-hard-knocks wisdom.

'Yeah.' Trish gave a tired shrug. 'They might change my shifts for a while, so I'm out of the way.' She didn't add, *of Ian*. She didn't need to.

'I'm sorry about how he spoke to you. It was... rude. He gets overwhelmed. It comes across as anger, when really he's just scared.'

Trish buttoned up her coat. 'Don't worry about it. Water under the bridge.' At the door she paused. 'But one piece of advice, Lizzie, for what it's worth... You need to stop apologising for things that aren't your fault.'

Chapter 11

TWO DAYS LATER Lizzie was discharged. There was no medical reason for her to stay in hospital.

It was not the homecoming either of them had envisaged.

The car journey home passed in silence. It was a short trip – back in time. Ian unlocked the front door and they stepped into their hall. She was home – to stay. The boys were still in the hospital.

Ian dropped her bag on the floor and pushed the door shut with his foot. He pulled Lizzie towards him and rested his head on her shoulder. It took her a few seconds to realise he was crying with relief that she was finally home. He was like this now – expressing his emotions in a totally new way. Affection, need, reliance: they had all been ingredients in their relationship before, but they had been her language, not his. Mick had been right; having a child changed things, and perhaps having two children increased the trajectory of that change. Whatever the truth, both of them were very different people from the ones who had left the house three weeks ago.

She stroked his back. It took him a minute or two to calm down. When he had, he took her hand and led her upstairs. Without a word he started to get undressed. She did the same. They got into bed in their underwear. It was the middle of the day. She wanted to be back in the hospital, on the ward, with her boys, but she was here, in their bedroom, with Ian. The sun shone through the window, full of promise.

For a long time he held her.

Welcomed her back.

Made her his again.

Afterwards, as they lay locked together, a couple once more, he described the life they would lead once the twins came home.

Chapter 12

PERHAPS IAN HAD MORE FAITH than she did, because barely a week later that hard-to-imagine family life came a giant step closer.

Lizzie came onto the ward early, as she always did – Ian dropped her off every morning on his way to work now – to see Nicky, one of the night-shift nurses, sitting in a chair with Oliver on her lap. It took Lizzie a second or two to realise that the breathing tube was gone.

Nicky smiled. 'We took it out last night, after you'd gone home. He's been doing grand.'

Lizzie looked down and saw her first-born son's face properly for the first time, free of tape and tubes. 'We thought you might like to try and give him a bottle. Cerys has just gone to get it. He had a feed in the night. Didn't you, little man? Took to it like a duck to water, but that's no great surprise, given the rate he's growing.'

Lizzie took Oliver into her arms and sat with him alongside Joseph's incubator. She stared down at him, marvelling at the sounds he was making. Normal, snuffly baby sounds. A little croaky perhaps, but after all the tubes he'd had forced down his throat in the past few weeks, that was to be expected. When she offered him the milk he guzzled. The strength of his suck, the way his hands reached up for the bottle, his liquid-clear eyes staring at her, the breaks for breath, the sheer glorious normality of it was astounding. When he'd finished she was able to rest him up on her shoulder and burp him, without a tangle of wires getting in the way – like you would any baby.

In that moment she finally believed he was going to be fine. Oliver was a baby who was going to become a toddler, a little boy, a schoolboy, a teenager and, at some point in the distant future, a fully grown man.

In the midst of her joy she looked across at Joseph and fell back to Earth.

She had one son on the path to his future.

And another not yet on the starting line.

Chapter 13

FROM THAT POINT ONWARDS, things changed rapidly.

Once on regular feeds, Oliver stormed ahead, gaining weight and strength at astonishing speed. Soon it looked odd seeing him in a room full of poorly babies. He was like the cuckoo in the nest. It made Lizzie feel uncomfortable, especially given the contrast with Joseph, but, as Helen pointed out, Oliver's strength and health were proof of what was possible. His was a good-news story. It gave everyone on the ward renewed faith in happy endings. Within the week there was talk of discharging him from the NICU.

Ian was over the moon.

Lizzie was deeply freaked out. 'What? You mean take him home?' She wasn't ready. Nowhere near, neither emotionally nor practically. How could she care for them both? She couldn't be in two places at once. Separating them was wrong; surely twins were supposed to stay together. They shouldn't break that bond. It could damage their relationship, for life. And the strongest argument of all, for Lizzie at least: the boys were safe in hospital. Why risk that? It was too big a step. The panic choked her.

But it also galvanised her.

She spoke to Helen. And Helen, as she had before, quietly, calmly and implacably came to Lizzie's rescue. She arranged for Lizzie to move into one of the precious family rooms along the corridor from the NICU, taking Oliver with her. This meant the paediatric team would be able to check that he was continuing to progress, and Lizzie would still be close to Joseph. Both boys would be where they should be – with their mum.

Lizzie was profoundly grateful.

Ian was deeply unhappy.

When they discussed it, his expression darkened. The stress he tried so hard to hide revealed itself in the tightness around his mouth and eyes. 'But this is what we've been dreaming of. Them coming home. For us to start living like a normal family.'

Lizzie steeled herself and leant into his frustration at her choosing her boys and her own needs over his. 'But it's not both of them. We can't leave Joseph behind and go home and play Happy Families without him.' Ian's warring emotions rendered him silent. As she watched his dreams crumble, Lizzie sought to placate him. 'Please, let's take up Helen's offer of the family room, just for now. It won't be for long. Another few weeks.' She saw him stiffen at the length of the delay. She hurried on. 'At most. You heard what Dr Seward said. Joseph is getting there. He simply needs a little more time. We'll be together soon. Both of them well. Won't that be better?'

'But Oliver is well enough to come home now!' The old stubbornness.

She matched it with her own. 'And Joseph isn't. They need to be together.'

Had they been at home, the debate would, no doubt, have gone differently, but as they were on the ward, with the nurses and the other families listening, Ian was under pressure to compromise, especially after his outburst at Trish.

After lots of soul-searching and some gentle, but sustained pressure from Helen, Ian eventually acquiesced to the plan. He really didn't have much choice. They had to do what was best for the twins. Lizzie was grateful and deeply relieved. Because despite Ian's very understandable disappointment, she had no intention of leaving the hospital without both of her boys.

Chapter 14

AND SHE WASN'T GOING to have to. Because sometimes miracles did happen.

At six weeks and two days old, Joseph was finally declared well enough to leave the NICU. It was evidence – and Lizzie had badly needed such proof – that life could be kind and could, sometimes, exceed your expectations. When it did, you had to rise to the challenge and make the most of it.

While they waited for Joseph to be brought to them, Lizzie sat, contentedly, watching Oliver. She never tired of it. He was sucking his fist noisily. He was always hungry – making up for lost time. Looking at Oliver's chubby legs thrashing and flexing, it was hard to believe he'd ever lain like a scatter of barely covered bones inside an incubator struggling for breath.

Unlike Lizzie, Ian couldn't settle. He paced, the impatience of the past few weeks compressed into each step. He hated being in the family room. She understood. To him it represented separation, lonely nights, an empty house, a partner who was never there. This room was a place where he did not belong. Lizzie did. To her it felt like home.

But in three or four days, possibly less, they would all be saying goodbye to it, and the hospital, for good.

Finally the door opened. They both stood up.

It was Helen. That pleased Lizzie. Helen had been there for them from that horrendous first day. It was fitting that she should be there for the beginning of the end. 'Here he is.' Helen glanced at Lizzie, seeking permission. Lizzie nodded and she passed Joseph over to Ian. 'It's all good. He's had a feed and a change in the past hour.' She reached out and gently touched the top of Joseph's head. 'We're going to miss him on the unit.'

Joseph wasn't simply another prem baby to Helen. Perhaps none of them were? Maybe that was what made her so good at her job – her capacity to remain professional and yet get involved. In some cases, more deeply than anyone had the right to hope or expect.

'I'll try to pop in over the next couple of days to check on him and get my little-man fix,' she smiled, 'but rest assured, he's doing great. Doc Seward is happy with him. She's ready to sign him off. Another few days and you won't need to see any of us, ever again.' At the door she paused. 'In case I don't get a chance to see you both together again, I just wanted to say... good luck.'

Lizzie heard the slight tremor in her voice. Ian appeared not to; he was too focused on Joseph. Helen nodded at Lizzie, then closed the door.

Lizzie's throat felt clogged with the pressure of too much pent-up emotion. She needed to do something. Without waiting for Ian to prompt her, she picked up his phone and began taking pictures – sealing the present into an imortant memory.

What she captured was her tall, strong, handsome partner cradling their child in his arms, his restless pacing reduced to a gentle sway – the image of devoted fatherhood. Ian's voice was low, measured, directed at Joseph, not her.

'Well, here you are at long last. Sorry it's taken so long to get you sprung, but it honestly wasn't for want of trying.' He kissed Joseph's head. 'Do you want to say "hello" to your big bro?' Ian moved over to Oliver and bent down. Tenderly he held Joseph alongside the Perspex side of the crib. 'There you go. Say "hi", boys.' He tilted Joseph towards Oliver. Joseph still looked so small in his hands. 'Now in the future you two will, no doubt, fight like cats and dogs. Who's got the best left foot? Who can do the most impressive wheelie? Who's got the best girlfriend? Who's stronger, fitter, taller, better-looking?' He laughed. 'That's okay. It's what brothers do. But none of that crap will matter. Because what's important – and what will never change – is that you two will always have each other.' He looked up, straight into the camera lens. 'And you'll always have me and your mum.'

As if in response, Oliver made a gurgling noise.

Ian laughed. 'Did you hear that? He'll be talking

before we know it.' He was buzzing with pride. 'Move Oliver over a little bit.'

Lizzie knew what he was going to do. She edged Oliver over to the right-hand side of the cot. Space created, Ian gently lowered Joseph down alongside his brother. They were finally back together after so many long, stressful weeks. Ian took his phone from her and zoomed in close.

Chapter 15

THEIR BAGS WERE PACKED and the car seats were lined up against the wall, ready and waiting. Lizzie had stripped the hospital bed and the cot for the last time. She'd folded the linen and cleaned the small bathroom. It had been something to do, as well as a small gesture of thanks for the kindness and understanding she'd been shown by everyone, not only the doctors and Helen, but also the other nurses and the small band of older ladies who worked as the ward orderlies, especially Trish. Her advice had been invaluable. Their parting the previous night had been bittersweet. She'd given Lizzie two leaving gifts. A bottle of gin and a last piece of typically robust advice. 'You need to back yourself, Lizzie, because no other bugger is going to.'

As Lizzie sat on the bare mattress and watched the boys shadow-boxing, it gave her heart to think of the huge number of people who had played their part in getting her family to this point.

Now it was really happening, she felt surprisingly calm. The long, anxious weeks since the boys' birth had been a strange, frightening, but ultimately positive time. They had helped to build her resolve and her confidence. In a peculiar way she supposed she'd been lucky, as she'd had longer than most women to get her head around how different her life was going to be, now that she was a mother. All the stress and fear – the lack of sleep and the overwhelming realisation that not one, but two lives wholly depended on her – were good preparation for what lay ahead.

The twins were dressed in matching jackets and woolly hats, outfits that had been knitted by Heather. It made them look like babies from a different era. She was fine with that. Two peas in a pod; one ripe and juicy, the other small, but just as sweet.

The nurses were right: the boys were happiest when they were together. Since Joseph had joined them in the family room, Oliver had been much more settled. They slept wedged together in the cot, creating their own warmth, with no need for lights and machinery. When they woke they would often not cry, but lay quietly, staring contentedly at each other, in no rush for Lizzie's presence. Even when she changed their nappies they liked to be side by side – they both fussed if they weren't. And when the nurses took one or the other away to be weighed or measured, the twin left behind always fretted. It wasn't her imagination, they really did need to be with each other, like twins should. It was a unity that she hoped would stand them in good stead for whatever challenges they faced in their lives.

In the quiet, stripped-bare room, Lizzie's thoughts turned to home: to the double buggy that totally blocked the hallway, to the pile of muslins folded neatly on the countertop, to the unopened gifts piled in the lounge – they were saving them to open together – to the nursery that had finally been finished and, inevitably, to Ian and his fizzing, barely contained excitement. He was coming to collect them at one o'clock. He'd already texted three times to reassure her they had plenty of food in the house and that he'd bought an extra couple of packs of the super-small nappies Joseph needed. He'd also told her exactly where he was going to park, and how he proposed that they manage getting the bags and the boys down to the car in one go. It was a military operation: an extraction he'd been planning ever since they'd had conformation that Joseph was being discharged.

Ian was taking two weeks' paternity leave. He was keen to get the boys settled into a good routine. They agreed it was important to start as they meant go on. He was also going to be in charge of managing the flood of visitors they were expecting – there was a lot of pent-up demand to see the twins. He'd drawn up a schedule. Lizzie's mother was top of the list. She'd been allotted two nights, arriving on Sunday, followed a few days later – to give them some time on their own in between – by Ian's mum. After that it was a blur of names, dates and times. Lizzie had pretended to listen to the timetable of visitors, but had, in all honesty, taken none of it in.

Regardless, it was all set up.

The grand homecoming.

The start of their lives.

Lizzie lowered her sights back to the actual centre of her universe. Her boys. They lay on the bed beside her, waving their arms and legs in the pale sunshine, oblivious to the fact that their next big adventure was about to begin. She reached out and stroked first Oliver's and then Joseph's cheek.

She hoped, for their sakes, that she was going to be up to it.

PART TWO

Chapter 16

SIXTEEN YEARS LATER

OLI WAS PISSED OFF, and that was not the mood he wanted to be in.

It was good that his sixteenth birthday had fallen on a Friday, but crap that it was a school day. He hadn't bothered asking his mum if he could take the day off, because he'd known she would say 'No', and would probably throw in a lecture about the importance of knuckling down for these last few months, for good measure. *GCSEs the path to college; good A levels the route to uni; uni the gateway to a world of opportunities* – implication… opportunities that she never had. Blah, blah, blah. To add to his aggravation, he was now sitting on a wall waiting for his brother. And, as always, Joe was taking for ever. Oli thought about pushing off, but they were both under strict instructions to arrive home together, at exactly the same time. A party, at home, at their age! He loved her, he really did, but there were times he wished she wasn't his mother.

The flood of uniformed bodies had slowed to a trickle.

It was amazing how quickly a school that held 1,600 kids could empty out at the end of a day. The last stragglers were the usual collection of oddbods, who obviously waited until the mass had dispersed before venturing out of the library, or whatever dark corner they hid in between lessons. It bothered Oli that his brother was one of the lurkers, but not that much. He and Joe moved in very separate, rarely overlapping circles at school. As a result, they barely saw each other – which was fine, with both of them. Because when they were together, even now, some idiot would invariably feel compelled to make a comment. It never ceased to surprise Oli how crass people could be.

He stared down the empty drive. Where the fuck was Joe? Oli found a stick and thrashed out his frustration on a clump of grass. The next few hours were going to be grim.

A family party – his mum really didn't get irony. Oli didn't know anyone who had less of a family than him and Joe, which meant that instead of relatives, the house would be full of his mother's embarrassing friends and, worse still, their neighbours. He wouldn't put it past her not to have made jelly in one of those sandcastle moulds, like she used to when they were kids. She loved all that stuff. It was strange really because if she ever spoke about the past, it was always about how tough things were when they were little, and yet she seemed, increasingly, to look back on those days with a kind of longing. It was hard not to conclude that she'd preferred him and his brother when they were young. It bugged Oli, but he never said anything. It would have upset her. Every family had its rules, and the key one in their house was that they had to be nice to their mum. It was what she was owed because she was, in everyone's opinion – including his own – a thoroughly good person. A ferociously hard worker and successful with it, kind, loyal, supportive, caring and, above all, thoughtful.

Oli whacked the top of a weed clean off. At least Auntie Sabine and Aleah would be at the party.

Sab was his mum's business partner, and her best and oldest friend. There was another thing that puzzled him: he'd never met two people so different – apart from him and his brother, of course. Auntie Sab was loud, spontaneous, sometimes deeply inappropriate. She liked a drink and a laugh and she seemed, genuinely, not to give a shit what people thought of her. Or at least not people who didn't matter to her – and there were a lot of those. As a result, Sab's relationship with Oli and Joe was great. She loved them, laughed with them, and often at them, and frequently slipped them the odd twenty to supplement their meagre allowance from their mother, but she never tried to influence them. She said they weren't worth the effort.

Sab exhibited the same sanguine philosophy when it came to her relationship with her own daughter. It was a dynamic that fascinated Oli and made him envious. She and Aleah were more like mates than mother and daughter. Whatever Aleah did, and she had pulled some real stunts in the past – having her navel pierced at eleven, hooking up with a boyfriend who was ten years older than her in the sixth form, dropping out of said sixth form after she dumped him to go to art school, only to jack that in when she got the bar work in Chicago, then coming back skint and moving back in with her mum again (hence her expected presence at the party today) – Auntie Sab simply rolled with it all. She appeared to love her daughter no more and, importantly, no less, no matter what she did.

Oli stood up and paced.

Where the hell was Joe? Another couple of minutes and he was heading home. Maybe he'd done a bunk, unable to face it? Nah, not a chance. That would be far too rebellious for his brother.

Thank God his mother wasn't on social media, which meant that at least their shame could be contained to their immediate circle. Perhaps surprisingly, for all her emphasis on memories and honouring where they came from, their mum wasn't one for capturing and broadcasting their lives. Indeed she was positively against it, forever cautioning Oli on the evils and risks of the Internet. Joe's online gaming seemed to trouble her far less – which only went to show how clueless most adults were.

Oli looked at his phone. Joe had better not have left without him. He messaged him. Got a response a minute later – Joe was slow doing everything: Coming now.

Five more minutes passed. By which point Oli wanted to hit more than just a bush with a stick. Then, finally, there Joe was, unmistakeable even from this distance.

Oli endured another interminable wait as Joe made his way up the drive. 'You took your time.'

'I didn't ask you to wait for me.' This was true.

'Yeah, but Mum did. The party, remember.'

Joe nodded and looked equally unenthused. They both hated her compulsion to squash them together at every opportunity, but neither of them had a choice. Being a twin was a curse. Oli lobbed the stick into the long grass. 'Shall we get this over with then?'

They set off, Joe a few paces behind Oli.

The one benefit of Joe taking for ever was that there was no one around to see them heading home together.

Chapter 17

THEIR BIRTHDAY CAKE was better than Beth had hoped. A half-and-half masterpiece. Joe's side was chocolate sponge with white icing and film-themed decorations. Oli's was carrot cake with green icing, topped with a pair of golden football boots and a ball. It was a complete clash, but very professionally done. It was much too artistic to ruin with candles, so Beth wrapped a potato in foil and stuck them in that instead. A birthday porcupine. She positioned the cake and the candle-spud in the middle of the table. There would be groans of embarrassment when the boys saw them. Tough!

Oli had promised they would be home by 4.30 p.m. and that he would stick around until 6 p.m. Beth had every intention of holding him to that. It gave him plenty of time to get ready for the party, which some girl called Emily, who lived over in Rayners Lane, was throwing. Beth was aware that Oli had liberated a half-full bottle of vodka from the cabinet in the back room a couple of days ago – which was forward planning, for him. She mustn't forget to take it off him before he left. She wasn't naïve enough to think she could stop Oli drinking when he was out with his friends, but she was damned if she was going to provide the booze. The only reason she hadn't raised the stolen vodka with him was because she hadn't wanted to risk creating 'an atmosphere'.

She knew neither of her boys wanted this party; the compulsion to celebrate was hers, not theirs, but sixteen was an important milestone and she was determined to mark it – as they had done every previous birthday. The added impetus this year was her awareness that she was running out of time. Beth also wasn't blind. She knew Joe and Oli weren't children anymore. That didn't trouble her too much – it was a natural progression to go from sharing the big occasions in your life with your parents, to wanting to be with your friends. No, what made it difficult for Beth was seeing one of her sons race full-tilt into adulthood, chin up, chest out, while the other edged forward hesitantly, head and heart down.

Beth looked around at the food and the decoration-laden room. She conceded – it was too much. Over-compensation. It was a habit of hers. She wandered to the window. Sab was in the garden, tying bunting to the fence, haphazardly. The sight made Beth smile.

It was Sab who had taught her the importance of celebrating. She was, and always had been, the bringer of laughter and lightness into their relationship, in both the good times and the bad.

Beth didn't need to close her eyes to conjure up their

inextricably shared past. The small, dark, damp flat in Harrow that they moved into as single mums, when the twins were eight months old and Aleah was seven, came to her mind readily, and often. It had been a life lived on a shoestring. Money had been so tight that they used to collect coppers in neat fifty-pence-worth piles on the kitchen windowsill. The condensation used to lift the dirt from the coins, so that every time Beth used one of the stacks to buy milk or bread from the corner shop, she'd had to wipe her fingers clean on the inside of her coat pocket. The taint of being poor – she would never forget it. Beth had many crystal-clear memories of their time in that small, shabby flat. Oli cruising around the crappy furniture, on the cusp of walking, babbling away to himself while Joe sat, propped in his bouncy chair, watching. The long, cold nights when she used to lift both of them into bed with her for warmth and comfort, conscious, even then, of the solid heft and resistance of Oli's little body compared with Joe's floppy, pliant limbs.

But – and it was a big 'but' – despite the lack of cash, the mounting concerns about Joe's development and their individual griefs and challenges, there had also been a lot of joy. Sab had insisted on it.

Images flickered through Beth's brain.

They'd celebrated the twins' first, second and third birthdays in the Harrow flat.

Beth remembered bargain balloons that had taken an Amazonian effort to blow up and had then drifted around the flat for weeks afterwards. A huge, pink 'Happy Second Birthday' (name scraped off) cake that Sab had blagged, for a knockdown price, from the baker's, after whoever had ordered it for their daughter failed to collect. There had always been plenty of toys – from the charity shop – garish paper plates and cups, a stack of white sliced bread, cheese-and-pickle sandwiches, party rings, monster bags of crisps and, in homage to Trish, a new bottle of gin for herself and Sab. She cherished her memories of Sab whacking the radio up loud and them dancing around the worn carpet, playing Musical Statues and Bumps when the boys turned three, with Aleah laughing fit to burst, until the miserable old bugger who lived upstairs banged on the floor.

They carried their traditions with them as they moved on and up together. Out of the Harrow Road flat to a marginally better one on Darley Street, then to the little house on Kent Avenue and next to the bigger house on The Limes.

So many birthdays and Christmases, so many good times, and quite a few hard ones as well. Sab had been there for her through it all.

She'd been at Beth's side when the letter arrived confirming what Beth had known all along – that her beloved son had cerebral palsy. And she'd stayed by her side for the complex, and at times emotionally draining, journey of discovering what that diagnosis really meant. Sab had put up with every home they'd ever shared being littered with disability aids, walking frames, exercise balls and specially adapted chairs; with their lives being regularly invaded by a parade of social workers, physios and therapists; and with Beth often needing Sab to care for Oli while she concentrated on Joe.

And, on the financial front, Sab had been a lifesaver as well. She'd accepted, without complaint, the disparity in what they both contributed. For the first five years Beth was only able to put her benefits into the pot. It was Sab who had earnt. She'd spent long days catching the bus to the land of affluence that existed not three miles from their doorstep, where she cleaned houses, for below the minimum wage, often supplying her own cleaning products. Even after Beth had found her niche – running the books in their burgeoning cleaning and housekeeping business – she'd never been able to match her friend's energy and focus. Sab often joked that she didn't need her to, that they needed at least one of them to be good at the *mothering thing,* but Beth knew she had been luckier than she'd had any right to be. She and Sab and the boys and Aleah had spent the best part of fifteen years living together as a family – *sans* men – and for that, and for the memories, Beth was deeply grateful.

Sab had finished hanging the bunting. It was wonky and the far end had already come untied, but it looked celebratory. As she headed back up the garden, she spotted Beth. She mock-bowed, demanding adulation for her efforts. Beth smiled, raised her hands and gave her best friend, business partner and saviour the ovation she deserved.

Chapter 18

THE HOUSE WAS, as Joe had feared, full of people.

Compelled to smile, talk and 'mingle', he did his best. Every way he turned, birthday cards were pressed into his hands. The gift-givers all seemed to expect him to open them on the spot, which he hated, but did. A couple of ten-pound notes fluttered to the carpet as he fumbled with his growing cache. There was something deeply unedifying about having to scramble around on the floor to retrieve cash. Heads and elbows collided painfully in the rush to help. It was a relief to make it across the room and sit down. Let them come to him, if they wanted to.

And they did, doing their duty with a brief chat, before moving off, with obvious relief, towards the food. Everyone asked how school was going. He said the same thing, over and over again: 'Well, thank you.' There was then a pause, followed by, 'So... what's next for you?' He replied, 'College, then uni, hopefully', which invariably prompted comments about how proud his mother was of him. Some added, 'Of both of you', depending on their academic or sporting bias.

Joe scanned the room for Oli. He was pinned near the food by a woman called Anthea? Alison? Alice? It was something beginning with an A. He was steadily eating his way through a platter of sandwiches and, by the look of it, trying to have an out-of-body experience. Joe watched his mum make her way over to his brother and hand him something. She then threaded her way through the bodies and sat down next to him.

'You okay?'

How many millions of times was she going to ask him that in his lifetime? he wondered. 'Yep. Fine. Thanks for all this.'

She smiled. 'Thank *you* for indulging me. I thought you might want to open this.' Another card, but this one had been posted, from Newcastle. Joe paused on seeing Mick's familiar blocky handwriting. He opened the envelope, taking care not to damage the card inside. On the front there was a cartoon rhino – an animal with a famously thick skin. It was a long-running joke. Inside the card, Mick's solitary signature floated untethered in a sea of white space. More than a year on and it still looked wrong seeing Mick's name without Heather's alongside it, his handwriting instead of hers.

Now Joe would happily have sat and talked to Mick for hours at any party. He and Heather had always come down from the North-East for his and Oli's birthday, in the past. It was a tradition; correction, *had* been a tradition before Heather got sick. Mick obviously wasn't up to visiting without his wife yet. That was understandable. He and Heather had been a team. Great stand-ins for the grandparents the twins didn't have. Joe glanced at his mum. Heather had been like a mother to her. Her death, though expected, had still been a shock. It was the saddest Joe had ever seen her.

She smiled, then tutted when she saw there was cash inside the card. A fold of twenties. 'That's so kind of him. I knew he wouldn't forget. You must text him to say "Thank you". Shall we do the cake now?'

Embarrassed by Mick's generosity, Joe opted for stuffing the notes inelegantly into the back pocket of his jeans. 'If you want.'

She must have picked up on his tone, because she added, 'We can give everyone a slice before they head home.'

'Sounds good to me.' The sooner this was over, the better.

There followed a call for hush from Sab. People quietened immediately – she had that sort of presence. His mum waved Oli over. He came, but with no great enthusiasm, and flopped down on the opposite sofa. There was a pregnant pause, then a terrible rendition of 'Happy Birthday' filled the air, as Auntie S brought the cake and a glowing ball of candles on a tray over to the coffee table. Not content with the obligatory sixteen candles, their mum had doubled up. It was a definite fire hazard.

The cake itself was huge, a strange psychedelic mash-up of football and film. For Joe, who was familiar with awkward moments, it was a new low, or high. Regardless, he smiled, and kept smiling. The countdown began. *One...* he and Oli leant forward and locked eyes. *Two...* Joe could tell that his brother was dying inside as well, but he wasn't attempting to cover it up. *Three...* Oli pretended to blow out the candles, but left it to Joe. An old, still-tiresome family tradition. It took Joe a few attempts to get them all out.

'Make a wish, but don't tell anyone,' their mother urged, as she did every year.

Joe did as prompted. He didn't need reminding to keep his wishes to himself. He had no intention of sharing his innermost desires with anyone.

As promised, with the cake cut, wrapped and distributed, thankfully people began to depart. After ten minutes there were only the three of them left, plus Auntie Sab and Aleah of course.

Oli must have known full well that it wasn't over, and yet still he tried to make his escape. 'Well, thanks, Mum.' He stood up. 'That was... nice. Is it okay if I go and get ready to go over to Em's now?'

'In a minute.'

They both knew what was coming. Resigned, Oli sat down again.

She disappeared upstairs and came back with two envelopes and two neatly wrapped parcels. Different wrapping paper from the gifts she'd already given them.

The atmosphere shifted. It took on an edge that would have been hard to read, if you didn't know their history.

She put the parcels on the table. They were fairly small and flat. The same present for each of them – again as tradition dictated. Oli reached for his, but she stopped him. 'Read your cards first.' She might have spoken softly, but her word was law when it came to this.

They picked up the envelopes and opened them at the same time.

A *To My Son on His 16th Birthday* card, the numbers picked out in gold. Joe barely glanced at the design. Inside there was the usual message – *Happy Birthday. Love, always, Dad xxx* – but on the facing page there was a whole paragraph of writing. She really had gone to town this year. Joe skim-read the message, feeling his mother's eyes on him, conscious of his brother sitting opposite, doing the same. It was emotional stuff. *Pride in all their hard work. Pleasure in their achievements. Respect for their different skills and talents. A reminder of how important their relationship as twins was, and always would be.* He knew the message in both their cards would be identical. Absolute parity was their family mantra, although that didn't mean life was fair.

What to say in response?

Nothing. There was absolutely nothing to say.

Oli reached for his gift, obviously wanting to hurry things along. Joe followed suit, equally happy to get it over with. The wrapping on Joe's parcel was only lightly stuck down. Another accommodation he was used to. It did help, but it infuriated him. He ripped off the paper. Inside was a Halifax passbook and card.

'It's okay to look inside.'

Joe did, his brain scrambling slightly to work out what he was looking at.

Seeing his confusion, Beth explained. 'Your dad believed you should save, even if it wasn't much. For rainy days... and sunny ones. I opened an account for you both when you were tiny. Now you're sixteen, I thought we should get them signed over into your names.'

'Wow. Mum, thank you.' Oli had obviously skipped to the last page.

Joe struggled with the pages slightly. There was line after line of entries, many of them small amounts, but eventually he found the final page: £4,000.

'I rounded it up. There should be enough for driving lessons, and a chunk to go towards a car, or to pay for the insurance. Or you could hold on to it for when you're at uni.'

It was too much.

But Oli seemed perfectly at ease with it. 'This is really thoughtful, Mum. Really. I promise I'll keep this somewhere safe. But... if you don't mind' – Joe both admired and resented his brother's balls – 'I need to be making tracks.'

Joe kept his head down. He heard movement, Oli standing up, a kissed cheek. He'd escaped – leaving Joe trapped with his mother and yet another thoughtful, kind, generous gift that felt like a burden.

Chapter 19

IN THE SHOWER OLI scrubbed at his hair and skin and tried not to think about this year's present from his father. Useful as the money would be – he couldn't wait to get driving – it was beginning to feel seriously weird, getting presents from a man who'd been dead for sixteen years.

As a kid, Oli had simply accepted this particular, peculiar birthday tradition, had liked it even. The presents had made him feel he wasn't missing out, not just on an extra gift, but on having a dad per se. Most of his friends had a father, so why shouldn't he and Joe? Even if theirs was a ghost.

Because, for them, his absence and yet his continued involvement in their lives was normal. Their dead father not only put in an appearance every birthday and Christmas; he was also present in their lives in a more day-to-day way as well. Never known and not remembered – at least not by Oli and Joe – he nevertheless lived on within their family, resurrected by their mother's memories, evocations and efforts. His values were taught at every opportunity, his views on things discussed as if he'd simply stepped into the next room, his allegiances in sports teams and politics handed on to them as naturally as such loyalties were in other families. As a result, their father's role in their lives was very much alive and kicking.

Of his death Oli knew very little, other than what his mother had told them. Which was: that he'd died in a freak accident the night before they were due to come home from hospital as newborn babies. He fell off a ladder, having gone into the loft to fetch something. Apparently it was pure bad luck that the fall had been awkward and had broken his neck. What their father had gone into the loft to retrieve, no one knew. It was, obviously, irrelevant in the grand scale of things, but for some reason the not-knowing bugged Oli more than it should have. Ian's sudden, unfortunate death had made a widow of their mother at the age of twenty-three, and them fatherless at barely two months old. The tragedy had driven their mum to pack up what little she owned and leave Newcastle to start again, from scratch, far away from such painful memories. It had been an awful tragedy.

But only in theory, for the boys.

Because as far as Oli was concerned, you couldn't grieve for what you'd never experienced. He'd never known his father, never known any family other than himself, Joe and their mum. Did it bother him that he didn't have a dad? Not so much. He honestly didn't feel the lack. Did it bother his brother? Probably. Joe was more sensitive about things, understandably, but it simply wasn't something they talked about. They were used to having a real mother and a phantom of a father. End of.

He blasted the last thoughts of family out of his head, shut off the water, dried himself and walked, naked, into his bedroom.

He looked at himself in the mirror and critiqued what he saw. It was an improvement. The gym sessions were beginning to pay off. Muscle was forming in the right places. His calves and abs were more defined. He looked strong. Oli was pleased. He got dressed: casual, expensive, non-obvious brands. He pulled a jacket out of his wardrobe. He wouldn't normally have bothered, but he needed somewhere to stash the vodka. Phone – check. Hair looking sharp – check. Breath minty-fresh – check. It was a party, after all. Libby and a bunch of her friends from the girls' high school were going to be there. Or so Dev had promised. A last once-over and Oli was sorted.

It was time to get his birthday started.

He took the stairs quickly, two at a time. Energy beginning to fizz inside him. The front door beckoned. Freedom. But he'd been brought up properly. It would be rude not to say goodbye, especially after all the effort his mum had put in, not to mention the four grand she'd just given him. Because, let's be honest, the money scrimped and saved in that passbook had nothing to do with his father and everything to do with her. He took a swerve into the lounge.

Joe was still sitting on the sofa, in exactly the same spot, the remnants of the party encircling him. Their mother was sitting next to him with a mug of tea. She was addicted, thought a brew could solve any problem, mental or physical. He couldn't abide the stuff. Sab was lying on the sofa, her shoes off, glass of red wine in hand. Aleah had gone. Good on her.

Joe flicked him a glance, his thoughts unreadable.

Oli wanted to ignore his brother. All Joe needed to do was get up and leave. There was nothing making him sit there like an obedient dog. The whole night lay ahead of him. But leave and do what? Oli knew Joe had nothing planned. No one to do it with. Irritation and sympathy surged through him. Two waves, crashing into each other. Equal and opposing and oh-so-familiar forces.

'I'm off now,' he announced.

'Have a good time.' His mother smiled. 'No later than midnight, remember. Text me when you're on your way home,' she nagged.

Sab lifted her free hand and waved it, regally and sarcastically. 'Behave yourself.'

Joe's eyes remained locked on Oli's.

No! This was his birthday. He'd done his duty. Oli was not going to get dragged into thinking about Joe's feelings. He was not his responsibility. Not tonight.

But it was his brother's birthday as well. 'Do you want to tag along?'

Joe blinked, shocked to be asked, but not half as shocked as Oli himself. Where the fuck had that come from? There was no taking it back now.

'To the party?' Joe asked.

'Yeah.' Even to his own ears, he didn't sound very enthusiastic, but that was because he wasn't. Joe didn't really know many of Oli's mates; he certainly didn't know them well enough for it not to be totally awkward. This was going to be a car crash.

Undeterred, Joe started getting to his feet. 'Yeah. That'd be good. I'll go and get changed.'

They were committed now.

What got to Oli the most was the look of delight on his mother's face. The fastest, most direct route to her heart was through Joe. Always had been. Always would be.

Chapter 20

THERE WAS A LOT to clear up, including a rubble of leftover cake.

Sab stayed back to help. It was nice pottering around, chatting. It reminded Beth of the old days, although there was now far more stuff to clean and wash and put away. It still shocked her how much she'd accrued over the years. Her life was now awash with possessions.

When it was all sorted, Sab hugged her goodnight. With her gone, the house felt empty, which was unusual because Joe was normally around in the evenings. Who was she kidding? He was always around in the evenings. They went about their daily lives as if Joe's cerebral palsy wasn't an issue, and most of the time it wasn't. He was super-bright, handsome, nice-natured, healthier than many with his condition, but his mobility problems did mark him out. Most sixteen-year-olds did not walk with sticks, or need a sit-down after being on their feet for longer than half an hour. They did not have to take a concoction of drugs every day just to keep them functioning. And as a result their lives, especially their social lives, were simply... easier.

Which was why Beth had been touched and surprised when Oli had invited Joe along to the house-party. So touched that she hadn't mentioned the vodka. It had felt precisely the right time to cut him some of the slack that Sab was endlessly advocating.

She glanced at the clock. There was a whole evening to fill.

She took herself off for a bath with her book. She was rereading *The Thorn Birds* – one of her many never-returned loans from Heather. Reacquainting herself with Father Ralph de Bricassart and Meggie was not only a bit of escapism, it was also an act of remembrance. Every one of Heather's paperbacks was a reminder of precious time spent together. Beth had never left her and Mick's house in Fenham without the 'loan' of another book.

When she came back downstairs an hour later she discovered she'd a missed call. She didn't recognise the number. Who would be phoning at 9.45 p.m. on a Friday night? No one, usually. Beth was aware of her own nun-like existence and was quite happy with it. She always thought nuns had it sussed, apart from the dedication-to-Christ stuff: land-owning, nice gardens, rosters for the boring domestic duties, a room of their own, no need to keep up with the latest fashions or diet, lifelong female friendship, no mobiles – she assumed – although perhaps the modern orders had moved with the times. Yeah, being banished to a nunnery didn't sound too bad to Beth.

It was probably an automated call. But as she reached for the TV remote, her ringtone sounded. Her maternal instincts stirred, uneasily. She picked up. 'Hello?'

'Is that Mrs Truman?' A young voice. Female. She didn't correct the caller. She never did.

'Yes.'

There was a pause. Beth listened. She could hear the wind blowing through some trees. No traffic. The girl was obviously outside. In a garden? There was music playing in the background. The party.

'I'm sorry to bother you.' The girl was very polite, and very hesitant. Beth detected other voices, again female, again young – contributing comments, adding to the confusion. 'We thought we should contact you.'

Beth's concern solidified. What had Oli done now?

'It's Joe,' the girl said.

That floored her. 'What's happened?' The alarm in her voice obviously rattled the girl, which wasn't helpful.

'He's okay. At least we think he is.' That was not reassuring. Beth restrained herself, waiting for her mystery caller to get to the point. 'He's just, well, he's had a bit too much to drink.' Relieved to have finally delivered her message, the girl became more articulate. 'He's been sick – a few times – but he's still quite...' She seemed torn by teenage solidarity as to what adjective to use. She plumped for 'out of it'. 'We found his phone in his pocket and we thought we'd better ring you.'

'Yes. Thank you. You did the right thing. I'll come and collect him. Can you text me the address, with the postcode?'

There was another pause, filled with talking. The girl eventually came back on the line. 'Yeah, I'll check with Emily and send you it.'

'Is his brother with him?'

'Oli?'

'Yes, Oli.'

'Um… no. Rachel and Lucy are with Joe, in the bathroom.'

Beth had a worrying mental image of Joe prone on a bathroom floor, his limbs in spasm, covered in vomit. Dehydration was an additional worry, as well as the damage the alcohol could do, on top of his meds.

'You made the right decision – calling me.'

'That's okay.' She sounded so young.

'What's your name, by the way?'

'Me? I'm Carrie.'

'Well, Carrie. Like I said, thank you very much for letting me know, and for looking out for him. I'll be there as soon as I can. Let me have that address. Don't forget. Oh, and if you can find Oli, can you let him know his brother isn't well.'

'I won't. I mean, I will. The address, and his brother.' The line went dead.

Beth's immediate thoughts, in order, were: thank God for sensible teenage girls; and what on earth had got into Joe? Followed by: what the hell was Oli playing at, letting his brother get into such a state?

Chapter 21

CARRIE WAS AS GOOD as her word, and the address came through as Beth was putting on her shoes.

Google said twelve minutes. She made it in ten.

She needn't have worried about locating the correct house. The staccato pulse of purple-and-red disco lights through the lounge window was a clear giveaway. The house was a semi with a neat front garden and a narrow driveway. A gang of kids decorated the front steps. They were drinking and laughing and having a good time. Unreasonably, she felt irritated.

Beth sat for a few seconds in her car watching them, sorry for what she was about to do, which was – sweep in, scoop up Joe in front of his friends, bundle him into the car and whisk him home. This was going to put a huge dent in his already-uncertain self-confidence. Being rescued by Mum was not cool at the best of times. For Joe, it would be a disaster.

But there was no avoiding it.

She took a steadying breath.

At the sound of her car door slamming, the kids on the steps paused their flirting. They stared at her, intrigued, as she made her way past the van parked in the driveway and walked up to them. No one moved for a second. Then, with exaggerated slowness, they shifted their entwined legs aside to let her pass. Foolish as it was, she was unnerved to hear them laughing behind her back. Sixteen was such a brutal age!

Inside the house was equally intimidating. It was less the volume of the music and more the human cacophony. The rooms reverberated with male yelling and high-pitched female screeching. There were kids everywhere. Beth got some funny looks as she walked further into the house, but no one said anything directly to her. Maybe, she hoped, it wasn't common knowledge that Joe was upstairs, in a state. Feeling like she was invading, she made her way up the stairs, away from the epicentre of the action.

On the landing she was greeted by the sight of three girls in micro-skirts, skinny vests and huge boots banging on the bathroom door. 'Let me in,' the head banshee screamed. 'If you don't, I'm gonna wet myself!' She thumped the door again. When it didn't yield she shouted, 'I ain't pissing in a bucket in the garden just because Joe fucking Truman can't handle his drink.' One last futile thump – black nails against the gloss paint – then she gave up. As she stormed along the landing and caught sight of Beth, her expression and manner flipped. Defiant to embarrassed in a split second. She obviously recognised Beth, although the recognition was not mutual. Beth's hopes for a quiet exit faded.

Beth waited for the girls to disappear downstairs before tapping at the door. Her more subtle approach worked. The door opened a crack and a young girl with way too much make-up obscuring her features peeped out.

'I'm Beth, Joe's mum,' Beth announced, somewhat redundantly, there weren't any other middle-aged woman roaming around the party.

The girl stepped back and opened up.

Joe was, as she'd imagined, sprawled on the floor, but instead of a frenzy of spasms, he was still. Absolutely still – which was not normal. The room smelt of vomit and perfume and air freshener.

'Joe. Your mum's here.' The girl kneeling next to him patted his arm ineffectually.

He wasn't merely drunk, he was totally out of it.

Beth crouched down in the tiny space between the bath and his body and looked at her son's face. It was slack, the features dragged to the left. He looked like he'd had a stroke.

'Joe.' The girl with copper-coloured hair tried again to rouse him, to no effect.

'It's okay.' Beth was grateful to both of them, but she wished they would leave her to it. He was her boy. Her responsibility. She needed to get him home. 'Joe!' she shouted. They all jumped. 'I need you to open your eyes and look at me.'

Painfully slowly, his lids fluttered and lifted.

'Joe!' This time with even more volume and feeling. 'You're on the floor in the bathroom at the party. You need to get up.' He shook his head, but at least that was proof of comprehension. Small victories. 'Have you managed to get him to drink any water?'

The standing girl nodded, the kneeling girl shook her head.

Beth went with the one closest to the action. 'Do you know what he's been drinking?'

'No, sorry. There's loads of stuff in the kitchen.' The copper-haired girl seemed disappointed in herself, bless her. She tried to make amends. 'But he has thrown up, loads. So I think a lot of it has come out.' Thank heavens for small mercies.

'Can one of you go and find Oli for me, please?'

They looked at each other. Playing nursemaid in a vomit-fragranced bathroom surprisingly seemed to hold more appeal than re-entering the noisy fray downstairs.

'I need him to help me get Joe into the car.'

Another glance passed between them. It was the standing girl who finally accepted the job. She pulled her skinny jersey dress down over her slim thighs and fluffed her hair. A quick check in the mirror and she set off.

It wasn't a big house, but it took more than ten minutes for her to find Oli or, possibly more accurately, for Oli to make it upstairs. He appeared in the doorway, took one look at his brother and said, 'Daft sod.'

With one girl in the bathroom and one out on the landing, Beth was very conscious they had an audience. 'Thank you so much for looking after him, but we'll take it from here.'

The sensible girl – Carrie? – stood up and edged past Oli; one backward glance and she left them to it. Oli came into the bathroom and hunkered down. 'Can he walk?' He was grinning, that's what really ticked Beth off.

'I don't know. I can't see his sticks anywhere. Do you know where they are?'

Oli shrugged, not bothered. Her irritation burnt. They would have to manage without them. Besides, given the state Joe was in, his sticks would be merely another hindrance.

'Didn't you know that he was up here? Like this?'

'No.'

'Well, you should have!'

Oli shrugged and the urge to berate him intensified, but Beth's more pressing priority was Joe. They squeezed in on either side of him and readied themselves. Beth could smell the booze on both their breaths. One sweet – Oli; one acrid – Joe.

Oli was still deeply unconcerned. 'He's just had a bit too much. He'll be fine after he sleeps it off.'

'Well, thank you for that, Dr Truman.' Beth switched her attention back to Joe. 'Joe, listen to me: on the count of three, we're going to stand you up and we're going to help you down to the car. Are you ready? You're going to need to help us.' Joe made a noise. Beth counted out loud, 'One, two, three.' The second countdown of his birthday.

They heaved. She stumbled and Oli had to bear most of the weight, but somehow they managed to get Joe up off the floor. He was astonishingly heavy. In what must have looked like a terrible episode of the Chuckle Brothers, they manoeuvred him out of the bathroom and along the landing, but Beth ground to a halt at the top of the stairs. The stairs were steep and narrow, impossible to go down two-abreast. Joe was a dead weight. What if they dropped him?

Oli, on the other hand, was blasé. 'What have you stopped for?'

'We can't get him down there.'

They held Joe's sagging frame between them. 'Well, what do you suggest, Mum? We can't stand here all night.'

She was panicking, sweating inside her coat. 'I don't know. Give me a minute to think.'

'Well, can you think a bit quicker – he's fucking heavy.' Oli would never normally swear in front of her.

She hadn't the energy to say anything. Besides, inside she was swearing herself.

Joe sank further, and Beth let him. Oli no longer looked amused. He looked pissed off. A lad came bounding up the stairs, glanced at them, smirked, edged past them and disappeared into the bathroom. No offer of help.

In the end they sat Joe down and, with Beth behind pushing and Oli in front pulling, they managed to get him to bottom-shuffle down the stairs. Their last struggle, down the drive and into the car, was watched by the audience on the front step. In that moment Beth hated them all.

She got in the car and gathered herself, expecting Oli to get in beside her, but he opened the door and stuck his head inside. 'Hope he's okay.' He started to withdraw.

'Wait. Aren't you coming home with me?'

'No, Mum. I'm not. It's my birthday and it's ten-fifteen. You said midnight.'

'But what about Joe?'

He shrugged. 'He'll be all right. He's just drunk. See you later.' And with that Oli walked away.

Chapter 22

IT WAS TYPICAL. HE should have known. Who was he kidding? Oli did know – from bitter experience. That was why he was so fucking mad. On what planet was it fair that he had to babysit his brother on his birthday? His anger sparked on the memories of birthdays past. There were plenty to choose from: having to pretend to blow out the candles on their joint birthday cakes *to let Joe have a chance*; his mum engineering Joe-wins when they played Musical Statues and Bumps; the time he really wanted to have a go-karting party, but was told 'no' *because of Joe*. And their birthday was simply a heightened example of the never-ending Joe Roadshow. It was the same the rest of the time – having to wait, having to be patient, having to fit their lives around Joe's CP. Oli couldn't wait to be old enough to leave home and become his own man. He was sick of it. Sod Joe! Sod his mum. In search of another drink, or three, he headed into the kitchen.

Danny was there, surrounded by a wodge of people,

Oli's best mates Tom and Aaron among them. They were looking at something on Danny's phone, laughing. Oli grabbed a bottle, not caring what it was. He popped the cap, drank deeply, big sweet-and-sour glugs. Cider. He hated the stuff. It was warm, but it was alcohol. It would do. After a few seconds they registered his presence. The laughing stopped, abruptly, and they split apart. Danny pocketed his phone like a fucking magician. Suspicion flared.

'What were ya looking at?' Casual, like – for now.

'Nothing, bro.'

That was Danny's first mistake. Oli felt the familiar prickle of his anger tightening. He was no one's 'bro'. He certainly wasn't Danny's. But some people just couldn't read the room. The stupid cunt went to put his arm around Oli's shoulders. That was his second mistake. Oli's anger hardened into sharp spikes. He shrugged Danny off. The atmosphere in the kitchen stiffened. 'Show me.'

Danny went to walk away. Now that was plain fucking disrespectful. Oli shoved him, hard. He was up for this, whatever 'this' was going to be. Danny smacked into the table. As it shunted across the kitchen floor it made a nasty, satisfying scraping noise.

'I said, "Show me".'

Then Tom started acting like a complete tool as well. 'Leave it, Ol. It was nothing.'

His snivelling only made Oli more determined, and more fucked off. 'If it's nothing, show me.'

Oli could tell Danny still wasn't taking him seriously – which was his third, and by far his biggest, mistake. Oli struck hard and fast. It was better that way. More effective. More rewarding. One punch, his thumb tucked in properly to avoid any possible damage to his hand – he had football in the morning.

Danny's head snapped back, then recoiled, like a cartoon character. Blood from both nostrils. His eyes popping with shock. But he could still talk, more's the pity. 'You fucking psycho!'

How stupid was this guy? The weird thing was that Oli always felt at his calmest just after the explosion. The lashing out obviously released something that was trapped inside him. 'One more time, Danny. Your phone?' He held out his hand. Smiled. 'Please.'

Tom, the worm, bailed Danny out of the corner he'd backed himself into. 'Give it to him, if he's so fucking desperate to see it.' It was pathetic how keen they all were to avoid a fight. Oli wasn't surprised. He was discovering that very few people, when it really came down to it, were prepared to step up. Despite his bleeding nose, Danny still seemed reluctant to comply, but eventually he offered it up, because he really didn't have a choice and he knew it.

It was, as Oli had suspected, a video of his brother. It showed him bum-shuffling his way down the stairs, then being dragged out of the house to the car by Oli and his mum. Oli could feel their eyes on him, waiting for his reaction. He kept them waiting. He watched the shaky footage, with its hurt-your-ears soundtrack of music, shouting and drunken laughter, three times. In the video Joe looked like a drunken sack of shit. A broken puppet. A joke. Pitiful. Pathetic. Pissed. All of those things.

He also looked like Oli.

And Oli hated it. He wished, not for the first time and, no doubt, not for the last, that he didn't have a twin. Hell, that he didn't have a brother – at least not one like Joe. That was shitty of him, but he was a bit of a shit. He deleted the video. Passed the phone back to Danny. The atmosphere quivered.

'Some people really can't handle their drink, can they?' He took a swig of his Dark Fruit.

The bubble of tension burst and they all laughed.

It was time Joe started fighting his own battles.

Chapter 23

BETH DROVE HOME WITH the window open to mitigate the dreadful smell and to keep Joe awake – the latter was more successful. Beth didn't know who she was more infuriated with: Joe for getting himself into such a state or Oli for letting him, then flatly refusing to come home with them.

Yes, it was Oli she was most mad at.

Joe she was worried about. His head kept dipping forward. Each time it did, she said something to him, not in expectation of a coherent response, but more to check he was still conscious. At the junction she contemplated turning left and heading for the hospital, but her rational side told her it wasn't necessary. He'd obviously been very, very sick, which must have cleared a lot of the alcohol out of his system.

At home Joe cooperated as best he could, but it was still difficult. Somehow she managed to manoeuvre him onto the sofa. She wasn't about to tackle any more stairs. She pulled off his trainers and his socks, with some difficulty, and threw them out of the back door. He could rescue them the next day if he wanted them badly enough. It felt invasive undoing and removing his belt, but she did it to make him more comfortable. She left him in his jeans, but struggled to work off his T-shirt because it was in a disgraceful state. She bagged and binned it. Two pillows under his head, his duvet draped over him, a sick bowl by his side. The relief of having him home and safe rinsed through her.

She made herself a mug of tea and brought it through to the lounge. Surprisingly, and reassuringly, he wasn't asleep. 'Sorry.' He sounded like he'd been yelling into the teeth of a storm.

'So you should be.'

He took a few clogged breaths. She revised her anger, knocking it down a couple of notches, but she was still running on adrenaline. 'What on earth possessed you?'

The normal exuberance – and stupidity – of youth? But Joe wasn't a normal, stupid youth. That was the one thing his CP ensured.

'It's my birthday, and I'll get pissed if I want to,' he sang. It was a weak attempt at bravado. 'I was celebrating.'

'I understand that, but why get into such a state?'

'I don't know.' She was surprised to hear an edge in his voice.

'What were you drinking?'

'Some cider, a beer, something blue, some Jack D, I think. Not sure.'

It was so out of character. Control was the be-all and end-all for Joe. It was his ingrained response.

'How are you feeling now?' She knew the answer to that.

He spoke to the ceiling. 'Crap. And totally humiliated.'

She let his admission land in the middle of their quiet, comfortable lamp-lit lounge. He was right; the events at the house had been humiliating and he would, no doubt, pay for them dearly. But she was his mum and, as such, she was pre-coded to try and make things better than they really were, even if it required her to lie. 'I'm not sure many people noticed.'

'Yeah, right.' The bitterness in his words stung.

'Hey.' She shrugged. 'We've all done it.' She hadn't, but it was something to say.

'But it's not as funny, is it? Who wouldn't want to see the local spaz getting wrecked and his mum turning up to take him home.'

Joe's obvious misery burnt off the last streaks of her residual anger. He didn't shift his position, but she could see the tension in his prone body. None of this was doing him any good, but she knew that telling him to calm down wasn't going to work. 'You mustn't—'

He interrupted her. 'What, Mum? What mustn't I? There's no getting away from it. I made a complete tit of myself tonight. And a lot of people saw me.'

In the low light she couldn't be sure, but she thought he might be on the verge of tears. Another humiliation. She looked away, to give him a chance to wipe his face. She scrabbled around for something positive to say. 'The girls seemed nice, especially the one who rang me.'

Joe groaned and rolled onto his side. 'Please, Mum. Can you just leave me alone.'

She had no choice but to do as he asked.

In bed she lay in the dark, worrying he was going to be sick and choke. She got up and opened her bedroom door wider, listened. She was reassured to hear him snoring. She climbed back into bed.

'Spaz.' It was such an appalling word – and to use it about yourself. Her stomach ached for him. Joe would never have said it if he hadn't been drunk. It was not a word that had ever been used in her house or, to her knowledge, in his hearing. It was offensive and outdated, but on a simplistic, brutal level it was accurate.

Spastic, meaning *related to or affected by muscle spasm* – the classic affliction of people with cerebral palsy. It explained Joe's crabbed left hand and the uneven CP swoop when he walked. The spasticity down the left side of his body was the reason he'd had to endure years of operations and painful physio. Why he was perpetually tired. Why his chest was always a concern. Why she worried so much.

Beth sat up and switched on the light in an attempt to put a stop to this train of thought. It was self-indulgent, redundant and totally unlike her. She was made of sterner stuff. As she looked round her oasis of a bedroom, it occurred to her that she hadn't heard Oli come in. She checked her phone. It was 1.13 a.m., way past his midnight curfew. Where the hell was he? Doing precisely what he wanted, as usual, she suspected. Getting drunk safely, having fun, no doubt with one of the girls. The ever-present contrast and conflict with regard to her boys reared its ugly head, yet again.

Identical twins were meant to be just that, weren't they? Exact copies of each other. And Joe and Oli did look remarkably similar, right down to the shape of their eyes and the way their hair curled up at the front if it was left to grow – like Ian's used to. But they were, and always had been, patently and markedly not the same. It was a dissonance that she and the boys were used to, but other people found it unnerving, and fascinating. Throughout the twins' lives she'd seen the curiosity flare in strangers' eyes. They'd glance, notice the striking similarities and the profound differences between the two of them, look away, then look back – their brains scrambling to accommodate the sight of two children who, although twins, were not the same. The disparity had obviously been there from birth, but what had started out as merely a differential in size had become a marked difference in capacity. On a couple of memorable occasions complete strangers had come up to Beth and openly sympathised with her about Joe, while cooing over Oli. And now they were grown, there was no getting around it: Oli was taller, stronger, fitter and, self-evidently, not disabled.

Beth switched off the light, lay on her back and looked at the ceiling. The house and the street outside were quiet. It was late, she was tired, she needed to get some sleep, but it eluded her. One son home and shattered, the other out and partying – she worried about them both.

Chapter 24

Joe hadn't slept. Or maybe he had, for a short while, but it hadn't been the annihilating blackout he'd been hoping for, more a stuttery sway between consciousness and blankness. He couldn't even get pissed properly. He hadn't needed the sick bowl his mother had left for him, he had nothing left to throw up – the burn in his throat was testimony to that – but the glass of water was welcome. He downed it.

Christ! What a cluster fuck.

And it had all started so well.

He'd been nervous in the Uber on the way over to the party, but being with Oli had helped. When Joe had gone to stash his sticks out of the way, behind the wheelie bins at the side of the house, Oli had said, 'You don't have to do that.'

Joe had responded, 'I know.'

Enough said. There were times when his brother's indifference was a blessing.

They'd walked into the party together and everything

had been okay. Oli's friends had raised their beer bottles and nodded. If they'd been surprised to see them out together, they'd covered it up well. The music was loud, which made talking unnecessary. That had been fine with Joe. He drank the beer that he was passed quickly, the second even faster, and by the third he started to relax. He recognised quite a few of the faces from school, but none were what you'd call friends. By his fourth drink he didn't care. He remembered wandering into the kitchen and getting into conversation with a girl with shiny black nails and a loud voice. She'd laughed a lot – at what, he couldn't remember. At some point a random guy came in, stripped off his T-shirt and insisted on showing his new tattoo to anyone and everyone, whether or not they were interested. Joe didn't think he'd danced. He hoped to fuck he hadn't. Then he'd started feeling ill.

After that it was less clear.

He couldn't remember how he got upstairs, never mind into the bathroom – the scene of his humiliation. The shame was like tar on his soul. Strangers' hands holding him as he vomited into the toilet. Girls? More than one? Looking after him, gently, kindly. His body heavy and unwieldy in their hands. They had smelt nice. He'd smelt rank. He remembered someone digging around in the pockets of his jeans. It occurred to him that they must have been looking for his phone, but he hadn't realised what they were doing at the time. It was the closest he'd ever got to the opposite sex. The intrusion of this thought appalled him.

At one point his leg had gone into spasm. His foot had connected with something soft. There had been a quiet 'oomph'. Christ, he'd kicked one of the girls. A voice had asked him to lift his face off the toilet seat. A warm flannel was wiped across his face as he dribbled and slobbered. The fragments were jumbled, but there were enough of them to form a very un-pretty picture. He remembered the swish of copper-coloured hair. The peeling label on the bottle of bleach on the floor beside the toilet. A sponge fish on the side of the bath, staring at him in disgust. Someone banging on the door. Screeching. The scenes, smells and sensations spooled through his brain relentlessly.

Then, just when he thought it couldn't get any worse, his mother had turned up.

She'd taken charge. But he hadn't complied with her instructions. He couldn't be arsed. Then Oli had appeared, looking down at him, hands in his pockets, a smirk on his face. Brotherly love cancelled. Joe remembered desperately wanting to go to sleep where he lay, but that hadn't been allowed. They'd yanked him to his feet, dragged him down the stairs and out of the house. The floor had tipped and swung wildly as the faces loomed in and out of his eyeline. Somehow he'd ended up in the car.

Back at home, tucked up safe and sound, he'd been a dick to his mum, saying stuff about his CP. Bitter, self-pitying crap. Had he cried? He wished he was dead. He rolled over and faced the back of the sofa, burrowed himself deep into the cushions, trying to muffle the shame. He didn't know whether it was the kindness of the girls, the mockery of the mob or the disappointment on his mother's face that was the worst. Yes, he did; it was the kindness. The girls had looked after him like he was a baby.

He would have to go back into school and face it down. By Monday morning the story would have had plenty of time to do the rounds. It had been bad enough before – the pity and the awkward efforts not to make his condition 'a thing', the special considerations – but now it would be a hundred times worse. He would be the butt of a juggernaut of whispered gossip.

He closed his eyes. Slept. But only for a little while. Then he was awake again. Unaware of what had woken him, until he heard the front door shut.

Oli.

His brother was quiet, trying not to disturb their mum no doubt. Shoes off the minute he stepped into the hall, his keys lowered onto the side-table as if they were made of glass. Then came the burglar-creep along the hall to the kitchen, the sound of the tap running. Joe heard each swallow. Rehydrating. It was a surprisingly sensible thing for Oli to do. Then Joe remembered – Oli had a match the next day; correction, this coming afternoon. Joe listened to his brother retrace his steps along the hall.

He lay still, closed his eyes. He sensed Oli stop in the doorway. They both held their breaths. What was he doing? Joe felt trapped and stupid and angry in equal measure. He waited for his brother to say something.

After what felt like for ever, he heard Oli walk away.

Chapter 25

IT WASN'T UNTIL late morning that Joe's hangover properly kicked in. By that point he'd made it upstairs into his own room, but even there he had very little peace. First he heard Oli thundering around the house getting ready for football, yelling about his shin pads, being deliberately noisy? Then his mum kept popping her head around his door, offering him drinks and snacks. Joe knew she wanted to talk about what had happened. He did not. He didn't want her empathy. Each time she came into his room he faked sleep. He was tired of pretending that everything was okay and he was fine, which is what she wanted to hear.

Eventually his own stink got to him. He hauled his ass out of bed and went for a shower. It helped. A bit. He was pulling on some clean clothes when the doorbell rang. He went out onto the landing and listened.

'Hello.' He could hear the caution in his mother's voice. She obviously didn't recognise whoever was on the doorstep. He couldn't hear the response, but something changed in her tone. 'Oh, of course. I'm so sorry I didn't recognise you. I was in such a fluster last night.'

Christ, now what?

'I found these in the garden, at Emily's house.' A girl's voice. There was a clatter – his sticks being returned. Joe peered over the banister into the hall.

'It's very kind of you to bring them round. We were wondering where they were. Would you like to come in for a drink?'

What was his mother playing at?

The girl stepped inside and bent down to unlace her Converse. A ripple of copper hair fell forward, obscuring her face. The girl from the bathroom?

'Please, don't bother.' His mum was doing her overly-friendly voice.

The girl wobbled slightly. 'No. It's okay.' She was struggling to get the second high-top off. Instinctively his mother reached out to steady her. Shoes off, the girl straightened up. 'How's he doing?'

Joe stepped back as if scalded.

His mum actually laughed. 'Not so bad, considering. He deserves to feel a lot worse.'

They moved away towards the kitchen.

Joe now had a dilemma. Leave his mother with the girl and allow the grilling to commence or head downstairs, face into the embarrassment, and try to limit the damage. Neither appealed, but he found himself on the stairs, then in the kitchen. They both turned round and looked at him as he entered.

'It walks among us.' His mum, trying to be funny.

The girl smiled, politely. She was strikingly pretty, although Joe knew she wouldn't have been considered fanciable by the lads at school – she was too individual-looking for that. She didn't have the straightened hair or the professional make-up that the rated girls had. She reminded Joe of Jennifer Lawrence, her manner as much as her looks. All these thoughts whizzed through his head as she sat still and composed, on one of the high stools in their kitchen. There was the longest, most awkward pause in history.

His mum filled the chasm. 'Carrie called round to check you weren't dead.'

Thank God his mum had said her name. Joe spread his arms wide, as if to prove his mother's point, and immediately thought better of it. He was wearing his *Chronicles of Riddick* T-shirt and a pair of saggy sweatpants. Worse, his feet were bare. He curled back in on himself, hid his left hand behind his back. No one wanted to see what he had to offer. They were both still looking at him, waiting, but for what?

'I think a "Thank you" might be in order... for last night.' He loved his mum, but sometimes he really didn't. 'Carrie was also kind enough to rescue your sticks. You left them at the house. Behind a wheelie bin, for some reason.'

'Thanks.' He sounded ungrateful, and pathetic – a tricky combo to carry off and yet he was managing it. He tried to toughen up, and soften his tone at the same time. 'From what I remember, I was in a bit of a state last night. Sorry about that.' He wished she'd leave, but no one seemed to be going anywhere.

'That's okay.' She smiled. Why the hell had she come round?

'What would you like, Carrie? Tea, coffee, we've got fresh juice and squash.' His mum was overdoing it, as always.

'Just a glass of water, please.'

Then his mother excelled herself. 'Why don't you take Carrie down to the den. I'll bring the drinks in a minute.' It was a glass of water, what was she going to do: go and collect it from the river?

Joe had no choice.

He was hyper-aware of Carrie walking behind him, holding back, as he made his way down to the den. Steps of any variety, even familiar ones, were always a challenge – the way his left foot turned in threw his balance. As a result he had to take it one stair at a time, like a pensioner or a stroke victim. He was so sodding slow, but at least he'd showered, so although he looked like a bag of washing, he didn't actually smell like one.

Once in the den, Joe became acutely conscious of the high register of nerdiness in the room. Sure, the massive screen for watching movies and gaming was cool, and the L-shaped sofa was perfect for whatever you might have on your mind, but he was highly conscious of the huge collection of games with their heavy emphasis on role-play, and of his models. They sat, pride of place – at his mother's insistence – on the shelves that ran along the back wall of the den. There were a lot of them.

He risked a glance at Carrie. She'd walked past him and was studying the display. Could it get any worse? With her back to him, he was free to study her. Her spine was straight, her shoulder blades discernible through her top; her legs were long and slim in her jeans. Even in her socks, she was definitely taller than him, but then again most people were. The precision of her limbs was unnerving. She had the posture of a dancer, or at least she stood like Joe imagined a dancer might stand. She turned round. Caught him looking. Where was his mum when he needed her?

'They're unusual. You collect them?' She indicated his models.

'No, I made them.' Full disclosure on the nerd front. She might as well know the extent of his geekdom.

She pointed to one of his Sirens of the Soul maquettes. 'I like these.' There were seven sirens, each possessing a different psychic power, clues to which were hidden about their bodies and on their clothing. The one Carrie liked was called Foresight. She was blind, but had eyes in the palms of her hands – like stigmata. 'What are they?'

Joe couldn't work out why she was bothering. He searched her expression for a clue to her motivation and found nothing, other than what looked like genuine curiosity. That was *not* what he normally saw in the faces of girls – or of most people when he talked about his interests, which was why he didn't.

She'd already seen him chuck up into a toilet. What had he to lose? 'They're characters in a fantasy series I'm developing. They're practice pieces. I want to work in animation. A lot of the studios like their animators to have model-making skills.' It was way too much detail. He was nailing his own coffin shut. Real life wasn't an episode of *The Big Bang Theory*.

She leant in closer, studying the Sirens. 'They're kind of creepy, but beautiful at the same time.' Which was exactly what he'd been aiming for.

And somehow that was it. The disgrace of the previous night was disposed of and they were having a normal conversation, which was the weirdest thing that had happened to Joe in a very long time.

Chapter 26

CARRIE KISSED JOE TWO weeks later, sitting on the bench in a bus shelter, on a day that felt like summer, despite the rain and the biting wind. He was so taken aback that he didn't react. She stopped, withdrew, looked confused. 'Sorry. I thought you wanted me to.'

Her retreat scared him. Had he stuffed it up before anything had even begun? He flustered. 'God. No. I mean, "yes"' I wanted you to. Want you to. I was just... surprised.'

She tilted her head. 'Why?'

His heart was battering. He wished he could rewind time by a few seconds, simply lean into her and kiss her back, like a normal human being. 'I don't know.' He did really. He deflected, started talking shite. 'Because you're taller than me.'

She frowned, then smiled. 'And height is a critical factor in fancying someone, is it?' She was mocking him, which was a lot better than her being mad at him.

'It is, for a lot of girls.'

'Not me.'

Joe heard what she was saying; he knew Carrie was offering him something he deeply, desperately wanted, but still he hesitated. The truth was he couldn't believe that his CP wasn't an issue. A turn-off.

'Joe?'

'I didn't think you liked me – not like that anyway.'

'Well,' she held his gaze, 'I do.'

She was so brave and fearless and unique and beautiful. His heartbeat dropped a notch. It no longer felt like he was having a cardiac arrest. He stared at the freckles on her nose. He wondered if she liked them. He did. 'That's nice to know.'

'Are you sure?' She was laughing now. Not at him, *with* him.

It allowed him to breathe. 'Yep.' He made himself sit still, tried to calm down. 'Yes. I'm sure.'

She stopped laughing and looked at his lips.

It was now or never.

He leant in and kissed her.

Chapter 27

CARRIE'S IMPROMPTU VISIT the day after Joe's birthday had a more positive effect than any combination of orange juice, paracetamol or maternal sympathy. The brittle shell of a boy that Beth had brought home from the party was transformed, after little more than an hour with this young woman, back into her son.

Beth had been at a loss to know where to go after Joe's 'spastic' comment, but to her relief she found she didn't have to 'go' anywhere, as Joe found his own way out of his slump. He went into school on the Monday, toughed it out through a couple of days of snide comments, and then they, and he, moved on. Just like that. It was a small, but glorious miracle. The incident didn't seem to have done any damage to his confidence at all. In fact, it – correction, his connection with Carrie – seemed to have the opposite effect.

Of course Beth's initial joy was qualified by a degree of worry. What would a girl as pretty as Carrie want with Joe: a shy sixteen-year-old with little conversation beyond gaming and films, who couldn't hold his drink and who had, to top it off, thrown up in front of, and on her?

But inauspicious as their first meeting had been, it soon became apparent that there was a genuine friendship developing between the two of them. Carrie came to the house often over the subsequent weeks. When she visited she always seemed happy to stay and talk to Beth for a little while, before disappearing with Joe into the den or his room. Beth, of course, fished for information whilst making sure Carrie felt welcome. Over tea and chocolate fingers, Beth found out that Carrie went to Belton Hall High, not Holroyd's, which was closer to her home, but was not an option because her mother taught English there; that she was clever, had a small but tight group of friends and was sporty – athletics and netball. She was close to her dad (his profession was not volunteered) and she had no siblings, which, Beth detected, was a regret. Beth also established that Carrie was sensible without being dull, in possession of plenty of opinions without the impulse always to share them, and was kind. Beth liked her. She could see why Joe liked her too. That Joe was forming a bond with such a sound young woman gladdened Beth's heart. A friend like Carrie was exactly what he needed.

Beth realised she'd got it all wrong when she walked in on them making pancakes one Sunday lunchtime. She sensed as much as saw that there was something different about the way they were moving around each other. The spaces between them seemed to have shrunk, a barrier removed. There was an ease and a synchronicity at play that was fascinating to watch. When she saw Joe rest his hand in the small of Carrie's back and lean his head on her shoulder, she knew they were more than friends.

Her surprise troubled her.

She said her hellos and left them to their brunch preparations, took herself upstairs, out of their way. There she sat on her bed and examined her conscience. It was murky. The deeply uncomfortable truth was that she'd assumed Carrie's friendship with Joe sprang from kindness, not attraction; and, even more shockingly, that because Carrie was pretty she couldn't be interested in Joe as a boyfriend. Beth flushed. Her own son, and she'd consigned him to the friend-zone.

Because?

Well, because he was normally shy around girls. To be honest, around most people.

Because he'd never expressed any interest in having a girlfriend.

Because he was a bit of a nerd, and nerds famously came late to relationships and sex, didn't they?

And – her face burnt hotter – because of his CP.

She thought of herself as Joe's staunchest advocate, and here she was reacting with the same narrow prejudice she would have been appalled to find in others.

She heard music from the kitchen. Carrie was into her music. How often had she and Joe sat, side-by-side in the back of her car, sharing headphones, when she dropped them into town or at the cinema? Christ, she had been blind. Why wouldn't Carrie think of Joe that way? He was lovely, creative, considerate, good-looking.

'Mum!'

She was being summoned. She went out onto the landing.

'Do you want a pancake? We've made loads.' She could hear the lightness in Joe's voice.

'Yeah. Thanks. I'll be down in a minute.'

He was happy.

Carrie was lovely.

Them going out together was a good thing. She just hoped it would last.

Chapter 28

TWO YEARS LATER

FOR THEIR EIGHTEENTH BIRTHDAY, Oli booked The Oyster. It was a fancy restaurant in Covent Garden, which Kieran, their team's number ten, had recommended. Kieran knew all the cool places, or least he claimed to. Oli had been determined to come up to town to celebrate. No more lame house-parties for him.

Of course Joe had pulled a face at having to travel 'all the way' into central London, but that was no surprise; when did he ever want to go anywhere or do anything different? He behaved like a forty-year-old. But sod him. Oli couldn't think of anywhere better to celebrate becoming an adult, legally, *and* realising his dream. His life was finally starting for real, and he wanted to mark the occasion with something special.

To kick off the proceedings in style he organised a limo to take them into town. He had the cash, so why not be flash? If there was an upside in terms of ease for his whiney little brother, so be it. Sometimes it was tricky to avoid doing something nice. It was great sitting in the clogged traffic around Piccadilly Circus sipping champagne, looking out through the tinted windows at the crowds. This was the way to travel.

To his relief, the restaurant looked bang-on. Proper fancy. It had a waterfall that cascaded down behind the bar from the mezzanine. According to Kieran, there was a private dining room on the upper floor that was regularly booked out by Premier League footballers and celebs who wanted to be seen looking good, but not be seen getting drunk and stuffing their faces with wagyu burgers. Leyla, Oli's current girlfriend, was on high alert, hoping to snap someone famous arriving or, better still, departing. She'd been buzzing for weeks about his birthday. She'd bought a new outfit – not that that was much of a departure from the norm – and had her nails and hair done specially. He smiled at her. She looked good. She didn't return his smile, she was too busy looking at the cocktail list. He encouraged everyone to choose whatever they wanted.

This was on him. His treat.

They were onto a second round of drinks by the time Auntie Sab turned up with Anton, her plus-one for the evening. Oli had expected Aleah to come to the meal with her mum (old habits and all that shit), but she'd declined – sent a deeply inappropriate video instead, which had made him snort toothpaste out of his nose, much to Leyla's disgust. Anton, Sab's current partner, was a nice bloke, easy-going, funny and obviously very into her, but that was no guarantee he would survive any longer than the others. Sab obviously liked male company, but seemed to lack commitment when it came to the opposite sex. She was more like a man than a woman. In fact, it suddenly occurred to Oli, she was quite male in the way she lived her life, full stop.

There were kisses all round. More chat. More congratulations. Then the waiter came to 'walk them through' the menu.

The food was fancy, artfully arranged on the plates. Oli thought, unkindly, that it must have seen as much tweezer action as Leyla's eyebrows. She was in her element, photographing every course from multiple angles, and posting live updates. She was very happy with the volume of likes, kept showing him the number tick upwards. He couldn't really be arsed with the social-media side of things himself – a legacy of his mum's aversion perhaps, and because he was a serious footballer, not some flash wannabe – but Leyla was all over it, which did no harm to his profile. He was, as she often pointed out, photogenic; and the more of a following he built up, the better the opportunities there would be for sponsorship and product placement.

Despite her looks, Leyla was really quite sharp commercially. That wasn't why Oli was with her, obviously. He liked Leyla, thought they suited each other. They had fun together, had shared interests – they were both gym addicts – and there was the sex, about which she was as enthusiastic as him. But as she moved his mum's wine glass out of the way to get a better shot of the salted-chocolate shards that had arrived with the coffee, he wondered how long they were going to last.

It was odd to have something in common with his forty-something-year-old non-auntie.

Oli glanced across at his brother. Joe had his arm draped along the back of Carrie's chair. The champagne and cocktails had obviously kicked in because he looked relaxed – well, at least as relaxed as he ever did. Seeing a version of his own face across the table provoked the usual mixed emotions in Oli, chief amongst them the old, oh-so-familiar frustration. Rationally, Oli knew it was unreasonable to feel resentment. Neither of them had chosen to be twins, it was simply a twist of biology, but he hated the constant comparisons, the unreasonable expectations about their relationship and the uncommented-on elephant in the room: his awareness that he'd been the lucky one. Oli switched his gaze away from his brother.

It was easier to look elsewhere. Carrie was talking to Sab, her face turned away from Joe. Carrie looked like she was really enjoying herself. She laughed at something Sab said with the same lack of self-consciousness that she had about everything. Oli watched Joe surreptitiously stroke her bare shoulder with his cramped left hand – touching base. It was a small, intimate gesture that made Oli feel uncomfortable. They were as tight as ever. He almost envied them.

He shifted his attention to his mum. She was looking around the restaurant. Her cheeks were tinged pink from the booze, her hair loose around her face. She was wearing what, for her, was a tight-fitting dark-blue dress. Oli was struck by how attractive she was. It wasn't a thought that had occurred to him before. Well, you didn't look at your own mum that way, did you? Not unless you were seriously sick. He had to think about how old she was. Had she turned forty-one or forty-two on her last birthday? He should know. Unlike Sab, Beth never dated, never mentioned men or relationships – not in connection with herself anyway. Ever. Why? he wondered. Should he ask? No, that would be too weird.

He gave himself a mental slap. Such reflections were hardly helping him get into the party vibe. Families – they were a load!

And that load wasn't about to get any lighter. Because after the consumption of the chocolate shards and espressos came the inevitable. His mother picked up her tiny sugar spoon and tapped it against her water glass, calling the table to attention. Sab had to shush Anton, who was in the middle of telling Leyla a joke. Thankfully, Beth didn't get to her feet, but she did sit up straight in her seat, which made her look out of place in the alcohol-oiled, chilled-out atmosphere of the restaurant. When she started talking, it became resoundingly clear why she'd stayed so resolutely single.

'First of all, I want to say a huge "thank you" to Oli for taking care of everything tonight. It's been lovely – really special.' Led by Sab, they all drummed their appreciation on the table. Oli liked the adoration. It felt good. 'Tonight, as you all know, is a double celebration.'

'When is it not!' Anton quipped, only to be glared into silence by Sab.

'First, we're here to celebrate Oli signing his full-time professional contract with AFC Wimbledon.' Leyla whooped at this point. Oli noticed that his mum had finally got the team name right. Beth smiled indulgently and carried on with her speech. 'Thereby achieving a childhood dream, and proving that sometimes kids really do know better than their parents.' There it was, the plural. She had never got over the death of their dad. She would always be a widow. 'I hope you know how proud I am of you, Oli, for everything you've achieved – and, I'm sure, will go on to achieve – with your football.'

There was more drumming, but Oli was acutely aware that despite how huge being signed by Wimbledon was, for his mother, it took second place to them celebrating their birthday.

'It's also, as you all know, Oli and Joe's eighteenth birthday.' Point proved. 'They are officially – as of,' she glanced at her watch, 'seven and a half hours ago – able to drink alcohol legally, which is a good job,' she indicated the collection of smeary glasses on the table, 'to vote, and to get married without my blessing.'

Anton glanced at Joe and Carrie. He looked poised to crack another funny, but the shift in mood around the table obviously made him think better of it. Looking at Sab's expression, Oli wondered if Anton realised his days were numbered.

'And, as much as I know it embarrasses you, I want to take this opportunity to tell you how proud I am... of *both* of you.'

Even-handedness was her mantra. And his fucking curse. Oli made a concerted effort to keep the smile on his face, but it was beginning to feel forced.

She went on, 'When you were born' – not this again! – 'you were both so poorly that I didn't allow myself to think about the future. But even then, as tiny prem babies, you were both fighters, both determined. And that determination has stood you in good stead as you've grown from boys to men.' This was more than embarrassing. Did she even realise that she'd just quoted a boy band? She still wasn't finished. 'Decent, honest, impressive young men.'

The room suddenly felt unbearably claustrophobic. People sitting at the nearby tables were watching and, worse, listening.

'And to mark the occasion,' she reached for her bag and extracted two small gift bags, 'these are for you.' She passed one of the bags to Joe and pushed the other across the table at Oli. 'From me' – here it came – 'and your dad.'

Oli saw Leyla turn round, perhaps expecting their father to make a surprise appearance. He hadn't gone into details with her about his family set-up and, to his relief, she hadn't asked. Now he was going to have to; he couldn't have her going around waiting for his dead dad to rock up.

Neither he nor Joe made a move. Leyla had no such qualms. She stretched out a manicured hand, picked up the gift bag and passed it to Oli. 'Open it, babe.'

Oli met Joe's eye. There were traditions to maintain. Synchronised present-unwrapping being one of them. The compulsion to accommodate each other's feelings had been drilled into them since childhood. With a barely perceptible nod, they went in.

Present out of its fancy bag.

Paper ripped off.

Posh box snapped open.

Inside – a watch.

A very nice watch, with a simple, clear face. Gold, by the look of it. A leather strap. Quality. Traditional. An apt metaphor for everything their mother endlessly strove to instil in them. Oli heard his mum whisper, 'Look at the back.' He prised the watch from its plush velvet cushion, turned it over and read the inscription. He knew the engravings on both watches would be identical. He leant over the table and kissed her. 'Thank you, Mum.' He heard Joe say the same.

The show was over and he, for one, wanted out.

Check, please! It was time for him to pay the bill and bounce.

They had a club to get to.

Chapter 29

'COME HERE.'

'You come here.' Carrie made Joe walk around the bed to her. Joe didn't mind. He would have walked to the ends of the Earth for her.

'Thank God that's over for another year.' He pulled her to him, but after the briefest of kisses, she wriggled free. He released her. He sat on the bed and watched Carrie take off her dress. He wanted to ask her to come to bed, naked; or, even better, to simply stand there with nothing on and let him look at her, but he didn't. She slipped off her fancy bra and knickers quickly and pulled on a T-shirt and shorts, took out her earrings – left first, then right. She always did it in the same sequence. When she was comfy, she climbed on the bed and sat cross-legged, facing him.

It both frustrated and excited him that Carrie had a force-field around her, a space only he got invited into. Her self-possession made their intimacy special and made him feel worthy, but it also meant he could never relax and simply assume. Her body was unequivocally hers, and the way she used it, when and how she shared it with him, was outside his control. That didn't stop him wanting; if anything, it increased his desire. T-shirt and cotton knickers or heels and a dress – he was crazy about her.

'I thought it was nice.' She started smoothing moisturiser onto her face.

'You think?'

'Yes. It was ritzy and fancy,' she grinned, 'and free. What more do you want from a night out?'

'You.' He leant towards her for another kiss, but she swotted him away.

'We're talking.' She lobbed the tube of moisturiser onto the bedside cabinet. 'Get your head out of your pants – or my pants, to be more accurate.'

He accepted that it was one of those nights. 'It was Oli showing off.'

'Well, why shouldn't he? He's made it as a professional footballer. That's huge.'

'I know. I'm just not comfortable in showy places.'

She looked at him, questioning. That was another thing about Carrie: she really paid attention. She listened to what you hadn't said as well as what you had, made a judgement on when you wanted to be asked about your feelings and when you didn't. Hence her next question wasn't about his self-consciousness, she was probably bored of that particular topic anyway. 'Your mum enjoyed it. Having everyone together. It's important to her, your birthday, isn't it?'

'You could say that.'

'Can I see it?'

He knew she meant the watch. 'I left it downstairs.'

'Joe!'

There was a pause – Carrie's awareness that he found the whole 'presents from his dad' thing totally awkward was warring with her natural curiosity. 'Go get it, if you want to.'

She scooched across the bed, ran off and came back holding the box. She resumed her yoga pose, took the watch out carefully. She dipped her head, reading the inscription: *To Joe. On his eighteenth. So proud of you. Love, Mum and Dad x.* He said nothing. 'It's a very nice watch. Very grown-up.' She held it against her slim wrist.

'It is.'

'But...'

'Nothing. It is, as you say, a nice watch.'

'And yet you don't want it.'

There it was again, her ability to reach behind his words and read his thoughts. 'I really appreciate the thought she puts in every year.'

'But it's too much?'

'Please, Carrie. Can we just leave it for tonight?'

'Okay.' She put the watch on the side, slid into bed and clicked off her lamp.

He got in beside her. The whole left side of his body hurt. Not cramping tonight, more a deep-down fatigue that made him feel ancient, and fucked. Could proximity to his super-fit, increasingly ripped brother really make his symptoms worse? Of course it couldn't, but it felt that way. His twin, the professional footballer. It was like life was rubbing Joe's nose in it.

He shuffled around, trying to find a position that didn't hurt. Couldn't. He tensed, then tried to relax his legs. It made no difference. He was filled with an impotent, but fierce rage. The physical challenges of his CP were his norm. His body had always been a pain. Joe was used to the physical tremors and spasms, managed them; it was the unpredictably of his emotional relationship with his CP that he found harder to deal with. Perhaps it was because sometimes they were ugly emotions that, bizarrely, tended to bubble up at the most inappropriate moments – like at a really cool restaurant with great food and thoughtful gifts, and all the people who mattered most in the world to him. Anger, frustration, jealousy. Who would want to be around a guy with that sort of bitterness swilling around inside him? He arched and flexed, conscious that he was keeping Carrie awake. Self-pity shoved its way onto the list of his many unattractive characteristics.

He felt her hands on his back.

She held them still for a few moments, then began to trail her fingertips back and forth across his shoulders, light pressure at first, then firmer, back to light. She held her body away from him, touched him without expectation. He took what she offered, grateful, focused on what felt good. Slowly he began to relax, hurt less, feel better. The pain retreated, the anger faded, replaced by pleasure.

She said nothing.

After a long time he rolled over to face her and said simply and truthfully, 'I love you.'

Chapter 30

MUCH, MUCH LATER – so much later that it was beginning to get light – Oli stood in the bathroom at Leyla's house. He didn't feel drunk because he wasn't. One upside of the purging was that it got rid of the alcohol as well as the calories. Leyla was flat out, mouth-open pissed in the bed. She would be monosyllabic when she woke, which wouldn't be for hours. When she was hungover she was grumpy and, for a change, quiet. Leyla's parents were relaxed about him staying over, had been from day one. He knew, because they'd told him so, that they saw him as a huge improvement on TJ, her previous boyfriend, but he never felt totally at ease in their house, especially if Leyla wasn't around to act as a buffer.

Suddenly he felt a bit down, which was pathetic. It had been a good night. Everyone had had a great time. The club had been banging. He looked at himself in the mirror. He still had a long way to go, but he would be getting the best of everything now. His fitness, his health, his weight – it would all be more closely scrutinised by people who really knew what they were doing. It would be even more relentless than it had been in the Academy. He knew it was going to be hard work, but he would hack it. He'd held his own against the other signings. He'd matched if not bested Addy, managed to muscle him off the ball a couple of times, and Addy was, as they all knew, the one to watch. Oli was anxious about it, of course he was, but who wouldn't be? Football was a ludicrously competitive career choice, and not only in terms of the opposition.

Out of nowhere, Oli suddenly thought about his dad. If he'd lived, there would have been someone to share this with, someone who would have understood the pressures as well as the pleasures. His mum, Sab, Leyla – even Carrie, bless her – were pleased for him, but football wasn't their world. They didn't get it. Neither did Joe. For a second or two Oli felt sad and acutely lonely. Or, more accurately, very alone. He hated the feeling. Hated himself for succumbing to it. He pulled one of the bath sheets off the rail and wrapped himself in it.

Maybe he was just hungry. Yeah, that was what it was. But he couldn't go crashing about in the Henshaws' kitchen at 6 a.m. making toast. He thought about going back to bed, trying to sleep, but didn't. He sat on the loo. His thoughts snagged, as they so often did, on his brother. Joe would have been tucked up in bed for hours with Carrie.

Carrie was part of the family now. She'd been staying over at the house for what felt like for ever.

When it became clear that Joe and she were in a full-on relationship, Oli had been surprised. First, that his brother had managed to get a girlfriend; second, that Joe was proper sleeping with her; and, third, that their mum seemed to approve or at least, if not approve, not object. It was so *not* her to be relaxed about sex under her roof. But, as ever, exceptions were made. Because this was Joe they were talking about, and Carrie was good for Joe, she made him happy, boosted his confidence, and therefore Carrie was given the red-carpet treatment.

He wondered what the reaction would be if he started bringing Leyla home.

Oli had invited Joe, and Carrie, to the club, but of course his brother had declined. Oli thought Carrie had looked disappointed, as if she'd fancied a proper night out for a change, instead of bed by 11 p.m. Oli would have been fine with her tagging along. Carrie was easy to talk to and she would have loved the club. Music was her thing. He'd heard her singing her way around the house when she hadn't realised anyone was listening. Her voice was good. Not sweet and light, like he'd expected, given her relentless niceness, but strong and distinctive, kind of raw. But they were never going to come out to the club – because of Joe. Dancing was one of the many things his brother didn't do and, therefore, she didn't do either. His brother was one lucky bastard. Carrie put up with a lot to be with him. Not that it was anything to do with Oli. Perhaps that was what love was – putting other people's needs before your own.

On that deep thought, he stood up, headed back to the bedroom.

Leyla had rolled onto her back and was sprawled out in the middle of the bed, dead to the world. He climbed in beside her and gently, but firmly, pushed her over onto her side. She muttered with irritation, didn't wake.

If love was all about compromise, then maybe it wasn't for him after all.

Chapter 31

THREE YEARS LATER

Sabine rocked up on Beth's doorstep at just gone 7 p.m., clutching a bottle of gin – the nice stuff – and a sack. 'Here.' She passed Beth the sack. It was full of logs. 'Thought we could get the fire-pit going. It's a nice night to sit out.'

Beth looked past her at the cloudy sky. 'We've been together at work all day.'

'Are you saying you're sick of me?' Sab mimed offence.

'No. Never.'

'I should bloody well think so.'

Sab got the fire started while Beth organised the drinks and the snacks, a division of labour that reflected their personalities, and their skills.

When they were sorted, Sab dove straight in. 'Are you all right? You've been in a strange mood all day.'

Beth deflected. 'I haven't. I was just busy.' They rented a large workspace in a converted mill building now, had desks that faced each other. The old double act alive and well, and making real money these days. Equal partners, at last. The office was plenty big enough to accommodate them, the six full-time members of staff they currently employed and the huge, very fancy coffee machine that Sab had insisted they buy, although Beth still preferred instant. The mill was a ten-minute drive from each of their houses.

'As you always are, but you're not normally mono-syllabic. Here.' Sab took her drink from Beth and raised it. They clinked rims. 'To the boys.'

It was the twins' twenty-first birthday and the first time, ever, that they'd not spent the day together. Sab pulled a chair up to the fire, kicked off her shoes and tucked a blanket over her knees. It wasn't *that* nice an evening. 'Have you heard from them?'

'Joe FaceTimed me earlier.'

'How's he doing?'

'He's fine.' As he had been for a good while now. Loving being at uni in Manchester, enjoying his Film and Media course, still with Carrie, his final exams on the horizon. He had a lot going on. Too much for him to make the long trip home for his birthday — which was precisely what she'd always wanted for him.

'And Oli?'

'A response to my text at lunchtime. Nothing since.'

Five mouthfuls and Sab's glass was already nearly empty. 'And how's he doing at the moment?'

'The same.'

'Meaning?'

Beth poked the fire, trying to stir some more energy and heat into the heart of it. 'Adrift. He's still struggling to get his head around them dropping him.'

'That was months ago.'

'Yes.' Long enough, in Beth's book at least, to have accepted the decision and to have started to move on. 'He still thinks one of the lower-league clubs will sign him. He keeps mentioning the names of scouts who've been in touch, and openings that might be perfect for him, but I have my doubts. He's in denial.'

'Well, it must be hard, to have it look like it's all happening for you and then for it to be snatched away.'

'Yes. It is. But that's precisely why I wanted him to stick at his studies, so that he would have something to fall back on. Very few of the lads, even the exceptional ones, ever make it as full-time professionals. Deep down, there was always a high probability it wouldn't work out. I warned him, but he didn't listen.'

'He had a decent shot at making his dream a reality. Of course he didn't listen, not when he had clubs clamouring to sign him.'

'Well, there's no one clamouring now. I worry that he got things far too easy, much too quickly.' Beth didn't add – because she hated to admit it, even to Sab – that she had her suspicions about the real reason Brentford had let him go. It was the age-old worry with Oli: his attitude. She'd seen him being subbed off early, to avoid another booking, too many times to be unaware of his struggles to keep his temper in check. The commitment and passion that drove him often tipped over into unfocused aggression on the pitch, and even, from what she'd heard, on the training ground with his teammates. That she hadn't raised this suspicion with Oli was revealing. The truth was she hadn't spoken to him about it precisely because she was afraid of his response.

There was a clink – Sab pouring herself another G&T. She offered Beth a top-up. She declined, but Sab leant over and splashed some more gin into her glass, regardless. 'That's a bit harsh. It wasn't easy for him. He worked hard. Trained hard. He earnt his success.' Sab didn't play favourites, but Beth noticed that she was always quick to defend Oli from criticism.

Beth softened her tone, but not her opinion. 'You know I love him dearly, but I worry that the success he had, going through the system as a kid, gave him too much self-belief. It fed certain strengths and masked his weaknesses. And, let's be honest, he was never lacking in self-confidence. I think that's why he's having such a hard time now that it looks likely he's not going to have a career in football.'

Sab was quiet for a few seconds. 'You are tough on him, you know.' She rested her head against the back of the chair, looked up at the sky. 'Give him time, I'm sure he'll sort himself out in the end.'

Beth wasn't so sure. It had been bad enough when Wimbledon moved Oli on, but being dropped by Brentford, that had sent him into a tailspin. And the spinning seemed to be speeding up rather than slowing down.

The alcohol, the crackle of the fire and the gathering darkness made voicing her worries easier. 'You think? He's not demonstrating a lot of common sense at the moment. He's still spending money like water, he's drinking, he's dossing around in that flat on his own. Or at least I think he's on his own. He won't countenance giving it up and moving back in here while he sorts himself out. Though that's the only sensible solution. It terrifies me how much debt he's getting into, but if I raise it, he snaps my head off. He lost it with me last weekend, and all I said was that I thought he should contact Guy and see if he had any casual work to tide him over.'

'Back on the building sites?'

'Yes. At least he would have something to do with his time, and he would be earning. He told me, in no uncertain terms, to butt out.'

'Well, maybe you should.'

A silence settled. It was hardly a celebratory atmosphere.

'Penny for them?'

Beth roused herself. Sab had made the effort to come round to try and cheer her up, the least she could do was talk. 'Sorry. I'm poor company tonight. I'll be fine tomorrow. I just miss them being here.' She didn't add 'all the time'. She didn't need to, Sab understood.

Sab stood up and hobbled over with the blanket

wrapped round her like a toga, bringing her glass with her. She threw a cushion on the floor, settled down on the ground and leant against Beth's legs. The warmth and weight of her were comforting.

'Do you remember that time Oli got suspended when he was at St Jude's?'

Beth had mislaid the memory, but Sab had dusted it off and handed it back to her. It was an odd recollection to choose, given that her aim was, patently, to defend Oli's reputation, but Beth knew why she'd gone for it. 'I do.'

It had been World Book Day and Oli had refused, point-blank, to go as anything other than a footballer. When Beth had challenged him to come up with something more book-based, he'd marched up to his room, dug out a *Shoot Annual* and defied her to say he couldn't wear his Tottenham kit. She'd given up and turned her attention to Joe. They'd opted for Wally from *Where's Wally* – because the costume was simple, low-key and there was a good chance that he wouldn't be the only kid in a striped jumper, dark glasses and a bobble hat? Understandably, Joe hadn't wanted to dress up in anything that would make him stand out.

It hadn't worked out quite as they'd hoped.

Beth had taken a call, mid-morning, requesting that she come into school, *at her earliest convenience*, and take both of the twins home. No explanation was given, at that point, as to why. When she arrived, the boys were in the corridor outside the Head's office – Joe sitting still, as no doubt instructed, while Oli roved up and down, scuffing the skirting board with the dusty toe of his school shoes. Joe had been pale and silent. In his hands he'd held the broken frames of his Wally glasses.

After ten minutes Beth had been called in to see Ms Gale, the Head. The boys were told to wait.

It transpired that there had been an incident, or rather two, in the playground at break time. Apparently there had been some rough and tumble and Joe had, accidentally, been knocked to the ground. His Wally glasses had been broken. It was nothing major. There'd been no injuries, other than a small rip in his trousers, hence the school hadn't phoned Beth. But just before the end of break, Oliver had been observed running across the playground and cannoning into another child. The boy had fallen to the ground. Oli had stood over him, shouted something and been seen to aim a kick at the prone child. The upshot was that the other child had received not only a nasty shock but, they suspected, would-be bruising to his knees and possibly his side. His parents had taken him home, in tears.

For a minute Beth's concentration had drifted and she wondered whether the Head meant the child or his parents had been crying. As Ms Gale spoke, she wore an expression that oscillated between disappointed and irritated. 'It appears to have been a wholly wilful act on Oliver's part and, as such, we are suspending him until the end of the week while we investigate further.'

Beth asked what Oli had shouted. Ms Gale said it

didn't matter. Beth suspected it did. But that was it – she and the twins were dismissed.

They drove home in silence. Once there, both boys retreated to their rooms without being told.

Beth chose to quiz Joe first. He was reticent, saying merely that a boy called Jonathan had bumped into him, he'd tripped, but he was fine.

Oli was more forthcoming. His opening gambit was, 'I'm not saying sorry... and you can't make me.'

Beth had sat on his bed. He'd remained standing. 'I'm not asking you to apologise, Oli – well, not yet – but I do need you to explain to me, honestly, what happened.'

He had crossed his arms, defensive and assertive at the same time. 'Jonathan Peat was being nasty to Joe. He kept calling him a wally.'

'But he was dressed as Wally.'

'No!' Oli looked exasperated. 'Not cos of his costume. Jonathan was being nasty. He's a bully. People are frightened of him, 'cos he can arm-wrestle Ben Crowther and he's in Year Four.'

'So you think this Jonathan boy tripped Joe up deliberately?'

There was an eyeroll of disbelief. 'No.'

'What? You're not making sense, Oli.'

He looked tearful with frustration. 'You're not listening. You never do. He didn't trip Joe up; he pushed him over and he stomped on his glasses.'

'Are you sure?'

'Yes.'

'So...?'

Oli stopped puffing and fidgeting and looked straight at her. 'So I taught him a lesson. No one else was going to.'

'So you hurt him?'

'Yes.' He lifted his chin.

'For Joe?'

There was a slight pause, then he said, 'Yes. He was picking on Joe, making him look stupid, calling him names, and that's not right.'

Beth was well aware that Oli was playing back to her the messages she'd drummed into him since he was old enough to understand. 'What did you say to Jonathan, Oli, after you'd knocked him down? Ms Gale said you shouted something.'

Before her eyes, she saw Oli straighten up and his chest expand. 'I told him he was a lowlife piece of shit.'

Beth found herself at a loss as to what to say to that.

A log collapsed in the fire-pit, sending sparks into the darkness. Sab laughed. It was a good sound. 'You didn't know whether to punish him or give him a medal, did you?'

'No.' Beth smiled. 'But that's Oli for you.'

'And what about the time they went into town with Aleah to go to Madame Tussauds and ended up wandering around the Elephant and Castle for hours, trying to find anything like a bunch of wax celebrities.'

Beth reached out, touched Sab's hair and laughed. 'I remember.'

They only stopped reminiscing when the fire was nothing more than a heap of grey ash. As they gathered up the glasses, blankets and cushions, Beth realised it was cold, and late. The boys' birthday was nearly over and she'd survived it, without them. More than that, she'd had a nice time.

Back in the centrally heated warmth of the house, Sab readily agreed to stay the night. It made no sense for her to go to the hassle of leaving her car and booking an Uber to take her the short journey home to her equally empty house. Sab was having one of her periodical sworn-off-men patches. Beth didn't expect it to last. Her bouts of abstinence never did. Sab claimed to be looking for love, but persisted in choosing blokes who were incapable of it. Her taste in men hadn't changed much over the years. She went for entertainment value over reliability, fun over the fundamentals. Perhaps she felt more in control that way.

Beth had watched a series of men come and go and, for a time, most of them made Sab happy, but her relationships never got serious. As a result, Beth didn't worry too much about her friend. In the twenty-plus years they'd known each other, Sab had never seemed in danger of losing her head, far less her heart.

'Time for a nightcap?' Sab asked, always the last woman standing.

Beth didn't want more alcohol, but she went to make a cup of tea, happy to do anything to prolong the closeness. Sab opted for a rum, something equally warming. When Beth came back into the lounge with their drinks, Sab was standing over by the corner unit looking through the small stack of cards and presents that had arrived for the boys.

'How's Mick doing?' She must have seen the cards from him.

Beth settled on the sofa, sipped her tea. 'Better. Busier. He's doing some volunteer work. Did I tell you he's selling the house?'

'Why?'

'To move closer to Claire.'

Sab nodded. She'd grown fond of Mick over the years, as did most people who spent any time with him. Although Beth saw Mick less frequently nowadays, he remained an important anchor in her life. He was the only surviving link with her past – the happy memories and the unhappy ones.

Sab's hand trailed across the presents, stopped at one of the photobooks Beth had put together for the boys – a carefully selected record of the two of them from birth to twenty-one. A cheesy present perhaps, but the act of picking out and ordering the photos had made her smile, and remember. She hoped the books would do the same for the boys – remind them of their old closeness. Sab flipped the gift tag over. Beth waited for her to make a comment. She didn't have to wait long.

'So you're still on with this nonsense, are you?'

Beth knew what she meant. 'It's not nonsense to me.'

Sab grimaced, took a sip of her rum. 'I'm not sure we agree on the definition of the word. Pretending that Ian is still around definitely falls into that category for me.'

'It's not pretending.'

'What is it then?'

'More a gesture. A way of letting them know they're loved.'

Sab made a despairing gesture. 'How many times, Beth! They are. By you!'

She and Sab had had different versions of this same conversation for years. They always had to agree to differ. 'This is the last year I'm doing it. They're adults now, I know that.'

Sab walked away from the stack of presents, but she didn't sit down. She paced, while Beth tracked her. She looked agitated, but when she spoke there was more bemusement than irritation in her voice. 'I've never understood your compulsion to keep him in their lives. I would've thought you'd want to forget, not remember.'

'It's never been about me. It's been for the boys. I didn't want them to feel they were missing out.'

'They haven't.'

'They have. Boys need father figures.' She ignored Sab's exasperation, ploughed on. 'Everything I've ever read, or heard, about raising boys says they struggle if they don't have positive male influences in their lives.'

She wanted to add... *Look at Oli.* 'It's different with girls, they look to their mothers for their blueprint, but boys look to their fathers. I didn't want Joe and Oli to have that disadvantage – not along with everything else.' She knew she was provoking Sab, but although she loved her friend, relied on her and would do anything for her, when it came to parenting they fundamentally disagreed.

Sab's relaxed, laissez-faire attitude had been tested over and over again by Aleah, but she'd stuck with it. It was an insouciance that Beth found fascinating and baffling. To her, your children were just that... *your* children. Stepping back and letting them make mistakes and choose paths that led towards trouble, rather than away from it, seemed a dereliction of your duty as a parent.

And yet, though it pained Beth to admit it, she could see that Sab and Aleah's relationship was strong – perhaps stronger than hers with the twins. There was love and trust between them as well as space. And despite Aleah's erratic path through life, Sab's daughter was, for the most part, happy and independent. She seemed to thrive on the chaos she created for herself, while Sab stood loyally on the sidelines cheering her, whether her daughter was soaring or falling.

Sab swallowed the last of her rum. Took a breath. 'With respect... that's total, utter bollocks.' She threw herself down on the sofa next to Beth. 'Oli and Joe have been lucky. They've had you. You are, and have been, the best parent they could have asked for. They have *never* needed Ian. At some point you're going to have to accept that you, alone, are enough.'

Her vehemence shocked Beth, though it was no surprise. Sab had always had more faith in her than she had in herself. 'Thank you for that vote of confidence.'

'You're welcome.' But Sab wasn't finished. She took Beth's face in her hands and stared into her eyes, transmitting a blaze of love and indignation. 'I want you to promise me this is the end of it, here and now, and that you're going to leave Ian in the past – where he belongs.'

After a beat Beth conceded. 'I will. I promise.'

'Good.' Still Sab didn't let go. 'And you're going to let the boys get on with their lives so that you can get on with yours.' Beth nodded. Finally Sab smiled. 'You have to say it. Out loud.'

Beth conceded. 'Okay, I will let them get on with their lives.'

'And?' Sab insisted.

Beth laughed. 'And I will get on with mine!'

Sab finally released her. 'Halleluiah. This calls for a toast.'

They'd finished their drinks, but it didn't matter – the hiccups in life rarely did, with Sab by your side. Undeterred, she raised her empty glass and declared, 'To... being enough.'

Beth raised her mug and they clinked rims. 'To...
enough.'

They both pretended to drink to that.

Chapter 32

TWO YEARS LATER

It was a spur-of-the-moment decision fuelled by a short, but lucky streak at the Blackjack table on the last night of his twenty-third birthday trip to Vegas, and by a deep-seated desire not to go back to his crappy recruitment job and his depressing flat. He had a brother with an apartment in the best city in the world, so why wouldn't he decide to dump his hungover, skint mates and catch a flight to New York? What else were you supposed to do, when you were young, free and single? He might be past it in football years, but not in real life. Or so he seriously hoped!

Oli emailed his boss from the departure lounge, made it sound like a family emergency. He left the nature of the problem vague. They knew his brother was abroad and disabled, which he hoped would mean they wouldn't be too narky about him taking a few extra days to go and visit him. Joe's condition did come in useful, sometimes. Oli knew he should wince at that truth, but he didn't. He'd lived with Joe's CP for as long as his brother had.

Disability didn't only affect the individual; it affected the whole family.

The one person who would be pleased by his unplanned swerve to New York was their mother. She was forever commenting, with a sad little frown, on how little contact they had with each other these days, how nice it would be if they spoke more. Well, this trip smacked of effort and brotherly love on their birthday – which was always when their mum was at her most sentimental. Double Brownie points.

His flight was called.

Oli stood, stretched and joined the queue for boarding.

Chapter 33

NEW YORK LOOKED EPIC out of the cabin window as they came in to land. A floating carnival fairground crammed full of distractions. Oli's curiosity to see how four months Stateside had changed his brother was a nice side-garnish. They had spoken of course, shared the occasional awkward three-way FaceTime with their mum; and, as much as he feigned indifference, Oli had seen every single one of Joe's interminable posts. His brother had never really bothered with his socials before, other than posting the occasional photo of him and Carrie – proof of enduring coupledom. There again, Joe had never had anything quite as cool as this, to fill his Insta feed. A secondment to an apparently big player in the games industry – the company was called something weird, like Buzzard – a salary bump, with generous expenses and a furnished apartment in Queens thrown in for the duration of his stay. He had well and truly landed on his feet, which, Oli mused a little fuzzily and more than a little bitterly, could be seen as ironic.

Only in America would such a thing as an Accessibility Consultant exist, never mind get paid what Joe claimed to be being paid. Who knew that drawing fairies and goblins and being good at waggling a games controller would prove so lucrative?

Oli asked for another beer to take the edge off, but the air hostess told him there wasn't time. It was time to *stow his table and return his seat to the upright position.*

The trip to Queens was a ball ache. He took the train. He had come away from Vegas up, but after buying his ticket to New York, and with the wedge he was no doubt going to drop over the next couple of days, he didn't want to risk exceeding the limit on his credit card – again. His quarterly bonus was usually decent, his approach worked well with prospective candidates and most clients; recruitment was mainly a question of establishing relationships quickly and of charming people into jobs they weren't sure they really wanted, but his base salary was crap. And life – even the boring everyday life he was now living – was expensive. It would be good to see if his little brother would put his hand in his pocket, for a change. Joe could, after all, afford it.

When Oli finally arrived at Joe's address, nearly two hours later, the beers on the flight were proving to have been a very bad idea. He had to press the buzzer for ages before his brother responded and let him inside the building. By the time Joe finally opened the door to his apartment on the sixth floor, Oli was bursting for a piss – which majorly detracted from the joy of seeing the look of shock on his brother's face. He'd obviously been in bed and asleep, judging by the state of him – tatty T-shirt, boxers, all-round gormless expression. 'Oli! What the hell?'

'Happy Birthday!' After a second or two of stunned nothing, Joe came in for a hug. Oli dodged it. 'No time for that. Where's your bathroom?'

Joe gestured vaguely towards the darkened interior of the apartment.

Oli launched himself through the first door he saw, which thankfully turned out to be the right one. As he peed, he took in his surroundings. They were shabby in an artsy, bare-brick walls kind of way. Contrary to the received wisdom about the superiority of American bathrooms, the shower over the bath looked feeble and the tub was stained, while the small window, set high in the wall, was cracked; and even if you had been able to see out of it, it would not, he guessed, provide a view of the iconic New York skyline. It was all very low-key and authentic. Joe, no doubt, loved it.

Above the sink there was a bathroom cabinet. Oli finished up, rinsed his hands, dried them. Then, with a casual gesture, he popped open the cabinet, curious, although about what he couldn't have said. He'd shared bathrooms with Joe for a good chunk of his life. He knew his deodorant brand, the spot-cream he'd put his faith in since being a teenager, his peculiar addiction to cotton buds and Listerine. Joe had always had a 'thing' about being uber-clean, inside and out. Inside the cabinet there was the usual jumble of stuff. Oli recognised the old electric razor that Joe had owned for years. From memory, it was a sixteenth-birthday present from Auntie S. Joe hadn't ever needed to use it more than a couple of times a week – though judging by the hipster stubble on his brother's face, the razor was now truly redundant. There was the usual extensive collection of Joe's meds. At a glance, he appeared to have migrated onto some American brands for his pain relief. Maybe they were stronger. Oli wondered, briefly, whether Joe's stomach was coping with the switch. All as expected, so far.

It was the contents of the middle shelf that caused Oli to do a double take.

He kicked the bathroom door shut with his foot, slid the lock – a precaution that he hadn't bothered with, to urinate – and pulled the light cord. There was the slap of flat white light so bright that it took his eyes a few seconds to adjust. When they did, there, as plain as day, were a woman's roll-on deodorant, an open box of tampons, a packet of floss and a half-full bottle of perfume – Yves Saint Laurent, Black Opium. Female paraphernalia that could, in theory, have been left by Carrie when she flew out to see Joe, for a long weekend, at the start of his secondment in January, but definitely weren't, because – and it slightly surprised Oli to realise this – he knew that Carrie used spray-on deodorant and she only ever wore Daisy by Marc Jacobs. It always threw him if he caught a trace of it on other women.

Whoever Joe's mystery female was, she was clearly American, she liked her perfume heavy and she obviously stayed over in the apartment regularly enough to need to leave her stuff here.

He was shocked. Didn't know whether he was impressed or disapproving. His brother with another woman. Not Carrie. It was difficult to compute. They seemed to have been going out for ever. Perhaps he was jumping to conclusions, filling in the blanks, based on his own history with women. Maybe there was a perfectly innocent explanation for why a woman was keeping her toiletries in Joe's bathroom cabinet, barely four months since he'd moved to the city. Not!

He clicked off the light and headed back down the narrow corridor to the living room, happy to explain his decision to rock up in New York, unannounced, in the middle of the night, but far less comfortable about asking his brother what the fuck he was playing at, sleeping with someone who wasn't Carrie.

Chapter 34

OLI TURNING UP, WITHOUT warning, had been a surprise – a good one, on balance – but it did complicate things for Joe.

For starters, Oli didn't seem to grasp that Joe couldn't simply drop everything the minute he rocked up, with his Vegas winnings, his dirty laundry and his desire to 'celebrate their birthday' – four days late. And so, while Oli slept on the uncomfortable sofa in the living-cum-kitchen area of the apartment, Joe set about reorganising his life to fit around his brother.

First off, he went into work even earlier than normal and reluctantly asked Emmanuel, his line manager, who was of course already in and working, for some leave. Joe had never seen people work so hard, or for such long hours, as they seemed to do in New York. Not that it bothered him. He was loving every minute of it. As he'd been told the first week there, the Blizzard way was *work hard, play hard, go again*. They hadn't been joking. There wasn't anyone over the age of thirty-five on their floor, and no one had kids – not that he was aware of anyway. If they did, they must hardly ever see them. Day or night, it didn't seem to matter, if they were hitting their stride they stayed and ran with it, in the office or out of it. And his team was great. A perfect combination of like-minded creative people who truly made the most of the city they had all, in their own very different ways, run away to.

He'd never been so tired, or so exhilarated.

Emmanuel was cool about him taking some time off, although he did ask Joe to update his work log, so they would know exactly where he was up to. Creative didn't mean flaky at Blizzard. One problem resolved, Joe moved on to the next. He messaged Brianna on his walk back to his apartment. It took him a while to get the phrasing right. New Yorkers seemed to like to collect people; they never seemed to have enough. There was every possibility she would suggest that they all meet up for a drink with some of the guys from work. The thought of Brianna meeting Oli made Joe feel nauseous.

But her response was swift and totally chilled. Have a good time with your bro. See you Friday? I'm free in the eve, if you are. x

For a minute Joe worried he'd come across as gauche, but he let that worry go, as he had so many others over the past couple of months. Caring less and enjoying more seemed so much easier in New York. The knowledge that Brianna had none of the usual curiosity about him being a twin brought a smile to his face.

Schedule rescheduled, Brianna warned off – at least until the end of the week – Joe strolled the last few blocks home, thinking about all the great things he could take his brother to see and do.

When he got back to the apartment, Oli was only just surfacing. 'Only three days! The tight bastards.'

As he hauled himself up from the sofa, Joe couldn't help but notice the physical changes in his brother. The honed, ripped torso was gone, replaced with an average-man bod. There was even the hint of a gut. Footballer to desk jockey, it was quite a turnaround. Joe knew his brother wasn't happy, hadn't been for a while, but it was a fact of life that was far easier to ignore when you were 3,000 miles away. Having the proof standing slap-bang in front of him made Joe even more determined to make sure they had a good time. 'We're lucky – Emmanuel is a sound guy. He could've said "no". People get much less holiday over here.'

For a moment Oli stopped stretching and scratching his backside and looked directly at Joe. 'Don't you want to hang out with me?'

Was that a touch of disappointment in his voice? Joe sought to reassure him. 'Of course I do. It'll be great to show you round. What do you wanna do first?'

Oli pulled on his crumpled shorts and T-shirt. The face that emerged through the neckline was far more like his brother of old. 'That's easy. Eat.'

They went to the deli on the corner. The F&D was classic Queens – small, busy, full of mismatched furniture and people. As good a first-morning introduction to

New York as any. Oli ordered a waffle stack with bacon, eggs and maple syrup. Joe went for a bagel. They both had coffee.

It felt odd having Oli pop up in the middle of his new life, but now that Joe had had a chance to acclimatise and reorganise things, he was genuinely pleased. He couldn't remember the last time the two of them had hung out together, on their own. It might do them good – some bonding time. And their mum would be delighted. He wondered if Oli had told her his plans. Guessed he hadn't. Oli wasn't big on communicating, with anyone. They should send her a photo. He smiled at the thought of making her happy and warmed, even more, to the idea of having a few days with his brother. 'Seriously, it's good to see you, man. How was Vegas?'

Oli grinned. 'Wicked.' A tale of late nights and blurry days spent recovering by the pool followed.

Joe chewed his way through his bagel as Oli talked. It was good – fresh, slathered in cream cheese and salmon; the food was always good at the F&D. Joe had discovered that if you lived in New York you had to develop, and voice, your loyalty to specific pizza places, bars, bodegas, coffee stands, even laundrettes. Having a list of absolute must go-to local joints was what marked you out as a resident rather than one of the thousands of tourists. He signalled the server, asking for more coffee. 'And how are things at home?'

Oli updated Joe on a load of mundane things he already knew. Joe spoke to his mum, and to Carrie, regularly;

well, maybe not quite as regularly as at first, but plenty enough to still be plugged into their lives. He noticed that Oli didn't mention Alice. Another relationship in the dust? He didn't ask. Didn't want to bring the mood down. Family matters dealt with, they raced to finish the remnants of their meals, just like in the old days. Despite his mountain of food, Oli won. He wiped his fingers on a clump of the wholly inadequate napkins from the dispenser on the countertop and sat back.

'So, spill. How are you finding living here, on your own?'

Joe had been waiting to be asked. 'It's great.'

Oli spread his hands. 'Elaborate?'

'You really want the full brag-fest?'

'Yeah, why not? Knock yourself out. My stomach's full and I'm sober for the first time in five days.'

'Well, look at it.' Joe gestured out of the window. 'The whole thing lives up to your expectations. When you live in a place like Queens, you start to get to know the city properly. You get a sense of what it's really like; not just Manhattan – which is exactly as big and loud and brash and exciting as you think it's going be – but each of the neighbourhoods are so different. And the food and the bars and the music scene and the cinemas: they're all better than anything we have at home, even in London. Nothing here is vanilla. And my job... ' He tailed off.

'Your job... what?'

Joe hesitated. No one loved working in recruitment. Oli worked to pay the bills nowadays – his dream well and truly dashed. Joe had no desire to rub his brother's nose in his own good luck, but it was hard not to. 'They're a good company and the people are all really interesting. A real diverse mix of backgrounds. They made me feel part of the team from the get-go.'

He saw Oli wince at 'get-go'. 'So you're glad you came?'

'Yes.' He was – 100 per cent, but that would do on the enthusiasm front. He wasn't an insensitive jerk.

Then Oli threw him off his stride. 'And how is it – you being here and Carrie being at home?'

Joe pushed the debris of his plate away and drew the bowl of sugar and sweetener sachets towards him, set about reorganising them. 'I miss her.' He did.

'But not like you thought you would?'

Joe couldn't work out where this was coming from. Maybe Oli hadn't broken up with Alice yet, but was thinking about it. Joe didn't think he should. Alice was nice. A lot nicer than many of Oli's previous girlfriends. He deflected. 'Why the sudden interest in my feelings?'

Oli shrugged. 'No real reason. It's just... I know you considered not coming. I thought it was because of Carrie.'

It was true. Joe had nearly turned the job offer down. And it had, partly, been because of the very real fear of being apart from Carrie for so long. But it had also been because he hadn't believed he was good enough – to do the job, to cope with being so far away, to live on his own, to be a fucking grown-up. The thought he'd nearly wimped out on the best thing that had ever happened to him now horrified him.

The things he would have missed.

'She encouraged me to come.' It was true; after the initial shock of discovering that he'd applied for the secondment, and got it, Carrie had urged him to take it. And, he thought, she still believed it was a smart move, job-wise. She'd also changed her March booking and flown out earlier than planned to help him through his initial wobble – although they'd explained that away on the basis of a too-cheap-to-be-missed flight deal rather than Joe's need to see her. All round, she had been super-supportive. He couldn't fault her – didn't. But thinking about Carrie complicated things and, as a result, it was something he tried not to do too often.

Indeed now that he was settled in New York, and at Blizzard, Joe had whole days, and nights, when he felt as if his old life in the UK simply didn't exist; or more accurately, that it existed, but was frozen in time, the clock stopped until he chose to restart it with a call or a text. Hence his initial confusion when Oli had appeared. The fact that his brother was currently sitting opposite him, scratching maple syrup off his shorts with his thumbnail, proved, disconcertingly, that both worlds – and all the lives within them – did overlap.

Oli stopped bothering about the state of his clothing and looked up. 'Hey, you don't have to convince me. I think it's good you're having some time apart.' Was that another prod?

Joe didn't respond. He stuffed the rest of the sachets back in the bowl and stood up, signalling the end of the conversation. 'Come on, let's get moving. It's nearly midday and so far we've made it a grand total of one block from my apartment.'

Chapter 35

FOR THE NEXT FEW days they behaved like complete tourists and had a great time.

They hired a boat in Central Park and spent the whole hour arguing about who was best at rowing.

They went to the Guggenheim, one of Joe's all-time favourite places, where Oli claimed that the exorbitantly expensive hot dog he insisted Joe buy him from the stand outside was better value than the tickets for the gallery.

They ate pasta and cannoli in Little Italy and bought salted pretzels and pizza slices from random street corners, for no reason other than that they saw other people eating.

Oli said 'no' to Ground Zero, but 'yes' to the Staten Island Ferry and a corn dog.

They got as far as looking through the glass frontage of MOMA, but Oli vetoed going in, saying he'd had more than enough art to last him a lifetime. He was immovable, even when Joe described how good the food in the café was.

They watched a college ball game in a sports bar, with chips and many, many jugs of beer, and got into an argument with a businessman from Illinois about Trump's chances of re-election.

They saw the entertainers in Washington Square, after which Joe dragged Oli into Barnes & Noble and made him buy a book for their mum. His choice, Oli was clueless. He went for *The Colossus of New York* by Colson Whitehead – a way of sharing the experience with her from afar.

They laughed and mucked about and bickered and enjoyed being together in a way they hadn't for years.

And it worked, perfectly, because neither of them brought up anything awkward.

Chapter 36

BEFORE THEY KNEW IT, their time was nearly up.

Oli was due out of Newark on an internal flight to Harry Reid, Nevada, the next day, then on to Heathrow. It was a total pain in the arse, but he couldn't afford a new ticket out of New York. He was dreading it: the tedious journey and the even more depressing arrival home. In contrast, his brother was obviously looking forward to going back to work.

They spent their last night in an upmarket whisky bar called the Flatiron Room on Twenty-Sixth Street. The bar had a curtained-off entrance with a dark-haired, forties-styled hostess and a bouncer who looked like William Perry, aka 'The Refrigerator'. Inside it was like a cave, with row upon row of backlit whisky bottles lining the walls and the ceiling. Joe joked it was dark so that punters weren't put off by the prices. The scene was completed by a Cuban jazz band and a Bond-esque army of beautiful waitresses. Their server introduced herself, without irony, as Madison. She brought them a meat-and-cheese sharing board with artisanal bread, and explained the drinks menu at length, asking them their taste preferences to help better direct their choices. Joe started with a twelve-year-old Abelour, Oli went for a measure of Heaven's Door. He picked it purely because he liked the name, and the promise it contained.

It was all very upmarket.

For long patches they sat in contented silence listening to the band. It was made up of five grizzled old men in straw trilbies. They played with an utter indifference to their audience. It was all very moody and cool, like starring in your own movie – a sensation that was enhanced by the tumblers of ten-, twelve- and twenty-year-old malt and rye whiskies they sipped and savoured, like experienced men of the world.

As they drank, Oli studied his brother. In addition to the stubble, his hair was longer and he looked like he'd put on a bit of weight, which on Joe's normally skinny frame was a good thing. The tan helped. Who didn't look better with a tan? His clothes were an improvement too. Trousers that actually fitted for a change, a decent shirt, even more decent trainers. The influence of the mystery woman?

Oli still couldn't make sense of it.

Carrie and Joe were the archetypal teenage sweethearts. No, they were more than archetypal; they were an uber-version of love's young dream. Loyal, loving, endlessly supportive – especially Carrie of Joe – and happy. Living proof that a relationship, started when you were little more than kids, could survive into adulthood and was even strong enough to accommodate one of them whooping it up in New York while the other was stuck teaching Shakespeare to barely literate teenagers in Brent Cross.

And yet the stuff in the bathroom cabinet said otherwise. The pack of dental floss, the deodorant, the tampons and the bottle of Black Opium might have vanished from it, but their existence definitely suggested that Joe was, or had been, cheating on Carrie. Joe spiriting the evidence away seemed to prove it.

And yet Oli still hadn't brought up the mystery girl.

His reluctance had complex roots, the deepest of which was his selfish desire to simply have a good time in New York. But there were other reasons for his ambivalence, including the realisation that he'd missed his brother. They'd had a great time together over the past few days. It had been easier somehow. Perhaps it was because they no longer lived in each other's pockets. As adults, with their own separate lives, the dynamic was different, more equal, less loaded. He'd not wanted to bugger up the relaxed vibe. He was also reluctant to have his suspicions about Joe being a love-rat confirmed. Whether this hesitation was because the tag didn't fit with his perception of his brother or because of the potential implications for Carrie, Oli wasn't sure.

Instead of thinking, he took another sip of expensive whisky, sat back and listened to the band. Yes, there were many very valid reasons for keeping his gob shut. The band was building up to a finale, the tempo of the music furious. Oli could see the sweat on the faces of the sax and horn players. They might be old, but they were good. He let the music drown out his thoughts.

With a crescendo the band ended their set. The audience got to their feet. They clapped wildly and whistled, it was all very American. An encore was demanded. The band played another couple of more mellow numbers, then exited the stage, leaving behind a pool of amber light that glinted on their abandoned instruments. In the lull that followed, the waitresses circulated, taking last orders.

When Madison surreptitiously presented them with the bill at the end of the evening – on a silver tray inside a leather folder – Joe flourished his card like a total fucking master of the universe. Living alongside the wolves of Wall Street was obviously rubbing off on him.

Oli let him pay. This type of brotherly showing-off had its upsides.

Chapter 37

THE WALK BACK TO the subway stop was Oli's last chance to take in the glittering, grubby contradictory glory that was Manhattan at night. Joe led the way past gyms where an insane, hollow-eyed Lycra army was still thrashing out the miles on treadmills, despite it being gone midnight, whilst two doors down far more rational New Yorkers lingered in bars over expensive cocktails. Most of the shops were still open and the traffic was as choked as ever. It wasn't so much a city that didn't sleep as one that never shut up. It was an obstacle course of people, cars and commerce. And yet it still seemed magical, despite the noise and the mess.

Oli could see why Joe loved it.

As they wandered along, Oli watched his brother. He could have sworn Joe's walking was better, more even, less rolling. But perhaps it was simply that they were both pleasantly pissed – which kind of levelled the playing field. Joe was certainly better at avoiding the omnipresent scaffolding that seemed to hold up every third building. Oli nearly knocked himself out, twice.

In the subway car – he was picking up the terminology – they sat side-by-side. Joe chatted shit the whole way back, while Oli half-listened, watching the lights and the graffiti fly by. It was soothingly hypnotic.

Back at the apartment, Joe was the one who didn't want to go to bed. He started digging around in the cupboards, searching for a bottle of bourbon that he claimed someone had left behind after a dinner party. How things had changed. Joe not only had friends now, he was hosting dinner parties! After a bit more scrabbling around, he spun round, triumphant, bearing aloft said bottle. His measures were drunkenly generous. They chose the floor rather than the chronically uncomfortable sofa.

'Cheers, little bro.' They drank. 'Thank you for a truly epic few days, mate.'

'My pleasure,' Joe slurred.

The leftover bourbon tasted very sweet after the good stuff in the jazz club, but they were both past caring. 'I'm really glad it's working out for you here.' Oli meant it.

'Ah, shucks. Thanks.' Joe pulled a cartoon dopey expression.

'No. Seriously. You seem properly happy.'

Joe stretched out, rested his head back against the sofa. 'I am.'

They listened to the sounds of Queens coming in through the ill-fitting windows of the apartment. Oli lost a minute or so. He wondered idly whether he, or Joe, might have nodded off. Then he realised that his brother was talking, so neither of them could really be asleep.

'I feel different here. Wanna know why?' Oli didn't need to respond, as Joe's speech had a momentum of its own. 'I'll tell you. Because here... no one gives a fuck about my CP.' He suddenly became animated. He pushed himself upright to give himself the space to wheel his arms around. 'They really don't, Oli.'

Oli hadn't argued with him, but whatever.

'They're not faking it, being polite, like people are at home. Here my CP is cool. I'm cool. How sick is that? I'm not shitting you, Oli. I'm really not.' He was very drunk. 'Maybe it's the industry I'm in, but they fucking love it. Can't get enough of it. Of me! I've had rooms of people... execs from Sony and Square Enix hanging on my every word, asking me questions, deferring to me. You see, I'm the expert. I'm the one who knows. It's all about accessibility these days.' Joe flung his arms wide. It was the most assertive Oli had ever seen him. 'And I'm the one getting the access – for a change.'

'That must feel good.'

'It fucking does.' Oli raised his glass to his brother in salute. But Joe wasn't finished. 'And I'm going to tell you something else, Ol, and this is a secret, so you must keep... shtum.' He put his finger to his lips and made a wet, shushing noise. 'Now get ready, because

181

this is going to mess with everything you know to be true.' He threw in a dramatic pause. 'Women in New York – the ones I've met anyway – they aren't bothered by it. By anything. Their whole attitude to sex is totally different. They're like *if you're not hurting anyone, what's the harm*?' Joe paused, gathered himself. 'And I'm not hurting anyone. I'm really not.'

Oli held himself still.

'You see, it doesn't mean anything. It's just fun.' Joe paused again, this time for longer, the grandiose gestures gone. When he spoke his voice, though still loose with whisky, was quieter. 'It's got nothing to do with how I feel about Carrie. You have to believe me, it really hasn't.' He turned to look at Oli.

It made Oli feel very uncomfortable. He suddenly didn't want to hear Joe's confession – because what would he do with it?

'I know Carrie is my... one.' Joe paused, stared with a wobbly intensity at Oli. 'But why do I have to have just one person who wants me?'

Oli kept his opinion on the subject to himself. There was more silence.

Joe was running out of steam, but he wasn't quite done. 'And do you know what, bro?' He reached out and punched Oli's shoulder with his free hand – a gesture of solidarity and conspiracy. The blow had no force. 'Leaving home, coming here, enjoying myself, meeting new people, getting... well, getting my chance.

It's normal,' he took a breath, 'and I refuse to feel guilty about it. Do you know why?' Joe didn't want, or wait for, an answer. 'Because,' he thumped himself in the middle of his chest with the base of his glass, 'for the first time in my fucking life, being fucking disabled is a fucking advantage.'

His head lolled back against the sofa.

Oli prised the empty glass from Joe's hand and pulled off his trainers. He took the cushions off the sofa and awkwardly manoeuvred his brother down onto them. Then he stood and watched him sleep.

The years melted away. Their sixteenth birthday. He'd watched Joe sleep that night as well. Then he'd pitied him. What did he feel about his brother now? Not pity, that was for sure. Envy? No, it was more complicated than that. What he felt was recognition. Joe was behaving like any normal bloke would, given a free pass for a year in the best city in the world. For the first time – probably ever – Joe was living like he didn't have CP. And Oli sure as hell wasn't going to criticise him for that. Their mother, and Carrie, everyone expected too much. Too much discipline, commitment, focus, good behaviour. They were twenty-three for fuck's sake.

Good on Joe for grabbing life by the balls for a change.

Oli fetched the spare duvet, draped it over his brother and left him to his drunken dreams – there was no point wasting a comfortable bed. He had a long day of travelling ahead of him. It was time for him to go back to his own dull-as-a-puddle life.

Chapter 38

IN THE MORNING THEY were both badly hungover. Oli was pleased that Joe was in a worse state than him, but it was a close-run thing. They moved around the apartment like old men. Silence suited their heads and their mood. Despite Oli telling Joe he didn't need to come and see him off, Joe insisted. He had, apparently, cleared it with the mythic, all-powerful Emmanuel. As the train carriage rattled along, viciously reminding them that copious amounts of Scotch and cheese should not be followed up with cheap bourbon, they barely spoke. It wasn't until they were in the terminal, looking up at the departures board, that Joe broached the previous night.

'You feeling human yet?'

'Nope. You?'

'No.'

They both laughed, but it was forced.

'Well, I hope you have a good trip.'

'Yeah.' Oli badly needed another bottle of water. 'Thanks for showing me the sights.'

'My pleasure.' There was a pause, but neither of them made a move. 'Oli?' Joe looked tense.

'Yeah.'

'You won't say anything, will you?'

They both knew what he was talking about.

Cruelly, and for reasons Oli wasn't too clear on, he paused. He had his brother on the hook. It was a novel situation. One to be savoured, but only briefly. He relented. 'No, course not.' He swapped his rucksack to his other shoulder.

Joe visibly relaxed. 'Well. Bye then. I'll see you soon. Not!'

They hugged, awkwardly. Oli brought the hug to an end by thumping his brother between his shoulder blades – tapping out like they used to when they fought as kids. Emotional airport goodbyes were overrated.

Before Joe had a chance to walk away, Oli asked, 'So, what's she called then?' The mystery woman's name would obviously mean nothing to him, but for some reason he suddenly really wanted to know it.

Their eyes met. Oli held Joe's gaze. He hesitated, then said, 'Brianna.'

Oli nodded. It was the proof he'd needed that his brother really had changed.

'Right. See you whenever, bro.' Joe was obviously keen to see the back of him now.

Oli raised his hand. 'Bye.'
With that, they parted.

Chapter 39

SEVEN MONTHS LATER

IT WAS GREAT BEING home. Everything was the same. His room, the house, all decked out for Christmas, the traditions – the bowl of nuts no one would touch, the dishes of chocolates they would, the same old TV shows, the mountains of home-cooked food and, most of all, the people, including Carrie.

Maintaining a long-distance relationship had been hard on both of them, but they were making it work. They'd had a glorious month together exploring the area around Rhode Island and Boston in the summer. Free as birds, with no one to answer to, no timetable to stick to. It had reminded him of their early days together. The re-emergence of their old passion had reassured Joe. It was a sign that they were still right for each other, in the long term.

His unplanned trip back to the UK at the end of September had obviously been very different, but even more important. Carrie's dad's passing had, unsurprisingly, hit her hard. She had been close to Rob, far closer than she was to her mother. His death, although not unexpected, had rocked her. It had been tricky for Joe to get the extra time off and expensive to fly home at such short notice, but it had been worth it. His visit had demonstrated his commitment to her.

Yes, there had been a lot to contend with over the past year – which was why Joe was so looking forward to having a chilled-out Christmas, back in the bosom of his family and his girlfriend.

It soon became apparent, however, that although Carrie was making an effort to throw herself into the spirit of things and into his homecoming, there was a part of her that was shut off from him. In the past he would have tried and tried, then tried again, until she let him in, but the knowledge that what she was guarding was a pool of sadness stopped him. Selfish as it was, he didn't want her low mood to taint his happiness.

Joe made up for his failure to lean into her distress by being more physically affectionate than usual and by saying lots of nice things to her. He told her how much he'd missed her, how appreciative he was of her ongoing support for what he was doing, how knowing that she was behind him made it all worthwhile. He said it so many times he almost convinced himself that him being in New York was good for both of them. But when he stared at his face in the bathroom mirror, he saw a coward. What Carrie really wanted was for him to want the whole of her, not only the parts that fitted around him – it was what she'd always wanted, and what they used to have. Yet he carried on regardless, protecting his own sense of contentment by putting off the conversation he knew they needed to have.

Despite the glue-like quality of time over the festive period, the days passed. They celebrated Christmas, slept through most of Boxing Day, walked and went to the pub on the dead days in between and, before he knew it, New Year's Eve came along. With it, Joe's awareness that time was running out sharpened and became more uncomfortable. His return flight was on 3rd January. He was scheduled to complete eight more weeks at Blizzard, just enough time to get his project signed off, then he was expected home – for good. He knew that once he was back permanently, his time in New York would be reduced to a few lines on his CV. It would become nothing more than a stepping stone to a better job, a bigger salary that would allow them to rent a decent flat or maybe even the little house Carrie dreamt of.

They celebrated New Year round at Sab's house. Oli came too. For the first time in years, he arrived without a date. They chatted briefly at the beginning, but managed to avoid each other for the rest of the evening – by chance or design, Joe wasn't sure. But he was fine with that. Being with Carrie in front of Oli made him feel self-conscious.

It was a good night. The house was full, the conversations easy, the music loud, the kitchen groaning with food and booze. The countdown to midnight was jolly and drunken. There were fireworks already going off further down the street – there was always someone, somewhere, who jumped the gun. On the stroke of twelve, Joe put his arms around Carrie and kissed her. He waited for the room to melt away, for their deep and special connection to blot out everything else.

It didn't.

He caught sight of his brother over Carrie's shoulder. Oli was watching them. He heard Sab and Aleah yelling 'Happy New Year' and the pop of corks. He felt the heat of other people's bodies pressing in around them. The jab of someone's elbow in his back. Across the room he saw his mum raise her glass to her lips and take a sip of champagne, her expression thoughtful.

It was the beginning of a new year. The start of another year of loving Carrie – amazingly, their seventh. One more step on the long path that led backwards through his life and stretched forward, without end.

He held Carrie a little tighter and kissed her again, a little harder. Joe knew how lucky he was to be with her. He loved Carrie, always had, but that didn't stop him, in that moment, wishing himself in his other life. In a bar with Lex, Mateus, Emmanuel and the others, drinking beer and talking crap. Or alone on Times Square, hemmed in by the heaving, shouting masses watching the ball drop. Or, God forgive him, in bed with Brianna in his tiny apartment, listening to the city go crazy while they drank champagne.

Someone started singing 'Auld Lang Syne'. He let go of Carrie and they joined in.

Chapter 40

JOE WOKE EARLY the following morning. He flexed his left foot. It was more painful than usual – all the standing around the previous night had taken its toll. It was pouring down outside. Miserable New Year's Day weather. The squalls sounded petulant against the window.

He got out of bed and reluctantly started his stretches. The rain must have disturbed Carrie because she stirred and rolled over, away from him. He cut his routine short and went downstairs. He made coffee. Instant. His mum wasn't bothered with *the provenance of the beans* or the *intensity of the roast*; to her, coffee was just caffeine. He was aware that he was thinking like a pretentious wanker, but he didn't mind. Twelve months ago he would have thought Starbucks was decent. The distance a person travelled could be measured in more than simply miles.

He climbed the stairs slowly.

Carrie was awake and sitting up in bed when he came back into the bedroom. In place of her usual T-shirt, there was bare skin. The sight of her hair skimming her pale shoulders got to him. She still had the power to stir him, although they hadn't seen in the New Year with sex, as they'd both been too tired. He passed her one of the mugs and climbed in beside her.

'Thank you.' Her voice was croaky from the party.

They blew on their drinks, drank. To Joe the silence, underscored by the rain against the window, felt uncomfortable, but the tension – as yet – was in him, not in the room. He knew he'd already used his free pass by taking the job in New York in the first place, then pushed his luck by extending his stay until the end of February. What he was about to ask was going to put even more strain on their relationship. But – and this shocked him – he found he was prepared to risk it.

He had the chance to stay Stateside until Easter, possibly until the summer. And that was too good an opportunity to turn down!

Emmanuel had called him in and had offered him a contract extension, just before he'd flown home – an early Christmas present. They wanted Joe to finish up his current project *and* consult on a new, blue-sky concept development piece for Microsoft. It was a real compliment to be asked. It spoke of their faith in him and the value he brought to the table.

That was what mattered: the career opportunities. It was about the skills he was gaining. The contacts he was making. The reputation he was building. Plus, with the references he'd have if he worked on the Microsoft job, he'd be able to apply to the big boys when he came back. Those sorts of credentials were gold dust. Worth the sacrifice of another few months apart. It wasn't about him wanting to hang onto his apartment in Queens, buying his coffee from the F&D every morning and spending his weekends in Brooklyn with his friends. It wasn't about living in the best city on the planet. And it certainly wasn't anything to do with having more time with Brianna. Those things were simply by-products.

He sipped his coffee. Two heaped teaspoons and it was still virtually tasteless.

But sensible as it was for him to stay on, from a career perspective and for their long-term prospects, he knew Carrie would be unhappy about it. She might very well be angry.

As she had every right to be.

But he also knew, or hoped, she would understand. And that she would wait for him. Because they loved each other and were destined to be together. And this was an investment in their future together – a future Joe wanted.

Just not yet.

Because once their destiny became their reality, that was it. When he came back to the UK for good, their coupledom would be sealed. This was his last assertion of self.

'Carrie.' The redundant use of her name must have triggered some concern in her, because she put down her mug and turned to him, her expression questioning.

'Yeah, what's up?' She waited for him to speak.

It was time to face into it. 'I want to talk to you about my job.'

Now she really was wary. 'What about it?'

He bit down on the bullet. 'Blizzard have offered me a contract extension.'

'I know. Until the end of February.'

'Not that.'

She stiffened and pulled the covers up around her shoulders as if suddenly cold. 'What do you mean?'

'They want me to work on a new project for them. For Microsoft.' Like that was going to sway her.

'From here?'

'No, out there.'

She went completely still.

He opted for full disclosure – well, almost. 'It would mean me staying out there until Easter.'

She bit her lip. 'And what did you say?'

'Well, I said I'd need to speak to you.'

'Why?'

'What do you mean, why?'

She stared at him.

He wished she wouldn't do that, force him to be explicit. He resisted her pressure. 'I know it's a lot to ask.'

She breathed out. A puff of deep exasperation. He simultaneously hated that he was upsetting her and chafed against his responsibility for her sadness. 'That's the problem, Joe. You're not asking. You're telling. Why else would you have said nothing about it until now? Be honest. You want to stay out there, don't you?'

He didn't say anything. Her expression stiffened. It was as if the anger she was feeling was trapped beneath her beautiful skin. It made her look different, less recognisable, less his Carrie.

'I'm guessing you've already said "yes", haven't you?'

He suddenly felt hard done by, and guilty. It was an unsettling combination. 'That's not fair. I am discussing it with you, now. I'm asking what you think we should do.'

'We?'

'Yes.'

She hugged the duvet tighter to her body. 'You know what I want.'

He did. And it wasn't what he wanted. Neither of them said anything for a few seconds. He tried again. 'It's only another few months, and I...' He didn't get to say more.

She climbed out of bed and spoke without turning around, her voice quiet and hard to hear above the rattle of the rain. He thought she said, 'Do what you want, Joe', but he couldn't be sure, and he couldn't very well ask her to repeat herself.

She walked across the bedroom, lifted her dressing gown off the back of the chair and disappeared into the en suite. She closed the door softly behind her, leaving him with nothing – no door slam, no drama, no tears, no accusations, and absolutely no idea of where he stood with her.

Chapter 41

APRIL WASN'T the cruellest month, January was. It went on for ever, the promise of the New Year stalled while everyone and everything waited for the days to lengthen and the weather to relent.

Without discussion, the three of them fell into a predictable weekend routine: food and accommodation provided by Beth, wine and beer by Oli, TV and film suggestions by Carrie. She knew her stuff. She had eclectic and quite challenging tastes. It was fun disagreeing about what constituted a classic, what made for a dud, what was funny but appalling and what was simply tragically bad. It was good to have the house full of conversation and laughter. Random takeaways and strong spirits sometimes supplemented, and prolonged, their get-togethers when Sab turned up, usually un-announced, but always welcome.

Beth suspected they were all aware that their gatherings were slightly odd: two mums, one son and the girlfriend of the absent son spending their Friday and often their Saturday nights together. But it felt comfortable; and besides, it was the month for retreating into your shell. Surely it was better to turn tortoise with other people than on your own.

Joe's announcement that he was going to stay on in New York had brought an abrupt end to their Christmas festivities. The last few days around the house had been awkward, strained even. When Beth had quizzed him about his decision, and the impact it would have on his relationship with Carrie, he claimed she was okay with it – started talking about some plan for her to fly out at half-term. He positioned it as a mutual decision, but the mood between the two of them said otherwise. By the last day it had been painful to watch. They'd barely said a word to each other, except goodbye.

And Oli had been weird about the news of Joe's extended stay as well. His actual response had been 'What a selfish prick!', said loudly and within earshot of his brother. His anger had seemed disproportionate to Beth, even allowing for sibling rivalry. She knew he was jealous of Joe's US stint, but she'd obviously underestimated how much.

Sadly, it had been a relief when Joe finally set off for Heathrow on 3rd January. As she watched him put his bags in the boot of the taxi, swiftly kiss Carrie goodbye and disappear out of their lives, again, Beth's sense that the boys were switching roles was acute and uncomfortable. It was, she realised, probably the first time she didn't approve of how Joe was behaving. And yet she said nothing.

Her emotions about her sons were further influenced by Oli's surprising post-Christmas willingness to spend most of his weekends with her. It was nice to have him home, but curious. She couldn't remember a time when he'd been around so much. Ever since he'd been old enough to take himself off, he had. Training, the gym, friends, girlfriends – they had all taken precedence over family life in the past. Now nothing seemed to make him happier than a home-cooked meal and a quiet night in, watching something subtitled and political, or arty and largely incomprehensible.

Tonight's planned viewing was *Borgen*: Season Three. They'd been saving it to watch together, but before they settled down they had one thing to do. Beth switched on the dishwasher and headed through to the lounge.

It was sod's law that Oli seemed to have chosen that precise moment to disappear upstairs.

Chapter 42

REALISATION DAWNED the minute Oli came back into the lounge and saw his mum's phone propped up against a stack of books on the table. If he'd remembered, he'd have stayed in the toilet for longer. Another bloody FaceTime with Joe.

But it was too late to back out now – they were both looking at him. Carrie patted the empty cushion next to her. Oli reluctantly took his place on the sofa. She smelt of her usual perfume. She always did. He had bought her a bottle for Christmas. He wondered if she'd started wearing it it yet. Her leg accidentally touched his. He moved away and steeled himself for an awkward ten minutes. The only upside was that he knew he wouldn't be called on to say much. His mother and Joe drove the conversation on these all-too-regular family calls. Oli had noticed that Carrie's contributions seemed to be waning as well. She joined in the chat, but rarely volunteered much about what was going on in her own life these days. Oli wondered if Joe knew she was looking for a new job, having lost patience with the Head at her current school; that she was having a rough time with her mother and it was getting her down – although she pretended it wasn't; and that the boiler in her rented house had been broken for a fortnight. No, Joe possibly knew none of these things and, even if he did, didn't seem to care. Oli placed his phone on the arm of the sofa, face-up, planning to surreptitiously keep an eye on the Arsenal–Liverpool match.

The call connected. Joe's voice boomed into the room, followed by a close-up of his face – still beardy, his hair fashionably too long. He looked more wanky than usual. Shrunk small on the phone screen, Joe's apartment looked like a film set full of self-conscious New York props. The clunky old air-conditioning unit, the framed MOMA poster, even Joe's insulated travel coffee mug, which was just in shot, looked contrived. Except that Oli knew it was all real, because he'd spent five days living there. Knowing that Joe was sitting on the same excruciatingly uncomfortable sofa he'd slept on brought back the memories even more sharply. He'd envied, even admired Joe back then. Not any longer. Oli wondered if Joe did a quick sweep around the apartment checking there wasn't anything belonging to Brianna on view, before he called home. He assumed she was still on the scene. Or someone else? Otherwise, why was the stupid bastard still out there?

They said their hellos, spoke about the weather – it was cold on both sides of the Atlantic, New York State had had a lot of snow – then Joe started banging on about some presentation he'd given to the vice-president of some such bollocks company. Oli tuned him out, stared blindly at his own phone.

With each one of these catch-up calls Oli grew more pissed off with his brother, and his promise to keep his mouth shut became more of a burden. He'd hadn't been close to Joe for years – they were too different – but he'd never before had him down as a selfish twat. And yet that was exactly how he was behaving: pursuing his own dream, with a side-order of commitment-free sex, while Carrie waited for him. Oli never called or messaged Joe outside these excruciating family calls anymore. He didn't want to, he had nothing to say to his brother, apart from... get your selfish, skinny arse home before something you're really going to regret happens.

Or don't.

It was Joe's loss.

In stark contrast, the more time Oli spent with Carrie, the more he liked her. He realised he'd never really thought of her as a person in her own right before. She'd been such a fixture in their lives – a fixture exclusively attached to his brother – that he'd never bothered to talk to her properly, or listen. But without Joe around, there had been more space and time to get to know her, for them to get to know each other. The first revelation was that she could be funny and sharp. He'd thought Carrie pappy, too nice to be interesting. He was wrong. She had a crackle to her that he'd not experienced before in a girl.

If you said something stupid, she looked you straight in the eye and laughed. It took some getting used to. And she was oddly comfortable with silence, which made a nice change.

Oli didn't like to admit it, but it was Carrie's presence that drew him home most weekends, more than his mother and her very good cooking. He'd even started skipping his Sunday-morning gym session in order to stay around for longer. And that was a sacrifice. He normally resented having to change his routine, for anyone or anything.

He must have been asked a question, because he realised they were all looking at him. To cover up his inattention he glanced at his phone, then at Joe. 'Sorry, mate. Salah has just scored.' No one would expect anything other than obsession with football from him.

Joe cleared his throat. 'I asked how things are with you?'

Oli shrugged. 'Me. Fine. Same old, same as.'

The conversation moved on. Oli's predictable response was sufficient reassurance that he'd been included. Yes, the truth was: Oli was now the boring twin, with nothing interesting going on in his life. Except a growing, but he hoped well-hidden, obsession with his brother's long-term girlfriend.

Chapter 43

IT WASN'T UNTIL he finally had a quiet night in, on his own, that Joe started to worry.

He checked his phone again. There was still nothing from Carrie. It had been three days. His concern was streaked with guilt – he should have been paying more attention, he should have acknowledged the slightly uneasy feeling he'd had all week and acted upon it.

Carrie had stopped communicating with him.

And he had ignored it.

He told himself to calm down. People were busy. He certainly was. Maybe she'd had a bad patch at work. But that didn't wash – when things were tough they talked more, not less, or at least they used to. Sitting on the bed, he scrolled through their exchanges. Their frequency, duration, content and timing told him any number of stories.

They were fine.

The tone of their messages was normal. She soun-ded like she always did. Maybe a little distracted, but there were no red flags. Fewer xx's maybe. No, the same amount.

He went back, read his own messages. He'd been a bit abrupt a few times, but nothing that couldn't be seen simply as someone with a lot of stuff on. He definitely hadn't let slip anything he shouldn't. Perhaps he hadn't asked Carrie enough questions? He checked. When he had asked her how things were going at her end, her replies had been short. It was a two-way thing; he couldn't be enthusiastic about stuff he didn't know about, could he? Had he been a bit insensitive regarding the contrast in their lives? Yes, maybe, on occasion.

They weren't fine.

They were in a rut. They were both tired of making the effort of keeping each other in the loop of their necessarily separate lives. Long-distance relationships were tough – everyone said so.

But it wasn't terminal. They were just missing each other, missing the reinforcement of physical affection and of simply being together. He vowed to get his arse into gear for Carrie's visit. He had been meaning to. It was only a few weeks away. Maybe he should send her some restaurant and theatre suggestions – that would get them back on-track.

But then it dawned on him – she hadn't actually confirmed that she'd booked her flights.

They were totally not fine.

Carrie had withdrawn from him, which meant she was thinking and, given the way things were between them – namely, rocky – such reflection was dangerous. So dangerous that Joe was frightened.

He was in deep shit.

She'd had enough of him being away. She was thinking about ending it. This could be it. The death of the most important thing in his life. He was going to be on his own. Really, truly on his own. The life he'd imagined picking back up when he returned to the UK was gone.

He threw his phone down, blaming it. The hundreds of messages and voicenotes, the random selfies, the funny little videos – they meant nothing. No, worse, they had provided the illusion of contact, of a sharing of the old closeness they used to have. But it was a false reassurance.

His body reacted accordingly. His heart clenched, restricting the flow of oxygen to his limbs, his left side went into spasm and the tremor in his hand worsened. In a rush of panic and self-pity, he mentally scanned himself and became aware of the nagging pain in his foot and calf and the constriction around his hips. It was as if the thought of losing Carrie had set free his CP. He told himself he was being ridiculous, that it was all psychosomatic, but his body didn't lie. It couldn't. Joe had had years of coming to terms with the irrefutable fact that his physiology was what it was – namely, ungovernable. And what his body was telling him, as he sat alone in his apartment 3,000 miles away from his girlfriend, was that he was in big trouble.

He needed to talk to her. He called.

She did not pick up.

He was reduced to texting her.

It took him twenty minutes to compose the message. What he ended up with was: Hi Carrie. I'm worried I haven't heard from you. I really need to hear your voice. I want us to talk, properly. Please ring me when you get chance. I'm around all evening. I love you. J x

He sent it, waited a few minutes, then in an overkill move, but one that left no chance she could miss his intent and his need, sent her an email as well.

Once dispatched, there was nothing he could do, but wait and worry.

Chapter 44

OLI WOKE WITH a heart thump. His phone was ringing. He knocked it on the floor, cursed, had to hang over the side of the bed and scrabble around the carpet to retrieve it. The screen flared into life in the darkness. 12.45 a.m. What the...? Joe's number. He answered, feeling... nothing good. 'Hello?'

There was no preamble. 'Why did you tell her?'

Oli knew instantly what Joe meant, but he played for time. 'What are you talking about?' He pushed himself upright. The room was cold and he still had the jitters from having been woken so abruptly.

Joe ignored him. 'I want to know!' The anger poured into Oli's ear, the miles between them shrank. 'What the fuck were you hoping to achieve?' Oli started to speak, but Joe cut him off. 'It was you. I know it was you! Don't you dare try and deny it.'

'I didn't tell her.'

'You fucking liar. She told me you two talked.'

They did, often, but why would she tell Joe that he'd said anything?

It sounded like Joe was crying, but that took none of the edge off his rambling fury. 'All those cosy evenings round at Mum's, and your nice little heart-to-hearts. Carrie told me how supportive you've been. You bastard!' It was a simple, sharp accusation.

Oli repeated himself, although he knew Joe wasn't listening. 'I swear I didn't.'

'Fucking liar!' Joe roared.

There was no hope of convincing him. This was the incendiary that was always going to explode. The fuse had been laid the moment Oli discovered Joe was cheating, but it had been buried, out of sight, no threat to anyone – until Christmas.

Christmas had changed everything.

Because it was over Christmas that Oli had started to see Carrie for who she really was. It was those feelings of recognition and desire that had lit the fuse, and the pressure of holding on to Joe's secret had been smouldering away and burning hotter and brighter ever since. So – as bad as this was going to be, and it *was* going to be bad – a big part of Oli was glad the blast had finally come.

'If you calm down, I'll tell you what happened.' There was a lull in the ragged breathing. Joe getting himself under control? Oli hoped so. 'I didn't tell Carrie about Brianna.'

Joe cursed again, but slightly less vehemently.

Oli ploughed on. 'I swear I didn't.'

'Well, she knows. How did she find out, if you didn't tell her? You're the only one who knew.'

The self-pity irritated Oli. 'Because she's not stupid.'

'Are you calling me stupid!'

Oli thought about denying it. Didn't. 'I wasn't, but yeah, why not?' It was time for some home truths for his 'sun shines out of his arse' twin brother. Joe had brought this on himself. 'You are fucking stupid. For messing around behind her back. For staying in New York when you knew Carrie wanted you home. For being a selfish prick. For treating her like shit.'

'Oh, now you're the expert on relationships, are you?' Oli didn't bother responding to that. Joe ploughed on. 'You're just jealous. You can't bear the thought that I'm doing better than you are, can you? That's why you had to go and stuff it up for me, didn't you?'

'Think what you like, little bro. But this isn't on me. And you know it. This car crash is your own fault.'

They both drew breath, ready to go again, but when Joe spoke his voice was quieter, some of the energy drained from it. 'You're right. It is my fault.' Oli let that hang. 'She said I'd changed. That you all thought the same.' Again Oli didn't say anything. 'I have. I thought it was a good thing.' The self-pity was back.

'Not if it leaves other people behind, Joe.'

'No.' There was a very long pause. Oli listened to his brother breathing. 'Carrie asked me why I didn't want to come home.'

'And what did you say?'

'I don't know, really. Stuff about my job.'

'But she guessed.'

Joe must have moved, because for a second or two the call dropped off. His voice re-emerged mid-sentence. '...wasn't ever serious. It really wasn't.'

'What? I didn't catch all that.'

'Don't believe me!' He was angry again. Irrational. Swinging through the emotions wildly, like a beaten boxer still trying to land a punch. His speech hitched.

It struck Oli that Joe had been drinking, or perhaps it was the stress. His speech was normally good, but it could let him down when he was really wound up. He interrupted him. 'Joe!'

'What?'

'If it wasn't serious with Brianna, then why did you keep sleeping with her?' Oli genuinely couldn't understand why he'd risked it. For what? For sex with someone who didn't matter, when Carrie so obviously did.

'I don't know.' Joe mumbled something else that Oli didn't catch. More bleating about finding himself, no doubt.

Oli lost patience with him. 'Carrie couldn't understand why you were prepared to sacrifice your relationship for a job, even if it was in New York. Once you told her you were staying out there for longer, she felt you were taking the piss.' That was his expression, not hers, but the sentiment was the same. And he'd encouraged it. 'She started thinking there had to be something else going on, or someone else; that you weren't staying on just because the job was going so well. She said if you were seeing someone, then it reflected how little you really cared about her.'

More silence. 'And you didn't reassure her.'

'About what, Joe?'

'That I loved her. Love her.'

Oli didn't hesitate. 'No, I fucking didn't. Because she deserves the truth, and you were lying to her.'

There was a beat of silence. Joe gathering himself. Then he spat, 'Well, fuck you!'

Oli was done. 'Yeah. Right back at you, bro.' He ended the call. Threw his phone down. Lay back in bed.

Bomb detonated.

Fallout to follow.

Chapter 45

OLI KNEW HE SHOULDN'T go anywhere near Carrie, not immediately – which he didn't, not for days and days. It took more discipline than he knew he had.

He messaged her, of course, as any good friend would, in the circumstances – which were left undefined. Neither of them mentioned Joe directly. How could they? In her infrequent texts to him she put on a brave front. She didn't rant or vent or say very much at all, which was her way; her quietly impressive, classy way. It was a restraint that contrasted starkly with the behaviour of many of the women and girls who had passed through Oli's life. The hook-up girls, whose names he'd barely learnt and had certainly forgotten, the girlfriends and the just-friends – he did know a few women he'd never spent the night with – most of them seemed to thrive on a diet of dramas and crises. They were like sharks, they had to keep emoting to survive.

Carrie, she was different, and she was hurting... because of his brother.

The not-knowing what she was feeling was intolerable. It messed with Oli's head. At work his concentration was shot and in the gym every evening, despite the music blasting directly into his brain, he couldn't stop thinking about her. Never before had he so wanted someone to open up to him.

His brother was, of course, no longer a conduit for information, and he was wary of asking his mother. She was struggling to absorb the shock of Joe and Carrie's imploding relationship. She'd called Oli as soon as she found out from Carrie herself that she'd ended it, which she had, two days after Joe's late-night call. It was classic Joe, avoiding the truth; classic Carrie to face into it. Despite their break-up, his mother seemed to think that their relationship was salvageable. *It had to be, surely*, went her circuitous logic, *because they loved each other, had from the very start. They would work it out – as long as Joe managed to get himself back home ASAP.*

Oli had started to ignore some of Beth's many calls, because hearing her fuss and fret about his brother irritated him. She was in full-on mum overdrive – loving, understanding, supportive... forgiving. But then, from what Oli could make out, she wasn't totally in the picture. No mention had been made of Brianna and the cheating. The fact that Carrie might still be protecting Joe, after the way he'd treated her, was beyond Oli's comprehension.

Free-weights routine finished, Oli climbed onto a bike and set the wheels spinning. As he built up his speed and a sweat, he thought about what love like that must feel like – if you were the recipient. It bothered him, far more than he cared to admit, that both his mother and Carrie were prepared to tolerate far more from Joe than anyone ever had from him. He whacked the level up on the bike, pedalled faster.

At what point did understanding tip into indulgence? When did empathy turn into excuses? He rose out of the saddle, put his head down and pushed hard.

Oli had realised Joe was special, in a way that he was not, from the moment he became conscious they were different people... so from about the age of two. He knew because of the way his mother treated them.

From the very beginning, Joe was the one who needed, and got, the most attention. Add in the CP – and all the accompanying hospital appointments, physios, specialist equipment, extra attention – and his status as exceptional was sealed. Although twins, born a mere twenty minutes apart, they'd always been set different targets, milestones and expectations. It had driven Oli mad as a kid that Joe's goals were always easier and, when reached, were greeted with a level of enthusiasm that Oli never enjoyed. Joe had been wrapped in their mother's praise and protection from everything, including criticism, for the whole of their lives. She had been his shield in a way that she'd never been Oli's.

And his mother wasn't the only one. Look at Carrie.

The instinct to protect and nurture had obviously played a huge part in her and Joe's relationship. How could it not? The power and the pleasure of being able to help someone believe in themselves, by simply loving them – he got it, he really did. But was such unconditional love healthy? Was it enough for the person doing the loving? How could it be? In the long run, didn't everyone deserve *mutual* support, affection, respect? Didn't the attraction and the love have to go both ways?

And as Oli pedalled as if his life depended on it, he pondered why no one had ever loved him the way his mother and Carrie loved Joe.

He whacked the stop button. Let his feet follow the loose spin of the pedals. He dropped his head. His breathing sounded like he was suffocating. Sweat dripped onto the bike and the floor. Why was he flogging himself like this? He couldn't exorcise the emotions that were tormenting him. He needed to act on them.

Chapter 46

Everyone else was asleep, or so it seemed. It was obviously easier to sleep and dream with a clear conscience. All Joe could hear was the hiss of the air being pumped around the plane, and the random coughs and contented snores of the other passengers.

He was on his way home.

The past few weeks had been the most miserable of his life – and the most embarrassing.

The speed with which his life had collapsed had shocked, but not surprised him. Carrie had been his anchor – without her, nothing held steady. Everyone he knew was pissed off with him. Justifiably. He had let them all down, in a myriad of ways: personally, professionally, emotionally.

Top of the list was, obviously, Carrie. But he turned away from thoughts of her. He still couldn't rationalise why he'd behaved the way he had. It was as if he'd been intent on wrecking their relationship – which made no sense, she had been the most important person in the world to him. She still was. Everything he'd done since that awful phone call had been for her, about her; had, in all honesty, been in pursuit of resurrecting 'them'. He had to believe it was possible. Life without Carrie on his side didn't bear thinking about, which was why he couldn't.

He'd handed in his resignation the day after their desperate conversation. The response had, understandably, not been good. Emmanuel had been very pissed off. He'd controlled it, because he was that kind of guy, but he was obviously – and totally understandably – unhappy. The hardest question to answer had been 'Why the sudden change of heart?'

The silence that followed had been deeply uncomfortable. To be honest or not? Joe chose something in between, tumbled out a flurry of apologies and half-truths and felt ashamed of himself. 'I've loved working here. Really. It's been fantastic. The people, the opportunities, but...' Emmanuel had waited. 'But things at home are difficult at the moment. My girlfriend...' Emmanuel had blinked, as well he might. Joe had said very little about Carrie at work, for obvious reasons. 'My mum...' Joe threw her in as a deflection. He stopped just short of adding... *my brother.* He was flailing, and they both knew it. 'I have to go back. I'm sorry to do this to you, and the team. I really am.' It was vague and unsatisfactory, but it was all he was prepared to say.

At this point Emmanuel had become brisk. 'Well, if that's the situation, there's not a lot we can do, is there?

I'll put it down to personal circumstances.' The cover story of a liar. 'We'll have to get a plan together for finishing off your work, and in terms of replacing you on the Microsoft project. That won't be straightforward, given we've already sold you in to them. I'll come back to you in a few days, when I've had time to sort it out, then we can agree your notice period, get you to sign the NDA...' He trailed off, as if already tired of him.

Joe had hoped to be released immediately, but he merely nodded mutely. Aware that he was in no position to argue.

The remaining fortnight had been grim – like serving time, which was precisely what he had been doing. Emmanuel was obviously not above impassively meting out some punishment.

Then there'd been the showdown with Brianna.

Word of his resignation unfortunately reached her before Joe had a chance to speak directly to her. She turned up at his apartment that evening in a storm of emotions. Listening to her rage, Joe heard uncomfortable echoes of his conversation with Carrie. The tone and accent were very different, but the underlying accusations were the same. He was selfish. He didn't consider other people. He was so wrapped up in his own wants and needs that there wasn't any space for anyone else. Their long, exhausting and tear-filled fight had confirmed it. He'd become a man who hurt people.

After that, New York lost its appeal.

His apartment was an airless box. Queens a place full of pseuds. Manhattan a nightmare. The non-stop noise grated on his nerves. The criss-crossing torrents of people made the simple act of walking a hazard. The kerbs were too high. The gutters too deep. The garbage overflowing. The smell of dope on every street corner oppressive. What he'd taken for energy was really aggression. The straight-talking was, in fact, rudeness. It was all too much. Within the space of twenty-four hours his love affair with the city was well and truly over. The branding lied, New York was heartless. He couldn't wait to leave.

But now that he had, Joe was dreading arriving home. Because once he got back, he would have to face his mother, his brother and the rest of his life.

The tiny digital plane that represented their flight showed them blipping their way across the wide, blank expanse of the Atlantic. Joe shifted in his seat, trying his best not to disturb the snoring woman to his left, the single man to his right and whoever was in the reclined seat in front of him. Being caged in so small a space was not good. He decided he could last another twenty minutes before he was going to have to get up and stretch. The woman wouldn't smile and make small talk when he had to wake her, not like she had all the way through the meal, despite the big hint – signalled by his headphones – that he wasn't interested in hearing about her trip to see her sister in Scranton.

Joe's thoughts turned to his own sibling.

Oli had not reached out since their deeply bad-tempered phone call, and neither had Joe. They were chalk and cheese in most things, but they were comparable when it came to stubbornness. Infuriated as he was with Oli, Joe felt his brother's absence. It was like a vague but persistent ache – and he was very familiar with how debilitating such low-level pain could be. When he got home they would have to see each other, speak, reconcile. They couldn't go on ignoring each other for the rest of their lives.

His feelings about seeing his mother were, if anything, even more complicated. He longed to be back home with her. She had been unbelievably – no, that was wrong – she had, totally predictably, been very supportive over the past fortnight. She'd been in touch most days with lots of practical advice and optimistic reassurance. She was adamant that he would get through this *rough patch* and, with luck and a huge effort on his part, that Carrie *would* forgive him. Precisely what Carrie would have to forgive had not been tackled. Joe hadn't told her about Brianna. He simply couldn't. The thought of his mother's disappointment in him was too stomach-clenching to contemplate. His guilt had been exacerbated by how hard Beth had tried to mask her own disappointment about their break-up, although he had heard it in her voice. He knew how close his mother was to Carrie. He wasn't the only one hurting at the very real prospect – whatever Beth might hope – that Carrie could be out of the picture, for ever.

It was no good. He had to move.

He tapped the woman's shoulder. No response. Tapped harder. Nothing. In the end he climbed over her awkwardly, praying she wouldn't wake and freak out to find him looming above her, his crotch in her face. Thankfully, she didn't stir. He could barely stand once he got into the aisle. The pain in his hips and knees was excruciating. He held onto the headrests and slowly dragged himself towards the front of the plane, forcing his muscles to obey his brain. Slowly he got some control, and the pain edged back to bearable. He needed to keep moving while he could, so he began making slow passes up and down the aisle, staring at the slumbering passengers and the occasional screen-staring fellow insomniac.

His attention inevitably snagged on the couples among the passengers. He was drawn to one pair in particular. Whereas everyone else had found whatever individual position they were comfortable in, these two were curled in on each other, face-to-face. His arm was draped across her body on top of the blanket, holding her safe. Even unconscious, and 40,000 feet above sea level, they were still a unit.

This was what he'd thrown away. The closeness, the trust, the inexplicable but essential protection of being loved, and loving someone else. The tragedy was that he and Carrie hadn't simply loved each other – they had understood each other. As Joe limped past the embracing couple for a third time, he wondered if they were as compatible as their sleeping pose suggested. Did the bloke know which earring his girlfriend always took out first at night? How her lips going pale was a sign that her period was due? That she would go quiet when she was angry, and talk more when she was tired? That she only sang in his presence when she was drunk, because she thought her voice was awful. Did they disagree on lots of things – music, breakfast cereal, the necessary frequency of hoovering – but never disrespect the other's view? Did they love each other like he and Carrie had?

He doubted it.

He and Carrie had spoken only once since she'd told him they were over. It had been awful. He'd been taken aback when she'd picked up, because all his other calls and messages had gone unanswered. Her abruptness had been harsh, but deserved. 'What?'

'Please, Carrie. I need to talk to you.'

'No, Joe. You don't *need* to, you *want* to. There's a difference.'

'Okay.' He'd been prepared to concede anything, if only she'd stay on the line. 'You're right. What I mean is, I *want* to talk to you. I want to try and explain, and to say I'm—'

She cut him off. 'What? Sorry?' The inadequacy of the word was crystal-clear.

But he had to try. 'Yes. And so much more. I know I don't have the right to expect you to listen to me, but...'

She made a choked, exasperated noise. It stopped him. He could hear her struggling to control her voice and her emotions. He waited. 'Too damn right, Joe.' She drew breath. 'You have no right to expect anything from me – ever again. Not my love, my patience, my support, my effort, my thoughts, my laughter, my sadness, my feelings... my body.' She gulped. 'And not... my stupid, misplaced, pathetic loyalty. You can't have any of it. Not anymore. You've fucked it all up, Joe. You! Not me.'

'Carrie. Please!' He was crying.

Perhaps she was too. But she was unrelenting. 'No. No more. I trusted you! I shouldn't have. Leave me alone.'

He stopped walking up and down the aisle and looked out across the rows of inert bodies. He was so tired – of the flight, of his whirring brain, of himself. He made it back to his row and stood over the snoring woman, willing her to wake. He didn't have the energy to climb over her. Of course she didn't stir, another immovable object in his path. In the end he shook her shoulder. She was not best pleased, but she did, grudgingly, stand up and let him back in. He thudded back into his seat. She into hers. At least there would be no chatting over breakfast now.

He checked their progress on the screen. The little digital plane was still making its lonely way across the Atlantic. Four more hours and they would be landing. He rested his head back against his seat, felt the reverberations of the engines and tried to contemplate his life without Carrie.

He couldn't.

Chapter 47

HE WENT WITHOUT WARNING, which was a considered tactic. He didn't want to be told to go away.

His heart was banging in his chest, and his mouth felt like it was full of chalk dust when he rang the bell. As he waited, he thought about how she'd look. He imagined her in her PJs and her eyes dark-shadowed. Beautiful as ever, but sad. And he couldn't help but imagine her surprise at seeing him. It would be awkward, he was prepared for that. How could it not be? There was stuff they'd have to work through. He would be patient, careful. He wanted to be patient – he'd been working on it. This was his opportunity to be there for her.

The door opened.

He was thrown.

Carrie looked – as she'd said in her texts – okay. More than okay, actually. She looked fine. Dressed in jeans and an oversized white shirt. Bare feet. Painted toenails. Some make-up. She never wore much, but what she wore was effective. Her eyes were her standout feature.

Lively. Intelligent. Eyes that were framed by thick, peaked eyebrows. 'Oli! Hi.'

'Hi.'

'I haven't missed a message from you, have I?'

He felt suddenly unsure. 'No. I just thought I'd call round. On the off-chance. I wanted to see... how you're doing.'

'I'm okay.' Her voice was sparky, for his benefit or her own; either way, it was good to hear. He'd been standing at her door too long. This was not how he'd envisaged it going. Then she smiled. 'Sorry. How rude. Come in. I'm having a beer, do you want one?'

He'd intended to stay away from the booze, he'd wanted to keep his sober inhibitions intact, but it would seem rude to refuse. 'Yeah. Great. Thanks.'

He followed her through to the galley kitchen at the back of the tiny house she shared with another girl. Laura? Oli had never met her housemate. Carrie's half-drunk Moretti was on the side. She fetched him one from the fridge, popped the cap and passed it to him. There was a chilli bubbling on the hob – food for more than one. She saw the direction of his glance. 'A couple of friends are coming round. Lara's out with Harry.' Lara. He'd been close. There was a defiant lilt in her voice. 'We thought we should line our stomachs before we go to the pub to drown our sorrows. You not got a date tonight?' She turned away from him and reached for the rice, measured some out into a mug.

It felt important how he answered, but the awareness of that made him clumsy. 'Me. Um, no.'

At that she raised an eyebrow, mocking. It hurt that she still had him stuck in player-mode. She chucked the rice into the pan. It hissed. She tasted the chilli, found it wanting, sprinkled some more cumin in. Oli watched her dance around the small space, moving out of her way as she opened drawers and cupboards, putting out bowls and cutlery. It felt warmly domestic. His bottle was empty, but he couldn't remember drinking it.

'Have you been all right?'

'Yes.'

'Seriously?'

'Yep.' She paused for a second, looked at him properly – finally. 'I've no choice, have I? Wallowing it in ain't going to change anything.'

'No. I suppose not.' He'd never sounded so lame in his life. He felt fifteen again. No, that wasn't true. He'd had more confidence at fifteen.

She noted his empty bottle. Hesitated. He had the awful sense that she wanted him to leave. The thought made him feel profoundly disappointed. But then she smiled. 'You're welcome to join us tonight, if you want to? One more sad singleton to add to the Valentine's fun.'

Chapter 48

THE OLD, ARROGANT PART of him could see why her friends, Fi and Lily, were on their own on the (allegedly) most romantic night of the year. Fi was funny and warm-hearted, but she was *very* into her politics – Oli imagined she would be hard work, if you spent any length of time with her. She was assertively plain in a 'this is me, take me or leave me' kind of way. And Lily, despite her prettiness and less combative views, had a nervy edge that hinted at past hurts and complicated current needs.

What one of those needs was became apparent as they got stuck into the first round of drinks at the pub, when she started touching Oli's leg. He ignored her. During the second round she went from 'accidental' touches to sustained pressure. After a not-immediately-dismissive few seconds, Oli moved his leg away. Thereon in, Lily stopped talking to him. Before the round was finished, she claimed to have a headache and had convinced Fi it was probably best that they order an Uber before it got really busy.

Oli politely kissed them both goodbye on the cheek, glad to see the back of them. Carrie hadn't joined in the conversation about going home.

'Do you want another one?' he asked her.

'No. I've had enough.' Well, that told him.

But she hadn't left with them. Wasn't moving now. They were both standing around awkwardly as people hovered nearby, waiting to grab their table. Oli was confused. 'So...?'

'I need some fresh air.'

'Yeah. Right. Good idea.' He reached over to grab her coat and held it open for her.

Carrie laughed. 'I didn't realise you were a maître d' in a previous life.' She stepped into the arc of his arms. 'Why, thank you.' Coat on, she wound her scarf around her neck and she was good to go.

Oli shrugged on his jacket and followed her out into the cold night.

There was something magical in the sudden change in sound, temperature and smell. It was like pushing a reset button. The lack of distraction seemed to render them both shy, but as they set off walking, Carrie slid her arm through his. Oli warned himself not to read too much into it. He'd noticed before how tactile she was. She was always hugging and touching people, even complete strangers. She didn't mean anything by it – it was simply her way. They walked in step, with her deciding the route. He was happy to follow her lead.

After a few minutes they reached the river. She stopped, but instead of looking down at the fast-flowing, glassy black depths, she looked up. He did likewise and saw, for the first time in a long time, that high above the murky haze of the street lights the sky was full of stars.

'It's fucking freezing, isn't it?' she declared. It wasn't the most romantic line, but she was right, it was in-your-bones cold, down by the water's edge.

'Yeah, it is. But it is' – he struggled to think of a description that would impress her – 'evocative.'

She laughed. 'Of what? A crime scene? Am I in danger?' She gave him a playful shove. It was a heady feeling, even through layers of clothing.

'I wasn't thinking anything quite so dark. We've been watching too much true crime.' His inarticulacy was surely a giveaway. He waited for her to say or do something, but she simply stayed where she was, a solid presence at his side, her face tilted upwards. It was a moment he wanted to last for ever, and yet to end and become something more.

The tone shift when it finally came was abrupt. 'Why didn't you tell me he was cheating, Oli? Joe said you found out about the other girl when you went to visit him. I'm struggling to understand how you could've known, all that time, and not say anything to me.' She sounded deeply disappointed in him.

Damn Joe! There'd been no need for him to tell Carrie exactly when he'd found out about Brianna. But, of course, Joe had. It was obviously revenge for his alleged betrayal. Oli knew Joe still believed that he'd told Carrie, or at least heavily hinted there was something going on. It bothered Oli, deeply, that he'd chosen the wrong loyalty all those months ago.

His hesitation brought a response. Carrie left the stars to their own devices and rounded on him. 'Oli?'

It was time to pick a side. He picked her. 'Joe made me promise not to say anything.'

Her expression flickered between pain and disgust. 'So you kept quiet out of sibling loyalty?'

Before his eyes Oli saw her feelings for him twist and blacken. He took a breath and piled in, pushing his brother further under the bus that had already run over him. 'Yes. And I regret it. I'm so sorry I didn't say anything.'

Carrie didn't look away, she wanted more. And he wanted to give her something that would help to excuse and, hopefully, redeem him.

'We really didn't talk about it when I visited him, or later. I presumed it was a fling.' Not quite true. 'I didn't know it was still going on.' That was true, although he'd had his suspicions. 'He shut me out.' Like he had her. They had things in common. Far more than just his brother. Oli desperately wanted her to focus on those shared interests, their similar sense of humour, the music, films, meals, good times they'd shared, not his betrayal of their friendship. 'Being in New York changed him.' Create some distance between them, that was Oli's play – although he really wasn't playing.

'Yeah. It did.' For the first time he heard bitterness in her voice, and he was glad.

'Carrie?'

'What?'

'Not that it makes any difference, but I think he's behaved like a complete tool. And I told him that, when he called me after you'd confronted him.' He didn't need to say *ended it*. They'd reached an impasse. Joe was a cheating bastard and he'd been complicit.

She started walking. He followed her.

'Carrie. Please. I honestly thought it wasn't serious. I thought he'd get it out of his system and come home, to you.'

'Yeah, well, he obviously had no intention of doing that, did he? Not any time soon. He'd still be out there now, living the dream, if I hadn't called him out.'

Oli reached out and took hold of her arm, slowing her pace. 'You're right, he's been unbelievably selfish. And that's on him.' It was now or never. 'I think he was a fucking idiot to choose to stay there rather than coming back to be with you.'

She walked on for a few more steps, then stopped. Before his eyes, she seemed to deflate. Her defiance trickled away. 'All that time, Oli. All those years. I thought what we had was... not special maybe, but at least real. I thought we had a future. But he threw it away the first opportunity he got. Just to sleep with someone else because – and I quote – he was *curious to see what it would be like!* He acted like it didn't matter. That somehow because it happened in New York, it wasn't real. Then he lied to me, for months. He made a total mug of me.'

Hesitantly he put his arms around Carrie and pulled her close, using his height to shelter her. She didn't resist. She said something, which he didn't catch because her face was level with his chest. She eased away from him, but not out of his embrace. She was calmer when she spoke. 'Why didn't you say anything to me when he went back after Christmas?'

'I didn't want to screw things up between the two of you.' That silenced her, but her expression was one of incredulity rather than understanding. He didn't blame her for being confused. It was fucked up. He hadn't realised how badly until New Year's Eve. Watching them dance had brought home to Oli quite how much he envied their relationship. How much he was drawn to Carrie, to her warmth, to the certainty that being with her would make the world better. *And* how impossible it was for him to interfere. Because he knew that if he was the one who said anything about Joe's infidelity, then everyone, including Carrie, would blame him for wrecking the relationship of the century. And for that, Oli had hated Joe.

She looked so sad. 'Well, it's well and truly screwed now.'

'Yeah, I know. And I'm sorry.'

'It's not you who should be sorry.'

The atmosphere between them changed again. Another reset button pushed. The tension hadn't lessened, but the charge was different.

The distance between them was achingly wide, and yet so small.

Regardless, she stepped into the gap. She brought her cold hands to his cheeks, held his face and his heart in her hands. They stared at each other, communicating without saying a word. She kissed him. He was confused. Was she forgiving him? Absolving him of his part in the deceit?

Then she kissed him again and he knew it wasn't forgiveness she was offering him.

Chapter 49

BETH HAD BEEN WRONG. Despite the cherry blossom, the heavy-headed tulips and the days of bright, cold sunshine, April *was* the cruellest month. It had all gone wrong, so quickly and so spectacularly, that it was hard to readjust.

Joe was home, and deeply depressed. His relationship with Carrie really seemed to be over. Finished. No coming back from it. All that love, understanding and potential written off, just like that. She blamed Joe, of course she did, he'd got over-confident, lost sight of what was important, taken Carrie for granted. But she also blamed New York, his employers at Blizzard – it was a stupid name for a company – and Joe's faceless, trendy new friends who had seduced him into forgetting what really mattered. And loath as she was to admit it, she also, ever so slightly, blamed Carrie. If she'd been more demonstrative, made her feelings more plainly known, if she'd objected more strongly when Joe said he was going to stay on until the summer, they might still be together.

The impact of their break-up was painful to see.

The Joe-at-Christmas – full of confidence and life – was long gone. Once home, he shrank back into himself. He was lost. No job, no girlfriend, no energy, no motivation, no self-belief. Once again she didn't know how to help one of her sons. Whatever she said was wrong. Leaving him alone didn't work. Trying to keep him occupied failed. Sympathising irritated him. Gently cajoling him to do something – anything – likewise. There were times when, despite her sympathy, she felt deeply discouraged, fearful that he was never going to haul himself out of the hole he'd fallen down. Or perhaps, more accurately, jumped into.

Carrie had not set foot in the house since he'd returned home. Beth understood, but she mourned her absence. Carrie hadn't only been good for Joe, she'd been good for Beth too. The painful truth was it was her laughter and energy that Beth missed most. At night, when she went around the house switching off the lights, she silently acknowledged that she was grieving as well, for the daughter-in-law she would never have and the grandchildren who would never be.

And just at the point when she and Joe needed him most, Oli had reverted to his old ways, barely coming to the house and hardly ever calling. Their cosy winter weekend get-togethers were a faint memory. And even when he did finally show his face, his impatience to get away again was hurtfully evident. Her appeals to him to try and support his brother while he was at his lowest ebb had been met with evasion and no action.

She felt angry and frustrated – with both of them.

And that wasn't good.

Their birthday was in ten days' time and, for the first time ever, Beth was dreading it.

Chapter 50

OLI WOKE UP ON his birthday – and his brother's birthday – in Carrie's bed.

He sensed she was awake, although neither of them moved or said anything. The weirdness that stalked their 'relationship', such as it was, pulsed stronger than ever. He held himself still, delaying the moment they would have to go back to pretending that what they were doing, and had been doing for the past month, was perfectly normal.

He was sleeping with his twin brother's long-term ex-girlfriend. It was the worst type of sleazy cliché.

But it didn't feel that way to him.

To him, it felt serious, *was* serious – more so than any other relationship he'd had before. When he was with Carrie, it was hot, heady and passionate, but it was when they were apart that he was most aware of the depth of his feelings for her. For the first time in his life, Oli had fantasies; not sexual ones, but powerful daydreams of spending the rest of his life with her. He imagined them living together, buying somewhere that needed doing up and them working together on it to make it their own. He longed to do all the mundane stuff with Carrie: wander around DIY stores, strip paint off skirting boards, make curries, watch TV, go to bed and simply hold her close. He wanted to be with her, properly.

He caught himself thinking about how and where he might propose to her. He pictured her shock, the long, agonising pause that would undoubtedly follow his proposal, then the joy when she eventually said 'yes'. He even imagined children. Their children. Carrie would be a fantastic mother. What sort of father would he be? Who knew? But he would do his best, and it would be enough, because they would be together.

Yeah, Oli was acutely aware he was in real, deep trouble – because he knew he was in love.

What he didn't know was how Carrie felt. Because although they were sleeping together, they were not *together*. If anything, the shift to becoming lovers had created more of a space between them. He caught her looking at him sometimes with a puzzled expression, as if she couldn't quite believe what she'd got herself into. After a second or two she would shiver herself out of whatever trance she was in. The sad smile that followed her mental retreats was somehow worse than the withdrawals. And yet she kept summoning him – into her life, into her house, into her bed, into her body, into their secret.

And he came willingly, knowing that he was leaving himself wide open.

They rarely went out. They never met up with anyone else. And, as far as he knew, she hadn't told anyone about them. Neither had he. It was an unspoken pact, designed to protect everyone involved, but it hurt him, because it made it very clear that whatever it was they were doing, it was an error: a repeated one, but no less wrong for that.

He understood, or tried to. She was conflicted – finishing a long, intense relationship with one brother, then taking up with the other so soon, and not just another brother, but that brother's twin who she'd known for years, must be confusing. Oli had to try very hard not to think about how it must be for her, touching, kissing, stroking, holding, cuddling, sleeping with someone who looked nearly the same as Joe, and yet who thought, felt, moved and fucked so differently. He knew that if he let himself think about it too much, they were doomed to fail, and so he didn't. But it took a lot of effort to block Joe out of the picture and make it simply about the two of them. The worry that he'd never escape his brother's shadow stalked him.

Oli couldn't pretend he was asleep any longer.

He stirred. Carrie did likewise. He wanted to put his arms around her and hold her, but he knew she would shrug him off. Their lovemaking took place in the dark, without words. In the daylight they were friends, nothing more. To remind him of the limits of their relationship, she sat up, creating space between them. At some point in the night she must have picked her T-shirt up off the floor and put it on – along, he was guessing, with her knickers. Her barriers were all firmly back up.

He matched her. Sat up. Leant back against the pillows. Reached for his phone. He flicked through his feeds. Faked indifference.

'Happy birthday.' Her voice was a clear giveaway that she'd been awake for a while. Waiting for him to leave? Creeping out while Lara was in the kitchen or the bathroom.

'Thank you.' No, nothing weird going on here, nothing at all.

'You got many messages?'

'A few.' He kept scrolling.

There was a name he didn't recognise. Ella H. He flipped through his mental list of girls met, flirted with, slept with, finished with – plus the ones who had got away. No, he couldn't recall an Ella H. He put his phone aside. He was so glad those days were behind him.

'Are you going see him today?' she asked.

Joe. It always came back to bloody Joe. 'Not specifically.' That was the other problem; Carrie knew all about their family habits and traditions. Christ, she'd been around for all their birthdays since they were sixteen.

'But you're going over to see your mum?' Did she sound wistful, even a little sad at the thought of his mother and the times they used to have, together? Oli swerved that train of thought as well. Maybe, with time,

Carrie would be able to reconnect with Beth, build back the closeness they used have – through him. It was hard to imagine.

'Yeah.' God, why did it have to be so awkward. 'There'll no doubt be the obligatory mountain of food and a cake, with twenty-four candles stuck in the top.'

'Oh, poor you!' She was right – he was being a brat. 'When are you going over?'

'Lunchtime.'

Neither of them said anything for a minute. It felt longer. Oli realised that the needy lover in him was waiting for a present or at least a card from her. He wanted to be *that man* in Carrie's life: the friend, the more-than-friend, the lover for whom she'd spent time and effort choosing the perfect gift.

He was out of luck.

'I'm off for a shower.' She slid out of the bed without so much as a kiss.

He picked up his phone again. There was nothing from his mum or Joe. 'Happy birthday, mate!' Self-pity, spoken out loud, to an empty bedroom.

He scrolled back to his mystery woman. Ella H.

He clicked on her message, out of curiosity, and fell through a rent in reality.

Chapter 51

JOE HAD HAD EVERY intention of going out when his mother told him Oli was coming round to celebrate their birthday – although he hadn't said anything to her. Her pained disappointment would have been too much to bear. Better to take the coward's route and sneak out while she was in the kitchen preparing lunch. He would endure the recriminations later. It was an appalling way to behave, but that was him now. Joe, the bastard who didn't give a toss about anyone else's feelings.

Or at least that had been the plan, until he'd opened a message on his phone from a girl called Ella H. No surname provided. A series of old photos were attached to the message. Photos that featured his mum, his dead dad and him and Oli as babies.

Joe peered closer at the images that had appeared, out of the blue, from some complete stranger, in a DM on his Insta feed. They'd all been taken in a hospital – Newcastle General, to be precise. That bit made sense. He'd seen such shots before, many times. There was one hanging in a frame at the turn on the stairs in the hallway, and his mum had included a couple of very similar ones in the photobooks she'd made for their birthday a few years back.

He zoomed in on the images of his dad. They showed a decent-looking bloke, despite the bad hairstyle and baggy polo shirt. The man's attention was not on the person taking the pictures, but on his newborn sons. There were photos of him holding them in turn, then one of him sitting in a blue vinyl chair with both of them in his arms – one big, pink, healthy baby – Oli; one puny white thing – Joe. Always the comparison, always the contrast. Their father's smile was wide, easy, unguarded. There was a strong sense of the potential of the life to come in these classic, proud-dad shots. The thought clogged Joe's throat. He looked away for a moment, composed himself, looked back. He guessed the photos must have been taken by their mother, not long before he and Oli had finally been passed fit to leave the hospital, and so a matter of days, maybe hours, before their father had died.

Ella H claimed that she was *family*.

What the hell did she mean by that? What sort of family? Joe couldn't remember his mother mentioning an Ella. But then again, she rarely spoke about anyone from her past. Even their father's ghost had been allowed to flicker and fade into the background in recent years. Except here he was, resurrected to youthful vigour by some photos, sent by some girl, who obviously wanted something, but was not prepared to come out and say what.

As Joe studied the photos an awful thought occurred to him. Why had this Ella H person chosen to message him rather than his brother or his mother? Had she seen the pictures of him, clocked his CP and decided he would be the soft touch? His paranoia drew a nice deep breath and inflated. He'd posted nothing since his break-up with Carrie, but maybe that absence had sent some sort of signal. 'She' – or whoever it was – could have been following him for months, lurking in the cyber-shadows, seeing all his braggy posts from New York. Perhaps she/they had worked out, from his sudden social-media silence, that he was in a bad way and had decided this was the most opportune moment to pop up and start claiming a connection.

Joe told himself to get a grip.

He reread her messages. She'd used 'you', which he'd interpreted as meaning just himself, but it could mean him and Oli. His brother could, at this very moment, be opening and reading the same claims. Why would you contact one twin and not the other?

Joe waited, but there was nothing from Oli. He'd been on his phone, Joe had checked, so perhaps this girl had only contacted Joe after all. He felt himself beginning to spiral again. Was he being targeted as part of some sort of scam?

To distract himself from the tight knot of emotions that had coagulated in his stomach, he went out onto the landing and listened. His mother was, of course, in the kitchen, her natural home. The radio was on and she was moving around, preparing lunch. All as you'd expect. All as normal as ever.

Joe returned to his room and sat on his bed in a stew of indecision. He contemplated sending the mystery Ella H a reply, but decided against it. He didn't want to prove himself quite as gullible as whoever was behind the messages thought him to be. He considered texting Oli, but couldn't bring himself to. He still felt a wave of anger every time he thought about or saw his brother. Crisis or not, he refused to be the first one to blink. There was really only one person he wanted to talk to. But he couldn't. He had well and truly burnt that bridge.

He looked at the photos again. Were they evidence of a long-lost relative reaching out or a cynical attempt to extort cash? There was nothing he could do other than sit and obsess, and wait for his brother to arrive.

Chapter 52

IT WAS PROGRESS, OF sorts.

Both of her sons together in the same room, being civil to each other, breaking bread, making small talk. She knew it was for her benefit rather than their own, but at least it was something. The distance between them frustrated her. She might have grown to question the myths about the special bond between twins, but she'd always believed their close relationship as children would stand them in good stead as adults. And yet look at them now, having to make an effort to get through a single meal amicably.

Hence, good as it was to have them together under her roof, Beth was secretly glad when the roast she'd lovingly cooked was consumed quickly and the offer of a piece of birthday cake was declined, with simultaneous claims of full stomachs. She could feel a wave of sadness building inside her that they'd been reduced to this. Though she had tried, neither of them would talk to her about what was really going on. Never before had she felt so shut out of their lives. To stem the self-pity, she went to fetch their birthday presents.

She no longer bought them the same gifts. They no longer waited for each other to begin ripping the paper off.

Let's face it, they no longer wanted to celebrate their birthday together.

And yet she persisted.

For Oli she'd bought a glossy, expensive coffee-table book, a compendium of the best films of the twentieth century, a nod to their much-missed film nights with Carrie. She'd struggled to think of an appropriate gift for Joe. After much deliberation she'd gone for a six-month gym membership, though she was worried that he'd see it as nagging, which, in truth, it was – although it came from a place of love.

'Thanks, Mum,' they said – almost in unison. They stood up to kiss her.

That was it. Their birthday celebrations done for another year. She was relieved it was over. As, no doubt, were they.

But then Joe offered to clear up in the kitchen, and Oli, to her surprise, offered to help.

She left them to it, hoping that some time together alone might help to slacken the tension between the two of them.

Chapter 53

IT TOOK UNTIL the roasting tin was clean before Joe finally got round to bringing up the messages. He'd been waiting for Oli to say something and, when he hadn't, Joe had convinced himself that the girl had only contacted him. He was going to have to deal with this on his own. The thought made him feel so weary that he blurted out, 'Have you had any weird texts today?'

Oli paused, then said, very simply, 'Yeah.'

Joe felt a rush of relief. 'Me too.'

Through the open window they could hear someone mowing their lawn and the sounds of the boys who lived two houses along arguing – something about an unfair overarm throw. It was all so cosily and predictably familiar.

'I presume Mum doesn't know anything.' Oli indicated their mother with a jerk of his head towards the sitting room.

Joe stacked the tray on the drainer. 'No. She's been completely normal.'

'So just you and me then?'

'Yeah.'

'And?'

'And what?' Joe honestly didn't know what he thought about it.

Out of nowhere, Oli snapped, 'Don't be such a dick.'

Joe flared back. 'Me? I'm not the one who's behaving like a dick.'

They stared at each other, trapped in their anger. Joe knew why he couldn't forgive Oli – his role in the break-up still stung, but he didn't understand why Oli was so pissed off with him. It was as if they were still stuck in the fraught emotion of that awful transatlantic phone call, neither of them able to move past it, or forget it.

But the aggro between them was getting them nowhere.

In the face of their inability to behave like rational adults, it seemed best to return to their old childhood dynamic – namely, Oli the top dog, Joe the also-ran – a time when things were simpler. Joe looked away first, conceding many things: his own guilt, his need for his brother and, crucially, Oli's superiority.

It worked. After a second or two, Oli reciprocated by saying, 'We need to talk.'

'Yeah, we do.'

The lawnmower spluttered to a stop. The silence was

loud. 'But not here. Not with Mum in the next room. The Owl, at eight p.m.?'

Joe nodded, although it wasn't how he'd hoped to be spending his twenty-fourth birthday.

Chapter 54

THEY SAT SIDE-BY-SIDE IN the pub, watching the other punters, who were, by and large, having a far better time than they were. Even the middle-aged couple in the corner, who hadn't said a word to each other since they'd sat down, looked content – the man with his half of pale ale, the woman with her fishbowl of gin and tonic.

Joe surprised Oli by diving straight in. 'I'm guessing she sent you the same pictures?'

They swopped phones, scrolled. Oli saw the same claims, and the same irrefutable photos. He was curious to observe how his brother was handling this. They returned each other's phone.

'They don't prove anything.'

So denial was Joe's considered reaction. Oli wasn't surprised, Joe's MO was usually full blinker-mode. Not so Oli. He liked to get to know his opposition, which was why he hadn't sat on his hands since lunchtime. When he'd got home he'd messaged Ella H and asked for proof of her actual existence and her connection to them.

What else would he have been doing on his birthday afternoon?

'No. Not on their own maybe.'

Joe looked puzzled, as well he might.

Oli found his conversation with Ella on WhatsApp and passed his phone back to his brother. 'But you need to take a look at the other pictures.'

Joe started scrolling. Ella had sent more evidence of, if nothing else, her access to a considerable stash of not only their baby photos, but shots neither of them had seen before, of their mum and dad as a young couple.

'She's got quite an impressive collection of photos, for some random nutter.' Oli watched a rerun of his own initial reactions ripple across his brother's face. Shock, confusion, doubt and, finally, concern that what he was looking at was, in some as-yet-unfathomable way, connected with their lives.

'You DM-ed her?' Joe asked.

'Yeah. I wanted to check her out.'

Joe clicked on her profile pic and enlarged it, exactly as Oli had. He was getting up to speed.

The picture showed a young girl. She looked about nineteen or twenty years old, certainly younger than they were. She had dark eyes and dark hair. A fringe. Big hoop earrings. A nice enough face. A slight smile. The definition of the girl next door. Her nose had a look of theirs. Perhaps her eyebrows were similar. The shape of her lips could be seen to have a look of theirs. But there was no striking resemblance.

Oli needed to tell him. 'She gave me her full name.' The clincher? 'She's called Ella Louise Hughes.' Their dad's surname. 'And she claims she's our half-sister.'

Joe slumped back against the vinyl banquette, his shoulder brushing Oli's. 'Shit!'

'Yep. Exactly. "Shit" just about covers it.' Oli let that thought drop and send out its ripple of consequences. 'As you can see from her messages, she was quite forthcoming when I challenged her. She gave me an address: seventeen Leyburn Avenue, Newcastle upon Tyne, NE7 8AP. It exists. I checked. And so does she. I've found profiles for the same girl on Snapchat and LinkedIn. She works at a medical-supplies company.'

'Have you tried to call to her?'

'No. Not yet. I wanted to talk to you first.' That was true. Whatever was going on between the two of them, and there was a lot – far more than Joe knew – this bullet had both their names on it.

Joe was still studying the girl's profile photo, processing what he was hearing and looking at.

Oli kept talking to give him time. 'And, apart from the extensive archive of old photos, she knows stuff. About Mum. About the time we spent in the special-care unit when we were born.'

'And about Dad?' There it was. Joe was getting up to speed.

It was a good question. How was it possible that they had a half-sister, a younger half-sister, living in Newcastle under their father's surname, if their dad had died twenty-four years ago – as they had been told, and always believed?

'She's cagey about him. When I asked any direct questions, she swerved them.'

'Because she's lying?'

Oli couldn't tell whether Joe wanted Ella's claims to be true or not. But that was no great surprise. He didn't know himself. A dead dad or a live one who'd had nothing to do with them all their lives? It wasn't much of a choice. 'I don't know.'

'But?'

'My instinct, from what she's said, is no.'

'So you think she's for real?' The million-dollar question.

Oli took a mouthful of his beer, set down his bottle slowly, putting off his verdict. 'Yeah. I think she might be.'

'Fuck!'

'Yeah.'

They fell silent for a moment.

Why *had* Oli gone from dismissing Ella H as some sort of crank to suspecting that what she was claiming might very well be true? Well, for a number of reasons. First, Ella's messages had been rational, detailed, well written and, so far, all she'd asked for was a meeting. And second, and this was a big *and*, when you thought about it – and Oli had, all day – their family history was hardly normal. In fact when you properly thought about it, you could say it was incredible.

Most people's fathers did not die a matter of hours before their newborn sons came home for the first time. Most people's mothers did not up sticks immediately afterwards and move to the other end of the country with twins, especially when one of them was not well. They did not go on to set up a life, and a business, with a woman they'd only just met. Nor was it natural for that woman to become, to all intents and purposes, the only family the boys had ever known. Because, let's not forget, neither Oli nor Joe had ever met a real aunt, uncle or cousin. (Oli had only vague memories of his grandma. He and Joe had been seven when she died.) How abnormal was that? Even for a small family. And most lads did not grow up in a house where the spectre of their father was summoned on a regular basis as a sort of role model, inspiration and threat to behave, all rolled into one.

So yes, Oli was inclined to believe this total stranger, who had reached out to them on their twenty-fourth birthday with news that their mother had been lying for the whole of their goddamn lives.

Which meant... it was possible – indeed probable – that their father had not been dead for the past quarter of a century. He was not an absence, a sorrow, a regret, a ghost. No. He was alive and well, and living in Newcastle.

And if that was the case, what the fuck had he and Joe been playing at?

Why hadn't they questioned any of this before? Why had they swallowed such an improbable chain of events without ever stopping to question the peculiarity of it all? How gullible had they been to believe, hook, line and sinker, such a mammoth, sustained lie?

'Very' was the answer.

But children are gullible, wasn't that the whole point of childhood? It was supposed to be a time of innocence when you could trust adults, especially your parents (or parent, in their case), to tell you the truth. But it looked like their mother, and Sab – the thought of her possible, indeed probable involvement had only just occurred to Oli – had exploited that faith. The two people who, until a few hours ago, he would have trusted with his life were, seemingly, consummate liars.

Joe was obviously still computing. He kept picking up and putting down his beer without drinking. Eventually he said, 'We need to talk to Mum.'

'Yep, we do.'

'Together,' Joe added.

Finally, ironically, here was something they agreed upon.

Oli downed his drink. Yes, they needed to talk to her, but more than that, they needed to confront her, find out what the fuck was going on – had gone on, all those years ago. The thought made him feel prickly with anxiety. A showdown with their mother, the nicest woman you could hope to meet, or so everyone thought, including, up until twelve hours ago, her own sons.

'You'll set it up then? At the house? As soon as you can?' Oli said.

Joe nodded again, miserably.

'And we agree that neither of us will say anything to her beforehand?' He detected a slight hesitation in his brother. 'I mean it, Joe. Nothing.'

The resentment was back. 'I heard you! There's no need to bang on about it.'

So Joe wasn't comfortable with them setting a trap for their mother. Tough. A trap was exactly what was called for. They needed to surprise her; that way there'd be no opportunity for any more carefully crafted lies. 'Okay.' Oli stood up. There was nothing left to say. 'Text me when it's sorted.'

'Yeah.'

At the door Oli stopped and looked back at his brother. He sat, on his own, in the middle of the busy pub, oblivious to his surroundings.

Their problem had been shared. But in no way had it been halved.

Chapter 55

After Oli left, Joe sat watching the ebb and flow of the other customers for a long time.

So long that one of the bar staff pointedly came over to collect his empty bottle and wipe down his table, but he simply couldn't face going home and making small talk with his mother. He didn't trust himself to be able to pretend nothing had changed, when it appeared everything had. Instead he went up to the bar and ordered a Scotch. His mood must have been obvious because, although the pub was busy, no one asked to share his table. Or perhaps it was the tremor every time he lifted his glass to his mouth that put them off. It wouldn't be the first time he'd been mistaken for a drunk.

The whisky was suitably astringent and harsh to swallow.

It was hard to credit that this was his life now. He was unemployed. Living at home. Sponging off his mother. He had lost – no, he had driven away – the person he loved most in the world. He'd already been standing on the edge of a precipice. And now this: the distinct possibility that his whole life had been built on an incomprehensible lie.

He downed his drink, grabbed his jacket and pushed his way out of the bar.

It was cold outside. He set off walking. It took him a few streets before he realised it was raining. The further he walked, the heavier the rain got. It soaked through his jacket to his shirt and his skin. The bottoms of his jeans sucked up water from the puddles as he crashed through them. He had no destination in mind; anywhere that was not home would do. He was hurting. He walked fast, not caring what he looked like. He'd had enough of endlessly trying to control his body and his emotions. He knew before he arrived where he was heading, of course he did. He was hardwired to turn to her in times of need.

Without waiting to give himself a chance to back out, he rang her doorbell.

There was a light on upstairs. She was in. Thank God. He heard her coming down the stairs. Saw her blurry silhouette through the glass panels in the door. The lock turned.

'Joe!'

'Sorry.' He was. More than he would ever be able to say.

'You're soaked.'

'Yeah.'

'Why are you here?'

'Because... I can't bear it.'

Carrie hesitated.

She looked like home. He waited for her to decide.

'You'd better come in.'

He'd never been so relieved and grateful in his life.

Chapter 56

THE PROMISE HAD BEEN to say nothing to *their mother*. But Sab? In Oli's opinion, she was fair game.

He headed to her house straight from the pub.

What else was he supposed to do? Carrie had made it clear that their Saturday night was – yet another – one-off. He couldn't talk to her about this, theirs was not that sort of relationship. In addition to which, as she'd told him, repeatedly, she was done with the complexities of their family.

But without anyone to offload on, the curiosity about his father was burning a hole in Oli's soul. Sussing out what Sab knew, and how long she'd known it, was one of the few things he *could* do. He knew there was a risk that she'd say something to his mother, but that didn't stop him.

Unsurprisingly, Sab was surprised to see him on her doorstep at 9.30 p.m. on his birthday. 'To what do I owe this honour? I thought you'd be out celebrating.'

'Nah, not my thing anymore.' He tried for a relaxed grin. Failed.

She seemed unfazed and smiled. 'Liar! Come on through.'

She'd obviously been working. There was a laptop on the countertop, as well as an open bottle of red wine.

Despite Sab's relaxed manner, Oli knew she still put long hours into the business. It was her nature never to be satisfied, she was always looking for new opportunities. Oli had grown up listening to her cajole his mother into taking the next step – the next, possibly lucrative risk. To date, her instincts had been proved right. From personally cleaning offices in Harrow for below-minimum wage, she and his mother now owned a franchise business that employed, indirectly, more than 350 people and made very healthy profits. It reminded Oli, not for the first time, that he owed a lot of the creature comforts in his life to Sab's drive and ambition. Without her, his mother would never have done it.

In his heightened state of mind Oli couldn't help wondering what else his mother might not have done without Sab by her side. She'd always been the dominant one in the relationship.

He clocked Sab watching him, waiting for an explanation for his impromptu house-call. To deflect any awkward questions, he wandered around the kitchen. It was a big, sleekly designed space with plenty of room to roam. Another random thought snuck into his head – he was awash with them. He wondered if Sab was lonely living in such a big house, on her own, and why she chose to remain single. She was attractive, full of life, well dressed, well off. And it wasn't due to any lack of attention. There'd been plenty of blokes, some of them keen, but none of them ever seemed to make it across the finishing line of the challenging obstacle course Sab set for them. With each relationship that ended, with a bang or a whimper, she would laugh and say she was too choosy to settle down with anyone. But was it really that? As Oli cruised nervily around her lovely, well-appointed kitchen, he contemplated whether Sab had other motivations for staying single, motives tied to her exceptionally close relationship with his mother and their shared past.

He was getting side-tracked, but that's what stirring up old shit did. It brought all manner of crap bobbing to the surface.

'I just thought I'd call in. I haven't seen you in a while.' There were the remnants of Sab's evening meal on the side: the end of a loaf of sourdough, something in a pan on the hob. Leftover stew? She was a good cook but, perhaps ironically, given their line of business, a slapdash housekeeper. He tore off a hunk of bread, dipped it in the sauce, chewed, swallowed, buying time. It tasted good. Mouthful eaten, he set off on another lap. 'I was chatting, a couple of days ago… with Carrie.' He winced at his own inarticulacy.

She raised an eyebrow at the mention of Carrie. Sab never bothered to hide her feelings, but, unlike his mother, she was much better at not always voicing them. Perhaps she believed her face was enough comment. It often was. He went on, pretending to be as casual as you like. 'We got talking about our childhoods. Stuff we didn't know about each other.' He was stepping near one bear trap, in order to set another. He stopped by the bread board and tore off another chunk, simply to give his hands something to do. Time for a downright lie. 'She asked me how you ended up being our pseudo-auntie.'

Sab lifted her heavy hank of hair from one shoulder to the other, as if it were a cat that needed resettling. 'Why on earth is she interested in that? It's ancient history.'

But it wasn't, was it? 'I don't know. But it made me realise I know very little about you and Mum in the early days. You always seem to have been... *just there*.'

She laughed, but Oli thought he saw a flicker of something guarded in her normally frank gaze – although, to be fair, he had been imagining all sorts of reactions since he and Carrie had started sleeping together. 'Thanks for that. You mean like an ugly, inherited sideboard or a bad smell in your drains.'

He tried to match her bantering tone. 'I would never describe you as ugly.' He left a pause for effect. He was shedding crumbs all over the worktop. He dropped what was left of his piece of bread. 'But seriously, it got me thinking, how did you two meet?'

She stretched out across the worktop and closed her laptop. 'Sorry, let me get this straight. You had a chat with Carrie, got nostalgic about your mum's past and decided to hightail it over here to ask me about it – on your birthday?'

He shrugged, going for cute. 'You know me, Auntie Sab. I'm impulsive, and these days I lead a very quiet social life.' The sympathy appeal might work – it did for Joe.

Sab pulled an expression that reflected many responses, but sympathy was not one of them.

Oli smiled even harder. 'Go on. Humour me. I'm bored and I've no one to play with.' Still nothing. He prompted her. 'I remember Mum mentioning some sort of single mothers' group.'

Sab finally relented. 'Yeah, that's right. We both went to the same, rather desperate support group for a while.'

Oli threw in a compliment, though it was also a truth. 'She said you owned the room, the minute you walked in.'

Sab shrugged. 'Your mum has always had a healthy appreciation of my magnificence. It's one of the many reasons we've stayed friends.'

Pleasant as all this joking around was, it wasn't helping Oli. It was simply making him even more aware of his deep ignorance about his mother's past, the real timeline of events and exactly where Sab fitted into the picture. 'So, you met in London?'

Sab gave a small non-committal nod, poured herself more wine and offered him some.

He declined and pushed on. 'I still don't get why she came down here from the North-East in the first place.'

'You know why. She wanted to get as far away as possible from what happened.'

'Yes, but why choose London, one of *the* most expensive places on Earth to live, with two small babies, no job and no family around to help?'

'There are cheap places to rent everywhere, even in London, if you're prepared to live in the nasty areas and eat a lot of pasta. As we did, for a long time.' Oli noticed she'd swerved the family issue. He said nothing, waited for more. She grudgingly obliged. 'Us living together made financial sense. We were able to split the bills and the childcare. It meant we could both work... which would have been impossible if we'd been on our own.'

'How old were we when she moved in with you?'

'She didn't *move in with me*, we found a flat together.' Sab was beginning to sound irritated. 'You were still babies.'

'And how long did we all live together?'

'A good few years. Until the business was established and we had enough to rent separately.'

'And then you lived round the corner?'

'Yes.' Her expression was growing increasingly guarded, and irritated. He didn't care.

'And you've stayed close – literally within streets of each other – ever since?'

'Yes.'

'That's seriously weird.'

'Thanks.' Sarcasm followed by a swig of wine.

Their conversation was not going as he'd hoped, but it was going the way he'd expected. They stared at each other. They weren't joking around anymore. Sab sat very straight and still, obviously deliberating. Her tone when she spoke was firm, revealing her repressed impatience. His questions were obviously pissing her off.

'It's not weird. Not in the slightest if...' she paused, 'you have the imagination and the empathy to understand what it was like trying to raise three small children on no money, and with very little help.' That jab went directly between his ribs. He knew he'd had a comfortable life. 'We were single mothers. We both needed someone who would have our backs. More importantly, we were friends. We relied on each other. Supported each other. Trusted each other. It made sense to stay close. It always has.'

She was warning him off, which only served to stir his suspicions. He was done with being subtle. 'Sab. What do you really know about my dad?'

The 'really' did not go down well, but she maintained her composure. 'What your mum's told me.'

'What has she told you?'

'Why are you asking about this now, Oli?'

'Do I need a reason?'

She shrugged. 'I suppose not. But I'm guessing there is one.'

He kept his motivations to himself, not yet ready to set that firework off indoors.

She sighed. 'I know the same as you. That he couldn't wait to be a father. That he was delighted when he found out Beth was carrying twin boys. He was around, a lot, after you were born, when you were both so poorly. He was a very involved dad. I've seen the same photos as you. What happened was a tragedy – for all of you.'

Her tone and stance softened. She slid off her stool and came towards him, reducing the physical and emotional gap between them. Oli sensed her wanting to reach out and touch him, but she hesitated, wary perhaps of his unpredictable mood.

'I know not having a father in your lives has been hard for both you and Joe. But trust me, you've been lucky. You couldn't have had a better parent than your mother. Her desire to raise you well, and with love, is the thing that drives her. She has done everything she could, every day of her life, to make up for that loss. And no matter what I say,' she smiled ruefully, 'she'll never stop.'

It was a pretty speech. The sentiments heartening. It was tempting to lean into her kind words and accept the hug she was offering him... but Oli declined. He deliberately hardened his stance. 'Yeah, it was a tragedy. To die in a *freak* accident' – he laid extra emphasis on the word 'freak' – 'the night before you're due to bring your wife and newborn sons home. How unlucky is that? And unusual.' She was obviously confused by the shift in his tone. 'Do you know how many people die falling off ladders in the UK every year, Sab?'

She took a step away from him. 'Of course I don't. And why would you?'

'Because I looked it up. It's fourteen.'

Sab blinked. 'Oli, what's this about?'

'As you said, Auntie Sab, an awful tragedy. But not the one my mother has been peddling.' There it was, blurted out because he couldn't hold it in any longer. He had shown his hand. That had not been the plan.

He didn't wait to see her reaction.

He brushed past her on his way out. He heard her following him, but he didn't turn round. There was no point talking to her. This was Sab, his mother's oldest friend. As she'd said... they relied on each other, trusted each other, supported each other.

And, on the evidence of this evening, lied for each other.

Chapter 57

Joe woke late.

It had been a long night and a late return home in the early hours of the morning. But he felt a lot calmer.

It was still raining.

He lay listening to it. Grateful. Without the rain, Carrie might have turned him away. He would never know. But she hadn't. She'd let him in. Let him talk. For the first time in months he'd felt a glimmer of hope.

Hope that she might, eventually, forgive him.

Hope that, if she forgave him, he could, perhaps, forgive himself.

Hope that he had a chance of becoming, once again, the man she'd believed he was. A decent man.

Starting as he now meant to go on, he got out of bed and did his exercises properly. The full routine, no shortcuts, because there weren't any, not if you wanted things to work. He'd always known that, in his heart. Stretching complete, he headed into the bathroom. He showered off the previous day's self-pity, wrapped himself in a towel, wiped the mirror clear of condensation and looked at his face. His mum and his brother, and his father, looked back at him. Decision made, he reached for his razor and got rid of the beard. When he'd finished, he stared at his own face for a while.

Whatever happened next, it was time for him to be himself.

Chapter 58

WHEN OLI WALKED into the lounge the following evening – Joe hadn't wasted any time arranging their little showdown – the first person he saw wasn't his mother, it was Sabine. His impromptu visit to her house and his clumsy questions had obviously raised one hell of a big red, flapping flag.

His irritation was intense. 'Why are you here?'

His mother stepped forward. 'I asked her to come.'

'What for: moral support?' He wasn't in the mood for politeness, however much his mother might value it.

'She has every right to be here. When Joe said we needed a... family meeting, my first thought was that Sab should be here. She *is* family after all.'

Oli bit back. 'An honorary member.'

Sab didn't look offended, but his mother flinched. 'Don't be so disrespectful, Oli.'

There was nothing to be gained by making an issue of it. 'Okay, if you want her here – as long as Joe is okay with it?'

Joe looked surprised to be asked; their relationship hadn't contained much mutual consideration of late. He indicated he was okay with Sabine being present, with a shrug. It took Oli a second or two to work out why his brother looked different. The fuzz was gone. It seemed an odd time to suddenly decide that personal grooming was a priority.

As they took their seats Oli wondered if his now clean-shaven brother had stuck to their pact. In the past he would have trusted Joe to keep his mouth shut – they might not have liked or understood each other for most of their lives, but they had always had each other's backs. But a lot had changed since Joe's stint in New York. The tight, restrictive lines of their loyalties had become twisted and stretched beyond recognition.

His mother and Sabine took the big sofa under the window. A united front. Oli sat opposite. Joe opted for the chair by the door.

'So, what's this all about?' His mother looked genuinely puzzled.

So Joe had kept shtum. But what had Sab told her? It would appear not much, other than that Oli was 'on one' about the past.

He kept his opening gambit simple. 'I've... sorry, we – Joe and I – have been contacted by a girl. On our birthday, of all days. Which is apt! She seems to know things about our family. Some very personal things.'

He watched his mother, closely. Her reaction, such as it was, was restrained. She pushed her glasses up the bridge of her nose, then dropped her hand back in her lap. 'I don't understand.'

'No, neither do we. That's why we need to talk to you.'

She glanced at Sabine. Sab looked at Oli. Joe looked from his mother back to him. It was a Mexican standoff, without the guns. Oli tried to read his mother's thoughts from her posture and her expression, but she'd have made a good gunslinger, because although he could see she was on edge, he couldn't identify whether the root cause was fear, anger or surprise. Whatever emotions she was holding onto, they were buried deep. 'What girl?'

'A girl called Ella.' He held back her surname. He saw Joe question this baiting of their mother with a raised eyebrow, but Oli wanted to test her. He needed to see what it would take to force the truth out of her.

'I don't know anyone called Ella.'

'And yet she seems to know us. Or, more specifically, she seems to know a lot about our birth and the time we spent in hospital as babies.' Oli was giving Beth an opportunity to come clean.

But she wasn't biting. 'How would she know about that? And why would she be interested?'

There was no reason to hold back any longer. The purpose of the meeting was, after all, to find out how much of what their mother was saying was true, and how much was false. Oli pulled the pin and threw the grenade. 'She knows our father.'

Their mother closed her eyes. Oli waited. It was like looking at a sphinx, but she couldn't hide inside herself for ever.

He pushed on. 'She claims to be his daughter. Which would make Ella Hughes our half-sister. Our *younger* sister.'

Sabine's composure disappeared and she let slip a loud 'Oh!' In contrast, their mother remained ominously silent.

'Mum!'

Finally, she opened her eyes.

'So could that be true? Could Joe and I really have a sister we know absolutely nothing about?'

She clenched her hands, her fingers crushing her thumbs into her palms, but she remained silent.

Oli was rapidly losing patience. 'How is that possible, Mum? Men don't normally go on having children after they're dead.'

Sabine stood up. 'That's enough, Oli!'

Oli got to his feet as well – Sab's indignation triggering his own. 'I really don't think it's up to you to decide what I can and can't say to my own mother.'

It was at this point that Joe finally entered the fray. 'Can we all just cool it? Getting worked up isn't going to help.' He sounded surprisingly calm. Oli, in contrast, felt like they were all tumbling down a very deep, very dark rabbit hole.

Sabine blinked first. She sat down.

Oli did likewise and said nothing more. He was afraid that if he opened his mouth the anger that had been festering inside him, since Ella had contacted him, would spill out and he would say something he would regret.

Joe stepped into the breach. He'd always been more conciliatory, always wanting to smooth things over rather than face them head-on. It used to drive Oli insane. It still did. 'We're as confused as you, Mum. But this girl has sent us photos that are exact copies of ones we have in this house, and she's told us things that seem strange, if not impossible, to know about our birth. That's why we wanted... we needed to talk to you. We can't make sense of any of it. We hope you can.'

His brother still seemed to be clinging onto the misplaced belief there was a rational explanation, and that their mother was about to supply it.

Oli was not. To him, her reticence spoke volumes. She was obviously stalling. It rubbed salt into the wound, to see her twist in her seat and whisper something to Sabine. Sab replied, at some length, her hand covering her mouth – two witches concocting a brew. Oli watched them with a building sense of rage, but whatever they'd discussed, at least it put an end to the procrastination.

Finally Beth spoke. 'The honest truth is... I don't know who this girl is.' Did he believe her? He didn't know. Her voice steadied. 'I don't know if she's your half-sister,' she took a shallow breath, 'but I can't discount it.' Then, for the first time since they'd stepped inside the house, their mother looked first Oli, then Joe squarely in the face. 'Because you're right. Dead men don't father children. Your dad could be alive.' She took another breath. 'He was, the day we left.'

PART THREE

Chapter 59

TWENTY-FOUR YEARS EARLIER

LIZZIE KNEW SHE WAS in trouble the moment she woke. The alarm clock on the side-table said it was 7.26 a.m. Ian was not in bed beside her. She'd overslept.

She scrambled out of bed, anxiety fluttering in her chest – a moth against a windowpane, battering away, to no effect. Sure enough, the radio was on in the kitchen. Shoving her arms into the sleeves of her dressing gown and her feet into her slippers, she hurried downstairs as fast as she safely could. At thirty-one weeks pregnant, she was no longer designed for speed. They always had breakfast together. It was one of the unspoken rules of their relationship.

She was out of breath by the time she made it into the kitchen. Ian was standing near the kettle, eating a piece of toast. She scanned the work surfaces. He'd already made himself a coffee. She pushed her hair off her face. 'Sorry' – for sleeping in, for not getting down to the kitchen before him to put the kettle on, for not having his breakfast ready and waiting for him. He said nothing, simply chewed. She smiled, willing him to let it go, reinforced her apology with an explanation. 'I didn't hear the alarm.'

He took his time swallowing what was in his mouth. 'I cancelled it. I've been awake for hours, thought I might as well get up.'

'Oh.' There was a beat. She needed to keep talking to stop the crust forming on the atmosphere. 'Didn't you sleep well, again?'

'No. That bloody dog was yapping. Didn't you hear it?'

She vaguely remembered the Durrants' puppy barking when it was let out for a wee.

'Sorry,' she said again. The mood in the room remained rigid.

He took another bite of his toast. Followed it with a swig of a coffee. Swallowed. Pushed his plate away. She hugged her dressing gown to her. He would be fine when he got back from work, her misstep would be forgotten.

She saw him put down his mug. Next stop, the fridge. How could she have forgotten to make his lunch as well? Tiredness of course, but that was no excuse, at least not one she could use. He would think she'd done it deliberately. He saw her panic and followed the direction of her gaze. He knew. He always knew. She made to edge past him. She could get some sandwiches together in a few minutes. It didn't need to be a big issue.

The next thing she knew she was on the floor, on all fours, every joint an exclamation.

The shock was profound. It shouldn't have been; he'd put her down before.

Her first instinct was her babies. Her belly hung heavy beneath the sagging bridge of her spine. She prayed that the arc of her body was strong enough to protect them. She lifted her head, but not much -- it wasn't wise. She focused on his socks and the bottom of his work trousers. They stayed like that: him standing over her, neither of them moving. She held her breath.

The seconds lasted minutes.

The radio burbled on. The travel news segued into the weather — it was going to be bright and cold. Some rain was forecast mid-afternoon. She kept her gaze lowered. Pretended she wasn't there. Silent defence — the only option open to her. A tune came on, something boppy and breezy.

He walked out of the kitchen without a word.

Still she didn't move. She couldn't. She knew from experience that the pain had to be allowed to run its course. It reverberated through her body, down her back, along her arms and legs, seeking an outlet. Her hands and knees had taken the brunt of her fall. They stung. She waited for a movement in her belly, but she couldn't feel anything other than the shock of the fall. From her prone position, cowering on her own kitchen floor, she listened to Ian walking around upstairs. He went into the bathroom and started brushing his teeth, as if nothing had happened.

At last she felt the push of a foot or a hand of one of the babies. They were okay.

She needed to get up. She had a packed lunch to prepare.

She pulled herself to standing using the drawer handles. No blood, no broken skin, this time, but she could feel the bruises brewing inside – a cruel tenderness that would take days to bud and bloom, then fade.

By the time he came downstairs she was standing by the door. He sat on the bottom stair and laced up his boots, ready for work. He took the offered lunch. 'Thank you.' Then, 'Are you all right? You look pale.'

She played her part. 'I'm fine.' How much to compromise? It was always a dilemma, but this needed fixing, and quickly. It couldn't be allowed to start up again. Not now. 'I must have caught my foot on something. These slippers need throwing out.'

For a split second he met her gaze, a tiny acknowledgement, not of his guilt, but of her culpability, then he shook his head in affectionate despair. 'What *are* you like? I'm going to have to keep an eye on you when these babies come. We don't want you dropping them on their heads, do we? I'll see you later. I'll text you when I'm on my way home.' He leant in and kissed her on the lips. Affirmation. Their pact intact. 'How about I buy some stuff and cook tonight? Save you the bother.'

'Yeah, that'd be nice.'

She stayed at her post by the door as he climbed into his van. She waved him off, listened for the sound of the engine long after it had died away. The pain still hummed in her joints and her skin. She closed the front door and walked back into the kitchen.

Before she did anything else, she wrote IAN'S PACKED LUNCH on the noticeboard stuck to the side of the fridge. She didn't want to risk making the same mistake twice.

Chapter 60

AFTER LIZZIE had tidied the kitchen, washed her face, brushed her teeth and got dressed she rang in sick. Then she sat on the edge of the bed, holding onto her belly and her sanity, as she watched the traitorous clock.

When she had first discovered she was pregnant she'd been anxious. It wasn't that she and Ian hadn't talked about having children. He'd spoken, often, about how he wanted the chance to be a better father than his own, how much he would love to have a son with whom he could have a good, healthy, loving relationship, but it had been a distant dream. One that would only be realised after the house was properly fixed up, after they'd got married, after they'd paid off their debts. And – for her – once his black moods and his sudden, fierce flashes of temper had become rare aberrations rather than an ever-present apprehension.

He was always deeply sorry afterwards – ashamed of himself and his actions. His contrition was genuine. A dark, crackling frustration was, unfortunately, the way he reacted to stress. It was an inherited trait. Growing up, he'd seen and absorbed a lot of anger. He'd learnt, from both his parents, that silence followed by a cathartic outburst was the way to deal with any uncomfortable emotions. It was an inheritance she was helping him put aside. The more Ian trusted her, the better it was. The better *he* was.

In a curious and complicated way, their love was strengthened by his struggles and her support. And besides, it was a small part of their relationship that she could cope with – while it was just her.

But an unplanned pregnancy seemed a huge risk, financially and otherwise.

For more than a fortnight she'd kept news of the pregnancy to herself. She needed to think and plan. Whenever she got the chance, she ran and reran the maths in a cheap lined notebook that she kept hidden behind the bread bin. She worried Ian might find it if she left it in her bag, he had been known to check through it – she was never sure what he was expecting to find. In her little black book, she worked and reworked their budget, trying to juggle their debts and repayments so that there would be a little more money left at the end of every week. She looked up what an average baby costs in its first year and calculated her potential maternity pay as best she could, assuming that she took as little leave as possible. She sketched out a list of things they could cut back on; buying some things second-hand would help.

All her equations underlined how imperative it was

that Ian hang onto his job, maybe take on some overtime. He'd moved around a lot, due to various problems with the management at the previous firms he'd been with. She even considered who might lend them money to tide them over, if things got sticky. Lizzie liked to have a contingency plan. The list of potential lenders was small. Her mother, Carol, was the only real option. She would probably help them, again, if she had to. Lizzie prayed she wouldn't have to ask, but feared she would. There was Heather and Mick, but she discounted that thought. She didn't want to believe that she – correction, they – would ever be that desperate.

After each round of her headache-inducing calculations Lizzie would close the notebook, wedge it back in its hiding place and hug her secret tightly. Until she told him, she still had options.

But keeping him in the dark was wrong.

It was Ian's child as much as hers. She couldn't, wouldn't deny him the one thing he wanted more than anything else in the world, aside from her. They would make it work; other couples did. A child could very well be the final step for him in leaving his past behind.

She told him at the weekend. No work. Less stress. More time to digest. He'd had a few beers the previous evening, but not too many. He'd slept late, showered, was heading out later with a mate who was thinking of buying a car and wanted his advice.

His reaction was pure, unadulterated delight. He whooped and cried and swung her around the kitchen with excitement. Then he talked non-stop. *The back bedroom would be perfect for a nursery, wouldn't it? When was her first scan? Were they going to find out the sex of the child? What did she want, a boy or a girl? He definitely wanted to be present for the birth. Did she want him to go to parenting classes with her? He would. He wanted to learn everything he could about her pregnancy and the birth.*

His reaction was lovely to see. Lizzie let herself be swept up in it. Joy was such a seductive emotion. There was no doubting that Ian had a huge capacity for love inside him, it was a big part of his attraction. Sharing in his excitement at the prospect of a baby – their baby – was a powerful counterbalance to the mean-spirited scrimping and worrying she'd been doing on her own ever since she'd stared in shock at the thin blue line on the pregnancy test. And the more he chattered and kissed her and made plans, the more she relaxed.

They were, in many ways, a good combination: his enthusiasm took the edge off her caution, her pragmatism tempered his wildness. Their child might luck out and inherit the best of both of them.

To her relief and amazement, although Ian's initial euphoria obviously faded, what replaced it had been a contentment she'd never seen before. He was happy, and his happiness rendered him softer. When she tentatively suggested they draw up a plan of how they were going to cope with the financial impact of a baby, he listened; and when she suggested cutbacks in their spending, he didn't bristle and resist. He even spoke to his boss, off his own bat, and asked to be put down for any available extra shifts. United on solid middle ground, Lizzie started to believe they would be okay, perhaps more than okay – she started to believe that they would be good.

Then came the bombshell.

It was not one baby, but two.

Even that didn't seem to faze him. 'Double the fun, in half the time!' he laughed. An instant family. It appealed to his impatience. At their next scan, when the midwife confirmed they were having twin boys, Ian's delight was complete.

The happy calm held through the first half of her pregnancy.

Ian read about the babies' development in the books she borrowed from the library, he went with her to her antenatal appointments when he could and, more valuable than all that, he stuck to their plan to save as much money as they could, while they could. Her due date, inked on the calendar in the kitchen, was a good incentive. It loomed large and immovable. The day they would become a family of four.

But perhaps it was the sheer effort of being the best possible version of himself that was the problem because, as her pregnancy progressed, Lizzie detected the dark shoots of old tensions pushing back up through the foundations of their relationship. She noticed that he was happy to talk about her pregnancy, as long as the news was good. She quickly learnt, without being told, that when he asked her how she was feeling, she needed to say 'fine'. And when she was tired and uncomfortable, as she often was, she had to pretend she wasn't. She didn't suffer from indigestion or persistent nagging backache or stretch marks or any anxiety about herself, or the twins, at all – as far as Ian was concerned.

Life was good. The babies were good. They were good.

But the more her body changed, the greater the pressure became. He took to touching her more and more often. He insisted on holding her hand when they were out in public, and if her pregnancy was ever mentioned in conversation, by friends or neighbours, he would always reach out and place a hand on her bump. She understood – he was proud, he wanted to claim the twins as being as much his as hers. People always smiled to see how involved he was. As did she. At home his attentiveness was even more pronounced. In the evenings he would lie on the sofa with his head resting heavily in the remaining space on her lap, waiting to feel the babies move. And if she went for a bath and a little peace, he would often come up and wash her back or her hair for her. It was all very loving, but Lizzie found it increasingly cloying and incessant.

On top of which, Ian still wanted to have sex as often as before, if not more. He claimed to understand her growing reticence, but that didn't reduce the frequency of his wordless approaches and his brooding silences if she rejected him.

By the end of her second trimester Lizzie was having to make a real effort, day and night, to accommodate his needs alongside – indeed, often ahead of – the growing demands of her pregnancy on her body and her brain. It was the only way to guarantee a peaceful life.

And she had, miraculously, managed to balance on that taut high-wire.

Until this morning.

When, with one small slip, she'd fallen further than the floor.

Chapter 61

Two hours later the pain and the shame still hissed inside Lizzie's body. In a bid to silence the disquiet, she went in search of Heather. Instead she found Mick.

Half an hour later she was in his car on her way to hospital.

Another hour and she was on an operating table. When she regained consciousness, the truth of her situation was undeniable.

She was a mother. Her babies were in intensive care. And Ian, for all his promises and protestations of love, was the cause.

Alone, and very afraid, she had no idea what she was going to do.

Chapter 62

THE ANSWER, at least initially, was to go on as before, fulfilling her role as a new mother alongside a man who truly believed he was a good partner and would be a good parent. His performance over those early fraught, stress-filled weeks was convincing.

The nurses, the doctors and the other parents all liked Ian. Why wouldn't they? His devotion to her and to the boys was exemplary. He was the model of a dedicated new father: gentle, patient, involved, working long hours and still being there by their side in the NICU every chance he had. Indeed, in contrast to her mute shock, his articulate care and concern were more convincing, certainly more appealing.

But every time he reached his hand into the incubators to touch either of the boys, Lizzie had to swallow hard to stop herself from screaming. She wanted to sink her nails into his arms and drag him away. She imagined pushing and pulling him off the ward, shouting and cursing, like the mad woman she now was inside. She wanted him out of the hospital, out of their lives.

Because it was Ian's fault that their sons lay struggling to breathe, their tiny bodies as breakable as porcelain. And hers. Because she had colluded in his dangerous fantasy.

When he'd put her down on the floor, she'd meekly got to her feet, made his lunch and kissed him goodbye – without a word of dissent. She'd let him get away with cruelty and violence and, as a consequence, she'd put the lives of her unborn children at risk. On the day of the twins' birth, and for all those years leading up to it, she'd allowed Ian to pretend to be a decent man and, in pretending, they had, between the two of them, created the exact opposite.

She was under such no illusion now, but as over-whelming as her situation was, at least while they were in the hospital they were safe. And, as desperate as those early weeks were, they were instructive. Watching her babies struggle, Lizzie learnt that the weak can fight. That physical frailty was no measure of strength. And that if you could cling on, there was a chance of recovery.

Chapter 63

LIZZIE'S HEART always beat faster as she waited to be buzzed back onto the ward. The fear that something bad might have happened in her absence, because of her absence, was hard to shake. But seeing Heather had been calming, reassuring – a glimpse of normality and so, for once, when she set foot back on the unit, she foolishly expected everything to be fine, or at least stable.

It wasn't.

The insistent beep of the alarm. The cluster of bodies around Joe's incubator. The air of restrained, intense concentration. Ian's stricken expression. Terror took hold.

Then as quickly as she'd plunged into the void, she resurfaced. Helen stepped away from the melee and said everything was okay. Joe was fine. It had been a false alarm – literally. Emotional whiplash. Lizzie was used to it by now.

Ian was not. She knew, even before the shouting started, that he'd been triggered. She'd seen this sudden switch from rational to wholly irrational enough times before. The ward staff and the other parents had not. She saw surprise on their faces, and unease. This was not the Ian they knew and liked. That Trish was the target of his rage only made Ian's fury seem even more disproportionate. Acting on muscle-memory, Lizzie stepped into the fray – prioritising his emotions over her own, absorbing his anger. Doing her job. By sheer act of will, she returned him to himself.

As always, it took it out of her.

When he was calm and she'd had time to check that both Joseph and Oliver were indeed fine, she excused herself and fled to the Ladies, where she locked herself inside one of the cubicles. She stayed in her small, less-than-fragrant sanctuary until she heard familiar footsteps.

Lizzie allowed herself ten minutes of respite with the world-weary, but robust wisdom of Trish, then she wiped away her tears and returned to her post.

The sight that greeted her was tranquil.

Ian was sitting in the armchair with Joseph tucked inside his shirt. The shouting bully had melted away, to be replaced by the loving, attentive man that Ian could be, and often was. Lizzie was surprised to feel a wave of anger rather than relief wash through her. Why should he be rewarded for his outburst? Why should he be allowed to touch, never mind hold, Joseph's fragile little body, when only moments ago he'd been ranting and raving? How was that acceptable? The rational part of her knew that the nurses had probably given him Joseph to hold in a bid to further pacify him and to reassure him that his son was stable, safe.

Lizzie forced herself to sit in the chair opposite Ian. She watched Joseph's little body inflating and deflating in double-quick time, fighting his battles in his own way, as he must. With every sinew in her exhausted body, she wanted to summon the nurses and get them to return Joseph to the security of his incubator. But she daren't.

After ten minutes of watching Ian contentedly snooze, the compulsion to say something was too intense to ignore. In the end she opted for a bland, 'Are you okay?' She meant *are you back in control?*, not *are you all right?*

He briefly opened his eyes. 'Yep.'

The sad, shocking truth was that he was back in control – of the situation, of the boys, and of her. As if to underline the fact, he raised his hand and stroked the back of Joseph's tiny head. The contrast in proportions was extreme. Heft versus fragility. Strength versus weakness. Status quo restored, Ian tipped his head back, shutting Lizzie out. The image of contentment.

Lizzie's eyes roved around the room, taking in the other babies and their panoply of equipment, but inexorably coming back to rest on Joseph and Ian.

Panic and inertia. Sympathy and loathing. Anger and affection. Love and hate. A cacophony of extreme emotions, with no compromise and no easy resolutions, rattled around inside her.

On her third sweep of the room her attention snagged on the boards above the twins' incubators. She'd never paid them much attention before, but there – in black on dirty white – was the boys' future, writ large and undeniable. *Oliver Hughes and Joseph Hughes*, in Ian's handwriting. Their father's surname. Their father's sons. His surname replacing hers. His rights usurping hers. She had carried the boys inside her, fed them, nurtured them, and her body would forever bear the scar of their birth, and yet Ian was claiming them. She steeled herself and looked directly at him.

He was no longer dozing. His eyes were open and he was staring at her across the top of Joseph's downy head. He seemed relaxed, but she could tell he was alert, aware of her awareness, waiting for her response to his overt assertion of ownership. She was accustomed to Ian observing her, anticipating her reaction to his unspoken, but clear intentions. She held his gaze. There was a fraction of a second when his face was utterly still, then he smiled, his charming, assumptive smile – which brooked no disagreement.

It was those four words, written in black Sharpie, that shunted Lizzie over the line.

Chapter 64

SHE SPOKE TO HELEN that evening when Ian had gone home. Asked for help. Stated, haltingly but accurately, and out loud for the first time, what had brought on her labour and what had been going on in the months and years leading up to her pregnancy. She explained that what Helen had witnessed on the ward was merely the briefest glimpse of how little control Ian had over his emotions and his temper.

Helen said very little, at first. She seemed to know that the best thing she could do was sit and listen. She didn't express shock or sympathy or outrage, or even surprise. Was that professionalism or, Lizzie would wonder later, familiarity with her tale – or at least different versions of it – from the other women she'd cared for so well? Helen had been a nurse for more than twenty years.

When Lizzie ran out of words and energy they sat in silence, letting the facts – because they were facts – settle. It was done. There was no going back. Lizzie felt shaky, with relief and fear. Nothing had changed, and yet everything had.

After a moment or two, Helen reached out and placed her hand briefly on Lizzie's forearm, grounding her. Lizzie focused on her simple wedding band. 'Okay. What happens next is... I raise what you've disclosed to me with one of the hospital social workers as a safeguarding concern. It's a legal requirement. Whatever you decide to do, or not do, I have a duty to report it. I'll make a short report tonight, and they'll follow it up in the next twenty-four hours. Or at least they should. There's always a bit of a backlog. They'll want to speak to me, and to you. They'll need to take statements and discuss protocols around keeping you, and the boys, safe.' She must have seen the panic ripple across Lizzie's face because she added, 'They're experienced in handling situations like this. They'll be very careful not to alert Ian, or anyone else who doesn't need to know — as will I, in everything I do or say from here on in.'

Lizzie nodded. She couldn't think about Ian finding out about her betrayal.

Helen stood up and Lizzie went to do likewise, but Helen waved her back into her seat. 'You wait here. I'm just going to fetch something.'

As she waited, Lizzie listened to the muted sounds of the ward, sounds she'd initially found frightening and now found soothing. Helen returned clutching a leaflet. She passed it to Lizzie, who stared at it in her hands, tangible proof that she was doing this, whatever 'this' was. Helen talked on, her voice low, her words plain and direct. 'The Women's Refuge people are a really useful resource. Their number's on there. They'd be good to talk to, sooner rather than later. They'll help you get your head straight, or as straight as it can be. They really know their stuff.' Again she responded with calmness to Lizzie's panic at the enormity of what she might be doing. 'They won't push you, Lizzie, but they will equip you with information and that's what you need. Okay?'

Lizzie nodded, although she couldn't envisage herself calling the number.

Now Helen did stand up. She still had another two hours of her shift to work. Other people's lives, patients and families were in her capable, but very human hands. Lizzie was simply one of her many responsibilities. 'You did the right thing talking to me. Remember, one small step at a time still gets you there in the long run.'

Lizzie felt a huge sense of debt to Helen. She had to at least try and reflect her faith that things would work out, somehow, in the end. 'Yeah. One step at a time.'

Even to her own ears, she didn't sound convincing.

Chapter 65

FROM THAT POINT ON, Lizzie found herself living a double life, which was bizarre and profoundly tiring. It was a duplicity that, despite what Helen had said, soon involved an ever-expanding number of people, many of whom remained disembodied voices on the other end of secretive phone calls.

Helen had been right: the women who staffed the helpline were experts in their very specific, very distressing field. They supplied Lizzie with a wealth – in fact a deluge – of information, suggestions and dire warnings about how precarious her situation was and how carefully she must prepare, *if* she was planning on extricating herself, and her boys, from her current relationship. The way they said 'current' struck Lizzie, it implied a life beyond Ian, and the prospect of hope. But the other stuff stuck as well; the statistics about the increase in frequency and intensity of abuse from partners during pregnancy and, even worse, the stark truth that it was at the point of leaving that women were most vulnerable.

Lizzie spent a lot of time over the following week locked in the end cubicle in the Ladies, clutching the phone they'd provided for her, reeling as the waves of good advice and the endless questions crashed down on her. There was so much to think about, so many conflicting and scary emotions to process, so much previously unspoken truth to be dug up and dragged into the light. It was too much. But after each snatched call, she washed her face and went back on the ward and looked after her boys. They were what kept her head above the waves. And when she was with Ian, on the ward and in bed at home, she acted the same as before.

It was like holding your breath and breathing at the same time.

Chapter 66

THE FIRST BIG STEP – and her first tangible act of defiance – came with the registration of the boys' birth.

Lizzie had no choice but to be brave, it was a legal requirement to register any child within forty-two days of birth, and the clock was ticking. The twins were, shockingly, now four weeks old, which gave her only another couple of weeks to sort it out.

The subterfuge required to keep Ian out of the process was made a little easier by the availability of a limited number of hospital registrar visits. It was a service provided to parents of babies spending time in intensive care. No one mentioned the obvious implication that it was really designed for those babies who were not expected to survive.

The thought that Joe might have been one of those babies haunted Lizzie – she knew that at some deep, irremovable level, it always would. Although he was now out of the woods – off the ventilator and making good, if slow, progress – Lizzie knew how close they'd come to losing him. It was a fact she made herself reflect on often. It gave her the courage to keep putting one step in front of the other.

The appointment with the registrar was booked for a Tuesday morning – a time deliberately chosen because it guaranteed Ian would be unable to attend. Lizzie didn't tell him it had been arranged until the day before. She claimed – as she and the social worker had agreed – that someone had cancelled at the last minute, which meant they, or rather she, could have the slot. Ian hadn't been pleased about having to miss it, but when Lizzie asked him to fill in the declaration-of-parentage form, he'd done it. He'd had little choice.

What she was going to do, or not do, with the form – well, that was another matter.

In the end the meeting was so mundane it felt like a let-down. The woman met Lizzie in the chapel on the ground floor of the hospital. She had a large leather folder, special pads of paper for recording and duplicating the necessary information and the manner of a bored parking attendant. Lizzie, who'd expected to be quizzed and who had, therefore, carefully prepared her answers, had been left to sit in near-silence for most of the twenty minutes it took to fill in the paperwork. It was such a routine process that when the woman asked for the details of the parents of the children, Lizzie simply passed over her and Ian's birth certificates and his form, without hesitation.

As a result, when the woman asked her to confirm the veracity of all the information provided, she was able to nod. The boys' father was Ian Richard Hughes. The boys' mother was Elizabeth Hannah Truman. And the boys were to be recorded as Joseph Truman and Oliver Truman.

'No middle names?'

Lizzie didn't hesitate. 'No.' She was not lumbering Oliver with Ian's father's name. If that robbed Joseph of her late-father's name, so be it. She thought he would have understood. Best to let them both simply be themselves.

There was more silence. More writing. Then it was done.

As Lizzie walked out of the chapel with the boys' names and parentage officially confirmed, her conscience was both guilty and clear. It would have been wrong to leave the box blank. The boys had a father. That father was Ian. There was no getting away from that.

But she could, perhaps, influence what his role in their lives would be.

Chapter 67

THE NEXT STEP, on the face of it, was easier – calling on a friend to help. The Refuge women recommended it, and Lizzie, like a good student working on a new, difficult topic, was doing exactly as advised. It was also harder, because by telling Heather the truth, Lizzie knew she was dragging her and Mick into the whole sorry mess.

She told Heather in the chapel – a safe place for dangerous secrets to be shared.

Lizzie started by telling her about what had really happened the morning Mick had rushed her into hospital: about the fall that was not a fall. Heather's response was impressively composed. She sat clutching her handbag on her lap and, as any good friend would, prompted Lizzie to say more.

And so she did.

She told Heather about the bursts of rage, the sudden shoves and slaps, the relentless pressure to do everything 'just so'. But she was honest as well. She spoke about Ian's desperate affection, the attraction of being so wanted, the love tainted by fear, the complexity of their relationship. And with Heather listening intently, Lizzie described Ian's assumption that she could, and would, bear the burden of his anger and his obsession, and go on absorbing it, without end. And in the retelling, Lizzie's belief in her own need to change her future, and that of her boys, strengthened.

When Heather did finally speak, it was to say something typically, reassuringly simple. Namely, 'What can I do?'

It was time to say it out loud. 'Help me leave him.'

Heather sat up straight and squared her shoulders, ready and willing. 'Mick and I will do whatever you need us to.'

Chapter 68

THE HARDEST FAREWELL was to Helen. She came to say goodbye to Lizzie at the end of her shift, in her civvies. They'd seen a lot less of each other since Lizzie and the boys had moved into the family room. In hindsight, the move had been part of a weaning-off process – a humane way of reducing Lizzie's reliance on Helen and on the support of the other nurses.

Lizzie was their mother. The boys were her responsibility. It was down to her now.

Without asking permission – they were well past that – Helen lifted Joseph out of the cot and settled him on her lap with a deep sigh of contentment, and tiredness. Oli stirred, sensing the loss of his brother from his side, and began sucking on his thumb noisily. They watched the sun rise, or at least they watched the light begin to glow on the concrete wall outside the window. The family room did not have a view, but it had given Lizzie a different perspective.

'So you're off today?'

'Yes.'

Both the boys had been passed fit and well. Finally ready for discharge – one week to the day before their due birth date. It was a miracle that meant the outside world, and all the decisions and challenges it contained, could not be held at bay any longer.

'Everything sorted?' Helen asked.

'I think so.'

Weeks of subterfuge and secret planning came down to this: one woman leaving hospital with her babies. It sounded so simple and natural. It was anything but.

The room was a warm pink, the sound of Oli sucking his thumb comforting. Helen was, as ever, a deeply reassuring presence. Leaving seemed an insane thing to do. Helen must have seen the doubt on Lizzie's face. 'I'm sure it'll be tough, to start with, but you'll get through it.'

'You think?'

'I know.'

'Thank you for the vote of confidence. Any last words of advice?'

Helen stroked Joseph's toes. It was strange to see her fingers and her neat, perfectly shaped fingernails. She always wore gloves when she was handling the babies on the ward, but she was no longer 'handling' Joseph, she was holding him, like a normal baby. A woman and a child, not a nurse and a patient. 'I think the most important thing will be... to ask for help.' Oli began to stir again. 'And don't forget, you've got one major advantage on your side – or should I say two – your boys are going to melt hearts, and soft hearts are going to be a lot more inclined to help than hard ones.' She was silent for a moment, gazing down at Joseph. 'Look after this little man for me.' Her voice thickened. 'He's special. I'm gonna miss him.'

Lizzie smiled. 'I will. I promise. And, Helen, thank you. For everything.'

Helen's normal professional briskness returned. She dropped a kiss on Joseph's head, then straightened up. 'I'm away to my bed.' She stood up and lowered him into the cot next to his brother. 'Bye-bye, Joseph. Goodbye Oliver. You two be good boys for your mum.' She stopped at the door. 'Bye, Lizzie. And good luck.' As the door closed behind her, Oli's grizzling turned into crying, which was taken up by Joseph, her boys' way of reminding her, should she be in any doubt, whose needs came first now.

Chapter 69

HEATHER AND MICK arrived an hour later.

As agreed, they'd waited until they saw Ian leave for work. He was going into the office to tie up his last bits of paperwork and hand in his time sheets before finishing for his paternity leave. He was expecting to pick Lizzie and the boys up at lunchtime. The previous evening he'd been buzzing with anticipation. Lizzie's brain kept returning to the memory of their parting. They'd talked about what they were going to cook to celebrate the boys coming home; what time her mother would be arriving at the weekend; when his mother and brother would come round. She'd even double-checked he'd bought the right size of nappies for Joseph, who still needed the extra-small ones. God forgive her!

Mick looked deeply uncomfortable standing in the family room. She didn't blame him. He wasn't a man designed for lying, and yet here he was helping her perpetrate a monstrous deceit.

Because it was poor Mick who had watched, made

sure Ian had set off for work, then had taken her keys and let himself into their house. Once inside, he'd extracted her secret pack of documents from the bottom drawer in the kitchen. It was Mick who'd had to drag her bag from behind the boiler in the bathroom and had collected the list of very specific items from the desk – some things weren't safe to remove until the very last minute. Having looked around in disbelief at what he was doing, and why, it was Mick who had left her house, locking the door behind him, feeling, no doubt, huge relief and a lot of guilt.

And here he was, standing awkwardly, smiling nervously at her, ready to help with the next part of the plan. 'Ready?'

She nodded, because what else could she do? This was happening, and it was happening now. There was no going back.

She strapped the boys into their car seats. Managed it without either of them fussing. She'd practised, believing, or rather hoping, that their peaceful compliance was some sort of tacit endorsement of what she was doing. She looked around the bare room. Was she ready? 'Yes.'

She carried Joseph, and Heather took Oliver, leaving Mick with the big wheelie suitcase and the bags. The suitcase, a gift from Mick and Heather, was another of the Refuge ladies' eminently practical suggestions. Good for rapid departures.

A couple of familiar faces saw them leaving, including Pete the porter, from that first night. He stopped briefly to say 'goodbye and good luck', but shockingly quickly they were outside, heading for the car park.

That was when the enormity of what Lizzie was doing hit home. Having Heather and Mick there helped. They got the boys strapped into the car and stowed her stuff in the boot. Then they all stood and looked at each other. Heather pulled Lizzie into a brief, fierce hug. 'Mick will look after you from here. When you can, call or text, just to let us know you're okay. And if there's anything – anything we can do...' She tailed off. 'I'm going to go now. I'm no good with goodbyes.' With that, Heather pushed Lizzie gently away, turned and hurried off. Mick and Lizzie watched her weave between the cars, heading quickly for the exit.

Lizzie gulped.

'She didn't want to upset you by getting upset herself,' Mick said. 'She's very proud of you.'

They watched until Heather disappeared from sight.

'Shall we?'

They climbed in, and Mick drove them out of the car park.

Chapter 70

THE MEETING POINT was, somewhat oddly, a retail park. The woman on the phone had explained that they used different pick-up spots – the busier and more mundane, the better. Women out shopping with their children, nothing unusual about that.

They were early. Mick parked near TK Maxx, as agreed. The boys were asleep. Lizzie and Mick watched the people wandering around with their takeaway coffees. Two cars along, an older chap sat staring into space, presumably waiting for his wife.

'I'm sorry.' Mick's voice startled her.

'What for?'

'For not realising.'

'How could you have?'

'Heather had her suspicions.'

'Did she? She never said anything.'

Mick shook his head ever so slightly. 'Not her place to. But she knew something wasn't right.'

Lizzie was surprised. She was fairly sure she'd never

said anything, or given anything away about the dark corners of her relationship with Ian, not to Heather or anyone. Her denial had been a form of protective cowardice. She hadn't wanted to acknowledge what was happening. Besides, she had once truly loved Ian.

At the thought of him, her stomach contracted. What was she doing? The panic threatened to overwhelm her.

Thankfully, Mick was there beside her, a solid, rational, kind, talking presence. He was still reflecting on what Heather had suspected. 'I think she'd had her doubts about him for a while. She liked you, from the moment she met you, but she was wary of him. I know she was shocked when you told her, but I don't think, deep down, she was surprised. Not like me.' He shook his head again. 'I thought he was a decent bloke. God help me, I shook his hand, offered to buy him a pint, when he told me the boys had been born.'

'Him', not 'Ian'. No, because Ian was no longer the ordinary man Mick had chatted to on the street, had lent tools to, had shared a drink with at Christmas.

'I can't get my head around how he can seem like such a nice bloke and, in reality, be the total opposite. It's beyond me. His own wife. His own unborn children.' Mick sounded disgusted – with Ian, and with himself. 'And you not feeling you could say anything until now. Until this. I'm so sorry.' He rubbed his hand over his face, roughly.

As it had before, Mick's thoughtful monologue helped to calm and strengthen Lizzie's resolve. Seeing your situation through the prism of other people's perceptions shed light on it when you were lost in the dark. 'Mick.' He was struggling, unable to look her full in the face. 'Mick. Please, look at me.' Finally he met her eye. 'This is not your fault. It's Ian's. And mine.' She held up her hand to stop him contradicting her. 'You and Heather have been my lifeline. Why else do you think I came to your house that morning? Why else was it Heather that I told, eventually? I knew I could trust you. Both of you. And there's not many people on that list. Even before all this. Knowing you were across the street from me was a comfort. You have never been anything other than good to me.'

He reached over and grasped her hand. 'I want to be able to say I'll go over and sort him out for you, but it's just not me.'

'And I don't want you to. Violence isn't any sort of answer.'

'But you leaving is?'

'Yes.'

'But you're having to abandon your own home, your friends, your whole life because of him.'

'Yes, but I'm not thinking about it like that. I'm leaving for the boys. And for me. We have to go, to have a chance at a better life.' That was the stark reality of her situation.

They sat holding hands. Five minutes passed. A dark-blue minivan pulled up. The correct licence plate. 'They're here.'

'Right.' He held onto her.

The van door opened and a middle-aged woman got out. She scanned the car park. With her free hand, Lizzie waved. The woman acknowledged her, but didn't come towards the car. It occurred to Lizzie that she must have done this sort of pick-up many times before. It wasn't much of a comfort, but it was some. 'I'd better go.'

He released her. 'You sort the twins. I'll get the bags.' Action always helped when emotions were too much to handle.

The boys woke as she set about unstrapping their car seats. Oliver began grizzling, but Joseph was quiet, his dark, unwavering gaze on Lizzie. She took Oliver across to the van first.

The woman smiled. 'Nice to meet you.' She briefly lifted a photo ID out of her jacket pocket and flashed it at Lizzie, proving she was legit. Blink and you'd have missed it. 'And which one is this?'

'Oli.'

She glanced down. 'Do they need a bottle before we set off?'

Lizzie wanted to get moving. 'No. They're not due a feed for another couple of hours.'

'Okay.' She held out her hands. 'Shall I pop him in then?'

Lizzie passed over her son to this total stranger. 'I'll go and fetch his brother.' She turned. Mick was hovering near the van with her case and her bags. 'This is Mick.'

The woman smiled. 'Hello, Mick. There's plenty of space in the back.'

By the time Lizzie had returned with the other car seat, her stuff had been stowed. The woman took Joe. Leaving Lizzie's hands, and her emotions, free.

Mick shuffled his feet. 'Well, love. I hope it all goes' – there was a fraction of a pause while he tried to think of the right word – 'to plan. We'll be thinking of you.'

It was an achingly good hug. As they parted, Mick pressed an envelope into her hand. She could tell by the feel of it that it contained a wedge of notes.

'No, Mick. You and Heather have done enough.'

He moved away. 'Take it. You're going to need it. And make sure that you take care of yourself as well as the twins. Shall I wait?'

The woman answered for her. 'There's no need. She's in good hands. We'll take it from here.' Lizzie belonged to this woman's world now, and that world did not include anyone or anything she knew.

Mick gave a small, awkward wave, then he walked away. Lizzie climbed into the minivan and slid the heavy door shut. The noise provoked another burst of crying from Oli. Joe remained silent. She stretched behind her and stroked Oli's cheek, trying to soothe him. He was not to be soothed.

The van rocked as the woman climbed into the front. 'A friend?'

'A neighbour, and a good friend.' Despite her best intentions the tears came and, with them, Lizzie lost control. The sound of her own and Oli's crying was loud inside the van. Lizzie was horrified, but she couldn't stop. The woman didn't make any attempt to stem the flood. She simply sat, placidly, letting Lizzie sob. There was a curious comfort in it. Sympathy would only have made things worse. After a minute or so the woman popped open the glove compartment and took out a battered box of tissues. She passed them to Lizzie. The mop-up commenced. Still the woman made no move to start the van.

'I'm okay now,' Lizzie managed. Oli's cries likewise were losing momentum. He now sounded more grumpy than distressed.

Some semblance of peace restored, the woman finally spoke. 'Of course you're not, love. Why would you be? You've just climbed into a minivan with two tiny babies, all your worldly goods stuffed into a suitcase, with no sodding idea where the hell you're going.' She smiled. 'But trust me, you've done the hardest part – the thing that takes the most courage. We've got you from here.'

All Lizzie could think to say was 'Thank you'.

The women switched on the engine. 'Ready?'

One last sniff. 'Ready.' Lizzie was surprised at the certainty in her voice.

They reversed out of their parking space and set off and, despite the whirlpool of fear that had opened up in Lizzie's soul since she'd first called the Domestic Abuse Helpline and set in train this dramatic, life-changing chain of events, she didn't panic. She stared straight ahead, with – as the woman had accurately said – absolutely no idea where she was going or how she was going to cope. But going she was, and she was taking her boys with her. As they approached the exit for the car park, the woman nudged Lizzie's elbow. 'Aren't you going to give him a wave?'

And there, standing at the junction with the main road, was Mick. He'd waited to see her off. When he spotted her, he started waving. Lizzie waved back. As they drove towards him, she fumbled to wind down the window. The woman pressed a button and the glass glided down. When they drew alongside, Mick flushed, reached into the van and briefly squeezed Lizzie's shoulder. 'You'll be grand. I know you will. Keep your chin up.' The van was on the move again. He let her go.

The indicator ticked, the van turned and they merged into the traffic.

Chapter 71

THE FIRST FEW WEEKS passed in a blur of tiredness.

Lizzie moved in with a woman called Margaret – she preferred Mags – and her husband, Steve. They lived in a semi in a suburb of Middlesbrough. Steve was rarely around and, when he was, he said very little. He worked as a cab driver: long shifts, late nights. To Lizzie's surprise, the house and her room were lovely. She had the whole top floor, a loft conversion with plenty of space and light. There was even a small en-suite bathroom. Mags's specialism was supporting teenage girls who'd decided to keep their babies and were sometimes, even more optimistically, trying to hang onto their teenage boyfriends as well. As a result, Mags had plenty of experience with newborns and frazzled mothers. It was down to her that Lizzie got the boys settled into a decent routine, that she coped when the boys both caught colds soon after they left hospital, and that she got used to turning up at the baby clinic and listening to the inevitable comparisons between Oli and Joe without bursting into tears. Indeed, it was Mags who supported Lizzie in insisting that those persistent concerns about Joe's development were converted into a referral to see a neurologist. In essence, Lizzie became a competent single mum because of Margaret.

Mags was also well versed in dealing with the labyrinthine complexities of the benefits system, on which Lizzie and the boys were now wholly dependent for their survival. Lizzie knew she was lucky to have been placed with such a sound and supportive woman and her patient, self-effacing husband.

But she didn't feel lucky.

What she felt was lonely, adrift and perpetually on edge. She was deeply anxious about her ability to do it all on her own, worried about Joe's development and, on top of all that, she was consumed by thoughts of what was going on with Ian. Every day she expected to be woken by a furious hammering at the door or to hear a voice screaming her name on the street. Ian had to be looking for them. He wouldn't simply let them go. How could he?

As advised, she'd reported Ian to the police for emotional and physical abuse. It was the necessary first step in protecting herself, and the beginning of the process that would ultimately lead to her applying for exclusive custody of the boys. The advice Lizzie was given was unequivocal: *her relationship was dead, Ian was a threat, she had to cut him out of her own and the boys' lives.*

But it felt wrong. She'd stolen his sons and, in doing so, had spirited away, in one fell swoop, the life he'd been expecting. Her actions must have broken his heart. What she'd done, by normal humane standards, was unforgivable. And now, by involving the police and the courts, she was going even further. She was smashing the mirage of the man he thought himself to be.

She spent a lot of time sitting on the bed in her lovely room in Mags's house trying to imagine the moment Ian realised she'd left him and had taken the twins with her. Right as her decision had been – and she had to believe it had been right, the alternative was unimaginable – she was tormented by the thought of the pain she'd caused, and by the fear of what his reaction to such a huge betrayal would be. In her heart she knew. Ian would be incandescent with rage. And his overriding instinct would be to hunt them down and bring them home, back where they belonged.

But with each day that passed, and every night they made it through, nothing happened.

The waiting was hard to live with. In the end it drove her to break the safety protocol and ring Heather.

She made the call from the garden, not wanting, irrationally, the boys to hear her speak ill of their father. Over the first few disorientating weeks Lizzie had kept in touch with Heather by text. Simple, short messages designed to reassure her and Mick that they were doing okay. The texts also allowed Lizzie to maintain at least one link with her past. Everything and everyone else was gone, out of reach. Apart from her mother, obviously, but that relationship, never good at the best of times, was sadly more a source of stress rather than comfort in her current situation.

Lizzie had phoned her mum as soon as she'd got settled at Mags's house, but Carol had been so shocked at the turn of events, and so upset about being kept out of the loop, that the conversation had not gone well. Lizzie discovered that Ian had already called her mother and had poured out his shock and grief to her – telling his side of the story first, and powerfully. This had obviously added to Carol's confusion and pain. Hearing the shadow of sympathy for Ian, in her mother's voice, had made Lizzie feel deeply let down. By the end of a fraught hour Lizzie had been left with the depressing impression that her own mother didn't fully believe what she was saying. Their subsequent, much shorter conversations had been equally difficult. The sad truth was, her mother still couldn't comprehend or accept what was going on.

There was no such hesitancy in Heather's support and love when Lizzie rang her. 'Hello, love.' Simply the sound of her voice was balm to Lizzie. 'How are you doing? It's lovely to hear from you.'

'Hi, Heather. We're doing okay.'

'You sure?' That was the difference: Heather could pick up and respond to an emotion without questioning it.

'Yes. Honestly.'

'Good. And the boys?'

'Doing fine.' There was no point in worrying her. What would be, would be, with Joe. Or so Lizzie told herself a hundred times a day. 'I'm calling about Ian.'

'Okay.' There was an immediate reticence in Heather's voice.

'I need to know what's happening with him.'

'You shouldn't be thinking about him. You need all your energy for yourself and the boys.'

'But it's impossible not to. Please.'

Heather paused. 'It won't do any good knowing.'

So it was as bad as she was imagining. 'But it's all I can think about.'

'Okay, if you insist.' Heather was one of the few people who treated Lizzie like a grown-up. 'He's still in a state.'

'He's been bothering you?'

'Don't worry about us. We're handling it.'

Lizzie's heart sank. She had brought this to Mick and Heather's door. She'd known there would be repercussions. How could there not be? But she hadn't intended her flight to hurt the two people who had supported her the most. 'Heather, I need you to tell me. All of it. From the beginning.'

Heather took a breath, buying time to collect her thoughts and edit them. 'Okay. But this changes nothing. Ian knows, or suspects, that we were involved in you leaving.' Lizzie felt a wave of shame. 'The first time he turned up was on the Friday afternoon – the day you left. I think he'd been waiting for us to come home. We'd stayed out deliberately, so it looked like a normal work day, as we planned. He was calm on the surface at first, but it was clear that he wasn't really. Mick kept him standing on the doorstep, just to be on the safe side. Ian asked us straight out what we knew. We said: about what? He said: about you disappearing and taking his boys with you. We replied that we didn't know anything. He accused us of lying. We said nothing else. He lost his temper, said he was going to get answers – from somebody. We gathered, as expected, that the hospital had refused to tell him anything, except to refer him to the police, as you had told us they would.'

It was cold rendition of something that had obviously been full of heat. 'And?'

'Lizzie... leave it.'

'No. I need to know. I should know.'

'Why? For some sort of punishment? Don't do that. Don't let him control you, not now you're away from him.'

'I want you to tell me. It can't be worse than what I've been imagining.' She sincerely hoped it wasn't.

Heather sighed. Conceded. 'There's not much to tell. He became agitated. It's okay, Mick sorted it.' Poor, quiet, peace-loving Mick. Heather stopped talking. Lizzie became aware of the sound of the wind-chime in the tree by the kitchen door. She was miles away from Ian and his anger. Mick and Heather lived across the street from him. There was no escape for them.

'And what's happened since?'

Her voice became firm. 'It's being dealt with.'

'He's been back?'

'Lizzie! All you need to know is that we are fine. You and the boys are safe where you are. You must stay out of it, for their sake and your own. It'll die down.' She refused to say anything else.

'I'm *so* sorry.' Lizzie heard Heather take a deep breath.

'Don't be. If you want to know what you can do, for us, it's this... Make this difficult time worthwhile. Forget about Fenham. Build a life for yourself and the boys. That's what Mick and I want.' Lizzie was too choked to say anything. 'And keep in touch.'

Heather ended the call, so Lizzie didn't have to.

Chapter 72

LIZZIE TRIED HER BEST to fulfil Heather's request. She cared for the boys, took them out and about, went regularly to the mother-and-baby clinic, talked and sang to them, rarely if ever let them cry. She even made some effort to look and sound okay herself, proof that she was coping.

Then, just as she started to get a grip on her new life, her resolve was tested, yet again, when her support worker, Lynne, came to the house unexpectedly. She sat down, tugged at her wrinkled dress, smiled fleetingly and, as it turned out, inappropriately and broke the news that Lizzie and the boys must move on. The reason given – ironically – was that she was doing so well. Apparently she'd passed 'her transition period' with 'flying colours'. Lizzie hadn't realised she was even being assessed. When she asked to be allowed to stay with Mags a little longer, Lynne smiled more fixedly, shook her head and said it was time for someone else to benefit from Margaret's support and experience.

With the pulse in her throat ticking, Lizzie asked where they were going.

The answer: a hostel in Sheffield.

Lynne explained that it was the next phase in Lizzie's journey. She also emphasised that it would be good for Lizzie's case. It would prove that she was taking the necessary steps in establishing an independent life for herself and her boys – one that was safe and sustainable. The pending court order to establish custody of the boys was yet another pressure. Apparently Lizzie didn't only have to be a good mum; she needed to prove it.

She was tired of it all. As Lynne went on and on about the practicalities of uprooting her, all Lizzie wanted to do was hoist the boys onto her lap, curl up on Mags's comfy sofa and go to sleep. Her life now consisted of nothing but an endless series of impossible steps.

But she couldn't stop. This was the path she had chosen. There was no going back.

The thought of moving again filled up a whole new reservoir of anxiety. They were being dispatched to a city she'd never been to and knew nothing about, to share a house with other traumatised women and children, even further away from home. Another new start. Another test she had to pass, on her own. Eventually Lynne stopped talking and left. Lizzie asked Mags to watch the twins for her. She needed a moment. She needed more than that in reality, but space and time were a luxury she no longer possessed.

She retreated to her sanctuary at the top of the house.

Standing under the skylight, with the warmth of the sun on her back, Lizzie looked around their lovely, cosy, safe room.

They were leaving. There was no putting it off.

She went to the wardrobe and pulled out the big wheeled suitcase and began, once again, to pack up her life and that of the boys.

Chapter 73

THIS TIME THE MINIVAN was white, but the driver reminded her of the first woman. She had the same short greying hair, the same brisk kindness. There was probably a battered box of tissues in the glove compartment of this van as well, but this time Lizzie didn't have any tears to dry.

She was toughening up.

She needed to.

She stared out of the window at the blurry scenery and simply accepted her fate.

Chapter 74

THE HOSTEL IN SHEFFIELD was on an ordinary street of red-brick houses, on a hill, with views down onto the city. It was the end property, bigger than the rest, with a wraparound garden. There were two kids playing outside with bottles of bubbles, watched by a woman who was presumably their mother. She sat on the doorstep in the sunshine, silent and unmoving. The bubbles drifted in batches out of the garden and away down the street. When Lizzie climbed down from the van and lifted out the twins, the woman on the step watched with naked curiosity. Lizzie smiled at her. To her relief, the woman smiled back.

Lizzie and the boys and all their stuff were inside the hostel within ten minutes.

Their room was on the first floor. It had a number stuck to the door. They all did. It gave the house the feel of an old-fashioned B&B. Lizzie's room was number three. It was at the front of the house – bare, basic, with a view. Not as nice as her room at Mags's, but she couldn't think about that. Forward was the only possible direction of travel. Bags dropped, Lizzie returned to the office where the hostel manager, Farida, was minding the twins for her. The office was tiny, especially with the twins' car seats wedged in it. It was also very messy. Farida smiled, but she looked hassled. 'Hi. Welcome to Holly House.' She moved a toy truck and an open pack of baby wipes off the desk. For want of anywhere to put them, she opted for the floor.

'Sorry about this.' She swept what looked like biscuit crumbs off the desk onto the carpet. 'The kids aren't supposed to come in here.' She shrugged as if conceding the hopelessness of imposing this house-rule. It was a gesture that Lizzie would grow very familiar with over the coming months. There were many rules and regulations in Holly House, but observance was, she would discover, often patchy. 'Are you okay to get the paperwork out of the way now?'

Lizzie was. What else was she going to do? The rest of the day, and all the days that would follow, stretched shapelessly in front of her. Two babies, one room, no Mags, no Heather, no support from her mother, not a clue what came next.

Farida produced a form. 'So let's start with the basics… I have you down as Elizabeth Truman, with Joseph and Oliver Truman. You go by Lizzie, I gather?'

Something possessed her. 'No!'

'Oh, sorry,' Farida looked up, 'that's what I was told.'

'Yes. I used to be Lizzie. But I'm not anymore.'

If she was going to survive this, she was going to have to become someone else, and what better place to start than with a new name. 'Can you call me Beth?'

For the first time Farida smiled naturally. 'We can call you whatever you like, Beth.'

Chapter 75

BY ITS VERY NATURE, Holly House contained a random mix of flotsam and jetsam. The women who lived there had all been swept up by events beyond their control and been beached together in the hostel on a hill, in a city few of them knew, with little notion or hope of escape. The miracle was that they just about managed to rub along together, despite the wildly fluctuating emotions that washed through the house on any given day. They might not all like each other or have much in common in terms of attitudes, parenting styles, drinking, smoking or even bathroom habits, but there was one thing they shared: abuse by someone they had thought loved them. That shared trauma gave them a solidarity, of sorts, to cling to.

To her dismay, Beth and the boys fitted in relatively easily, that was, she supposed, no great surprise – she was such a woman now. But she was still profoundly lonely, purposeless and anxious most of the time. Not great emotions to be carrying when trying to care for two still-tiny babies.

That changed with the arrival of the new woman.

She arrived at Holly House in the middle of the night. Beth heard the light come on in the room next to hers. She wasn't asleep. The boys were, after their late feed and final change of the night.

Room two had been empty for all of three days. It had been a blessed, but short respite. Talia's son had stayed up late, much too late for a four-year-old, and had been prone to sudden outbursts of inconsolable screaming. It was understandable, but hard to live with. Hence Beth was not, initially, overjoyed to hear movement in the room next door. She squinted at her watch. It was just after midnight. There was a murmur of voices. She strained, listening out for clues as to her new neighbour. One child or two? It was hard to tell. She heard a tap running briefly, the creak of the bed, a loud click – the light being switched off – then nothing. It was an impressively swift, silent landing.

Beth rolled over and tried to go back to sleep, aware of the presence of other lives on the other side of the wall and, at that point, simply grateful that the woman and her child were quieter than Talia and her wailing son.

Chapter 76

BETH MET THE NEW woman properly at the 'house huddle' the following day.

It was a baptism all new residents had to go through. You were inducted into the 'family' quickly at the hostel. Beth's own immersion had been barely a month ago, but it felt longer. Time crawled at Holly House. She vaguely remembered the patting of a variety of ringless hands on her bare arm, a general clucking of sympathy and a lot of oohing and aahing over the boys. It had felt welcoming and supportive, but deeply disorientating.

She now knew the format of the meetings and could attach names to all the faces round the table, although whether they were real names or expedient pseudonyms, she hadn't a clue. Her own shift from Lizzie to Beth had, in hindsight, been a typical act of timidity – a small, feeble nod rather than a grand gesture. Even now she sometimes didn't respond when her name was called. No one seemed to care. Beth/Lizzie, Angela/Cinderella, their names made little difference. And besides, manners were not that highly prized in Holly House. But she did now know which children belonged to which woman and the personalities of the main players. She knew who was messy in the kitchen – Lucie. Who talked the most – Jess. Who the least – Elena. Who made the most sense – perhaps, somewhat surprisingly, Cinderella. Who listened best – Hannah. Who cried a lot – that was most of them. And who never shed a single tear, at least not in front of anyone else – that award went to Kirsty. Yes, Beth was already a fully paid-up member of this peculiar, dysfunctional family. And now there was a new member who needed to be inducted. The woman from room two.

She arrived late for the house meeting.

It was a wise move. Nothing happened on time in the hostel. The challenge of herding the toddlers into the makeshift crèche in the back room and leaving them to cry, and of settling the older kids in the lounge with an adequate supply of snacks and an acceptable choice of programmes or games, always took for ever. Despite knowing that deadlines slipped and slid all over the place at Holly House, Beth was always one of the first to arrive for the weekly huddle, having first deposited the fed-and-changed twins in the back room. It felt wrong leaving them to the tender mercies of whichever member of staff had drawn the short straw, but those were the rules. In advance of this morning's meeting, as she had for the past few, she cleared the crap off the table, boiled the kettle and set out the mugs, as one by one the women drifted onto the assembled chairs. Someone always went into the side-alley for a smoke just at the point they were ready to start, which invariably triggered others to float away. It was during this slow settling that the new woman finally put in an appearance.

She was tall, mixed-race, with dark eyes. A strong face full of features that didn't apologise and hide. She was wearing the uniform of the hastily packed. Grey sweatpants and a creased T-shirt, her copious hair pulled back in a ponytail. The only incongruous element was her slippers. They were purple, feather-trimmed – not what Beth would have considered an essential item when fleeing abuse.

The woman from room two assessed the room and its inmates, then came over to the table, her slippers slapping against the bare soles of her feet and the sticky lino floor. 'Hi, I'm Sabine. Okay if I park myself here?' It sounded like a London accent. She laid her hand on the back of Jess's chair. They all had their spots. No one said a word. She sat down and crossed her legs. The slipper dangled from her raised foot. Beth noticed her toenails were painted a shimmery silver. Another incongruity. The most striking thing about her, though, was that she seemed utterly at ease.

Farida seemed slightly fazed. The norm was for new arrivals to sit in stunned silence for at least their first couple of meetings. One of the pleasures for the staff was drawing out new residents; they seemed to see it as a measure of their professional skill. But it didn't appear that Sabine was going to need anyone to be speaking on her behalf. The last two stragglers came in – Jess was one of them. She glanced at Sabine in her seat, but said nothing, which was a first.

Farida recouped and began by reminding them all of the importance of regular attendance at the huddle. There had been a poor showing the previous week, a consequence of a small, but alcohol-heavy party for Sheila's birthday. Escaping a violent marriage at the age of sixty-seven was something the girls had unanimously decided needed celebrating. Beth had shown her face for a short while, but not stayed, pleading, as she always did, the twins. They had jokingly given her a hard time about it. 'And this is Sabine.' There was a mumble of hellos and nods. 'She arrived with her daughter, Leah, last night. They're taking room two. Next door to you, Beth.'

Beth smiled a welcome to the bright-eyed newcomer.

Once up and running, Farida battled on, despite the many interruptions. The agenda was unwaveringly the same. An update on housing opportunities or, more accurately, the lack of them; a tedious section on benefits; then a long list of responses to the myriad of complaints that were raised at every meeting: the lack of hot water, the battered state of the toys, the pigeon crap in the back yard, how noisy the bin men were, people stealing milk, ham, a multi-pack of crisps that had definitely been full the previous day and *were NOT for communal consumption*, etc. The challenge, which some rose to and most failed, was for each woman to have the patience to listen to the other women's priorities and problems.

Gripes listened to, Farida turned her attention to their new arrival. This was, in all honesty, one of the real motivations for attending the huddle: fresh meat. The chance, however awful it sounded, to pick over a new tale of woe and, in doing so, measure their own troubles against it. Beth had noticed how some of the women seemed to want any newcomer's tale to be worse than their own. Perhaps it made them feel better about themselves. Others appeared to want the new resident to have experienced nothing nearly as bad as themselves, thereby cementing their life as more tragic. She understood both reactions. She had listened to each of their tales and felt such emotions herself.

'Is there anything you would like to tell us about yourself, Sabine? Anything at all? We find that the more we share with each other, the stronger we are as a group.'

Some of the women actually leant forward.

There was a pause, then Sabine replied, 'No. Not today, thank you', as if she was refusing a squirt of perfume in a department store. There was a slight pause. 'Except my daughter's name is Aleah. Not Leah.'

Farida looked slightly thrown. 'My apologies.' She moved swiftly on to informing them about some planned work on the kitchen to replace some broken tiles.

At the end of the meeting the women scattered noisily. Beth started to collect up the dirty mugs. She was surprised and delighted when Sabine, without prompting, filled the sink with water and began to wash up.

Chapter 77

IT WAS APPROPRIATE, in hindsight, that their bond was sealed over soapy water and other people's dirty pots. But, of course, it wasn't simply their domestic skills that brought Sabine and Beth together. It was far more than that.

For Beth, it was Sab's strength of character, her unflinching honesty and her unflagging belief in herself and her daughter that attracted her. Sabine was the only woman in the hostel who seemed hopeful. She possessed, apparently without forcing or faking it, an absolute confidence that things would get better. It was a view on life that Beth wanted to be near and absorb.

And yet Sabine's backstory was not so different from anyone else's.

A partner with great charm and well-hidden flaws, who she'd fallen for while young. A relationship begun with passion that had descended, incrementally, into something far darker. An emotional and financial dependency sealed by the birth of a daughter. The slow-dawning realisation that her vulnerability was real and dangerous. An escalation that had frightened her into action, for the sake of her child, and her own sanity. It was the same sorry tale.

And yet Sabine seemed, to Beth and the other women, to be invincible.

Her resilience alienated some of the Holly House residents, intimidated others and attracted Beth. And the joy was... Sabine reciprocated.

Why Sabine singled her out, Beth didn't know and she didn't analyse it too much, for fear of jinxing it. But within a few days of Sabine arriving, they were friends, comfortable in each other's company, in and out of each other's room all the time, happy to let the other step in with their child/children. Having another pair of hands – in fact two, because Aleah was amazing for a seven-year-old, just like her mother – was a huge relief for Beth. Finally, Oli and Joe were getting the attention they deserved, and she was getting the company she so badly needed. Almost overnight being the mum of twins stopped feeling like a never-ending treadmill and became, for the first time since they'd been born, a pleasure.

Effectively she and Sabine drew a circle around themselves and their children that, although made of nothing more substantial than liking and laughter, was impregnable.

To most things.

Chapter 78

DECEMBER WAS ALWAYS a difficult month at Holly House. The year Beth and Sab were living there was no different. Because what was Christmas really, other than a publicly sanctioned excuse for over-the-top demonstrations of one's love for one's children? It was also the time that families were *supposed* to be together. But for the residents of Holly House neither activities were possible or advisable. Which was why, in the weeks leading up to the big day, the staff and residents had to be extra-vigilant. Husbands and boyfriends denied access to their partners were often angry, and fathers denied access to their children could be inventive, especially if, as had happened in the past, any of the women weakened and became sentimental.

Thankfully, they made it to Christmas Eve without any major incidents, but the mood in the house on the hill was far from festive. There was a lot of crying, disputes broke out over the smallest thing – the location of the Sellotape triggered a full-scale row, with the threat of violence if it wasn't *back on the kitchen table in five fucking minutes* – and there was an increased amount of door-banging, not all of it by the children. One minute the women were clutching their wriggling toddlers to their breasts, and the next they were screaming that they were *sick to the back teeth of being cooped up like fucking battery chickens.* Even wearing a tinsel halo, Jess had a good line in expletive-rich imagery.

As the atmosphere thickened and soured, Sabine and Beth retreated to Sab's room. It was identical to Beth's, but nicer. Probably because she'd made more of an effort. There were cushions on the bed and floor, a batik wall hanging bought from a flea market and a selection of house plants that she'd somehow charmed the guy at the market to give her, along with a real Christmas tree. The tree was small and a little lopsided, but it didn't matter. The overall effect was eclectic, but cosy.

Aleah was lying on the rug, again not the standard-issue version, but a funky bargain bought from the local B&M. She was reading *The Tiger Who Came to Tea* to the twins, complete with tiger-ish growls. Aleah loved the boys. She spent hours watching over them, chatting to them about unicorns and road safety and the purpose of belly buttons. She had views on a wide range of topics and was confident in expressing them. Beth was a little in awe of her. At seven, Aleah had more confidence than Beth had at twenty-three. That was obviously down to Sabine. Who wouldn't believe in their own power to conquer the world, with a mother like Sab?

Another door slammed somewhere in the house, rattling the windows. 'It's getting crazy out there.'

'Crazier than normal, you mean.' Sabine was bending over the low table, finishing off the last of the bracelets. Jewellery-making was one of her many side-hustles. She'd taken quite a bit of cash off the staff and other residents in the run-up to Christmas. The bracelets were pretty and cheap. The perfect gift from, and for, women with very little. The previous month the front lounge had been commandeered as 'Sab's Salon' and the same beads had been used for hair-braiding. Beth had offered to help with both enterprises, but Sabine had declined with a laugh, saying that Beth had her hands full enough with the twins. A kind way of saying she'd be crap at it.

For a few moments Beth listened to the tiger *drinking all the milk in the milk jug and eating all the food in the fridge.*

Sabine paused in her work and looked at the kids lined up on the rug. She picked up her phone. 'Do you mind if I take one?'

'No, of course not.'

Sabine snapped a pic. Studied it.

'She's really quite something.' Beth spoke quietly. Aleah had big ears and although Sab wanted her daughter to be confident, Beth saw how quick she was to quash any signs of arrogance. 'She seems so unaffected by it all. I think you've done an amazing job.'

Sab rocked back on her heels and made a huffing sound. Dissent. Her expression clouded. 'No, I haven't.

I stuck around way too long.' Beth was shocked by the fierceness of her tone. Oli started grizzling. Aleah sat up and hoisted him, like a bag of potatoes, onto her lap. He didn't object. She then reached out, took a different book from the pile and carried on reading – the picture of competence and contentment. Sab continued in a whisper. 'She came home from school one day. It was during a good patch. We'd been doing okay, or what I thought was okay. We were eating and she suddenly said, out of nowhere, "Why do you let Daddy be nasty to you?" Just like that. Five years old, and she knew what was going on... and this is the thing: she knew it was wrong. I couldn't answer her. Couldn't even look her in the eyes. Because it was a totally valid, rational question. I was letting him.'

'Is that what prompted you to leave him?'

'Yes. It made me realise that enough was enough.'

'That was brave of you.'

Sab laughed, bitterly. 'No, it wasn't.' She looked away as if the sight of Aleah was too much. 'I kept her in that flat, around him, for another year and a half.'

'Because you were scared. We all were. We all *are*.'

'No. I stayed because, despite everything – the lying, the gambling, the violence – I wanted to be with him. I was selfish. I stayed for me.' She let that sink in.

'But in the end you did the hard thing. You left.'

'Yeah. Eventually.' Another harsh laugh. 'But that first night here I sat in the dark, on this very chair, watching Aleah sleep, our stuff in bin bags by the door, and I thought, I can't do this. I was all set to go back to him. How bad is that? I was prepared to take her back into that environment because I couldn't imagine life without him.'

Aleah was now onto the Very Hungry Caterpillar munching his way through his litany of tasty fruit.

'I only came downstairs that first morning to get Farida off my back. I'd already looked up the train times back to London.'

'So what changed?'

Sab laughed again, this time properly. Aleah looked up from her book and grinned at her mother. 'I met you, you dumb-ass!'

'Mummy!' Aleah scolded.

Sab held up her hands. 'My bad. Sorry, Aleah.'

Her daughter looked serious. 'It's not me you need to say sorry to, Mummy, it's Beth.'

'Sorry, Beth.' Sab pulled an exaggeratedly contrite expression.

Satisfied with her mother's apology, Aleah moved on to the caterpillar's unhealthy diet of Swiss cheese, salami and lollipops.

'You stayed behind after the huddle, every other bugger had just upped and left, and we washed up and we got talking, and I thought: if she can do it, so can I. Leaving like you did with the twins, right off the bat so soon after their birth, no dithering about, all on your own, with things the way they are with Joe, because you knew you had to – that's real bravery.'

Beth was about to disagree, but she stopped herself. She had been brave; braver than she'd thought possible.

They smiled at each other.

The moment held.

The stillness brought Beth a sense of calm she'd not felt for a very long time – not since before Ian. And a glimmer of belief in her own brand of strength.

But a second later the peace was shattered. There was a loud bang. The sound of breaking glass. A volley of shouting. There was nothing unusual about breakages and raised voices inside Holly House, but this time the voice was male.

Beth's heart thudded. *Ian?*

She held herself completely still. Was this her comeuppance for having the temerity to leave? For taking the boys? Was this her wronged, rage-filled man, or someone else's? Self-preservation made her pray, with every fibre in her body, that this threat belonged to one of the other women – even Sab. She wasn't strong enough. If Ian made it up the stairs, if he opened the door and walked into the room, she wouldn't be able to resist him. He would take the twins and push her back down onto the floor.

The shouting got louder, with more of the women joining the fray. Were they making it worse by fronting him up? Or buying time? It was too chaotic to discern an accent. It occurred to Beth that them being in Sab's room was a good thing. But it wouldn't really make a difference, would it? There was no way out. When Ian got upstairs, he would search until he found them. Beth watched Sab cross the room to Aleah. She crouched low, her arms encircling all three of the children, providing reassurance, but she didn't promise it would be okay, because Sab never lied to her daughter.

Farida's voice cut through the cacophony. The shouting petered out. A fist-clenched quiet descended. It felt as if the whole house was holding its breath. Beth strained to work out what was happening.

But there was nothing.

No footsteps on the stairs.

No slowly opening door.

No Ian looking at her with utter disgust.

Not this time.

Chapter 79

MUCH, MUCH LATER – after the police had departed, taking Jess's by-then-crying and apologetic partner with them, and after the women had hashed and rehashed the events of the day many times over and the staff had sought to calm the hysteria, and after the kids had been cuddled and fed sausages and beans, and been given a selection box each as a treat for being so good, and after some semblance of normality had finally been restored – the women all slunk off to their individual rooms to settle their children, as best they could, on *the most magical night of the year*. But even then, inside the cocoon of Sab's room, with the twins asleep in their car seats and Aleah snuggled down in her bed, Beth still didn't feel safe.

Sab patted the mattress and Beth climbed gratefully into bed beside her. They listened to the sounds of the house settling. Benign sounds now. The flushing of a toilet, the TV in Kirsty's room on too loud, as always, and someone moving around in the kitchen, making yet another brew – someone who *was* supposed to be there this time, not an intruder. Not a sudden, sharp reminder that their pasts could erupt in their present at any moment. Not Ian.

Sab voiced Beth's thoughts. 'We can't stay here.'

'No.' Aleah started snoring. It was a soft, snuffly sound. 'It's not just today.' Beth knew she could say anything to Sab, even if it felt disloyal and ungrateful. 'It's being surrounded by everyone else's troubles. All the sadness.'

'I hear you.'

'And the anger.' The very thing she'd fled. 'Sometimes I listen to how we all talk, in front of the kids, about life and men. It's so brutal and bitter. I get it, I do. Everyone is hurting. But it can't be good for the kids. It isn't how life should be.'

'I agree.' Sab shifted on the bed, sat up straight. 'Which is why we need to get out of here.' She was always so pragmatic and direct.

'But where can we go? You know what the waiting list for accommodation is like.'

'That's if we wait for them to find us something.'

'What alternative is there?'

Sab was staring at the opposite wall, seemingly at nothing, but Beth realised she was seeing something other than grubby cream paint, a wonky Christmas tree and thin curtains drawn against the dark.

'There's always an alternative.' She took hold of Beth's hand. 'If you're prepared to look hard enough.'

Chapter 80

SABINE WAS AS GOOD as her word.

Before January was out she announced she'd found them somewhere to live.

A flat in north London. Owned by a friend of a cousin of an uncle. Home territory for Sab. She was vibrating with excitement. 'It's perfect, by which I mean it's cheap. But if we're really going to do this, we need to do it quickly. It's available now, but he won't hold it for us for long.'

A new year, a new home, a new life. It was all happening too fast for Beth. 'Aren't you frightened Leon will find you?'

Sab stopped sorting the pile of laundry on the bed. 'London is a big place, Beth. His manor is south London. Leon thought his head would blow up if he went north of the Thames. Besides, I've had enough of hiding. Fuck him, I want to go home.'

Beth admired her courage, but doubted her own. Another move, another huge step, even further away from the North-East – no safety net this time. The fear returned.

'Earth to Beth.' Sab waved her hands in Beth's face. 'So? Are we doing this?'

Beth couldn't bring herself to say anything.

Sab waited for a second or two, then quietly but very clearly said, 'I've sorted us a flat. I can get work. It will be tight, but we will be okay.' She went back to folding the clothes. 'If you decide to stay, I'll understand, but I can't.' She swallowed. 'I don't want to do it without you, Beth, but I will, if I have to. It's time to be brave. Again.'

Chapter 81

FACED WITH SUCH a huge decision, Beth turned to the one person she trusted to give her sound advice. She called Heather and told her about Sab's ultimatum.

For a couple of seconds the line went quiet.

'You don't think I should do it?' Beth asked.

'No. It's not that.' It wasn't the most ringing endorsement. 'You've been so much happier since Sabine and Aleah arrived. I can hear it in your voice – your confidence coming back. It's good that you have a friend you can trust and rely on. It's just that London is such a long way to go.'

'I know.' It was, and in her heart Beth knew it was a move that, once made, there would be very little chance of coming back from. She would, to all intents and purposes, be shutting down her old life completely. The boys would grow up as Londoners, with southern accents. Not Geordie boys at all. And she would be moving even further away from her mother, which would weaken their already-strained relationship.

Heather broke into her thoughts. 'What about Joe?'

That was preying on Beth's mind as well. He was still waiting for his appointment with the neurologist. Moving would mean a whole new cycle of getting him registered with a new paediatrician, then waiting for him to be seen and assessed. It would delay the CP diagnosis, which she was sure they were going to confirm, even further. Sab had waved away Beth's concerns by pointing out that the best paediatric specialists were all in London. 'Sab reckons he would be referred to Great Ormond Street or one of the other big hospitals. That, in the long term, it would be the best place for us to live, if it is CP.'

'I can see that.'

There was a lull.

'And it won't make any difference to the custody case?' Heather asked.

Beth hadn't yet broached the proposed move with her solicitor. It was another hurdle to be got over. 'I don't think so.' There was one last obstacle, the biggest of them all, the one she'd left squarely and unfairly on Heather and Mick's doorstep. 'Then there's Ian?'

Heather's response was swift. 'What about him?'

'I can't just leave you dealing with him.'

'It's calmed down a lot.'

'Has it, really?'

'Yes.' A flat, sharp assertion. Heather wasn't designed for lying, but Beth knew she lied whenever they spoke about Ian.

'Heather?'

Beth heard her draw breath. 'Beth, if this feels the right thing for you and the boys, then you should do it.' She and Mick had always had her back. 'And if moving to London has the added benefit of getting you as far away as possible from Ian, then I, for one, am totally, wholeheartedly in favour of it.'

Chapter 82

Six days later, against the advice of their social workers, the staff at Holly House, the team at Women's Aid and Beth's solicitor, and after a long, tiring trip by taxi, train and white van – Sab's uncle met them at St Pancras – Beth and Sab moved into 1246 Harrow Road.

Their new home was a small, dark ground-floor flat in a featureless pebble-dashed block, on a busy, traffic-choked road. Between them they had six bin bags, one wheelie suitcase, a batik hanging, a jazzy rug, some plants, a small collection of battered children's books, three kids and £178 in cash.

As uninspiring as their new home was, they were excited. The flat was the best thing that had happened to both of them in a very long time.

PART FOUR

Chapter 83

TWENTY-FOUR YEARS LATER

'But that isn't the whole story, is it, Mum?' Oli heard the hard edge in his voice.

Beth started, as if she'd forgotten that he and Joe had been sitting there, listening, as she led them through the maze of her past. 'Sorry. What else do you want to know?' She sounded tired.

Oli felt a storm of emotions. There was sympathy and love, as well as an undeniable sense of pride in what she'd achieved in her life from such difficult beginnings, but he also felt horribly short-changed. Her story – *their* story – was shocking, and sad, and inspiring, but it was like listening to the retelling of someone else's life. Fitting this version of his and Joe's early childhood together with the half-arsed version their mother had peddled for nearly a quarter of a century wasn't going to be easy.

'I understand why you left, admire you for doing it, but you didn't really resolve anything, did you? You just left it all behind. Dad, the lives we might... we were supposed to have. Then, and this is the bit that makes absolutely no sense to me,' Oli felt his grip on his anger slipping, 'you pretended none of it happened.'

Sab stepped in. 'She did it to protect you. Haven't you listened to a word she's said!'

Sabine's intervention infuriated Oli. 'That may be true.' Sab snorted, but wisely refrained from saying anything else. 'But why not tell us the truth? If not as kids, then when we were older? Presumably there must have been some sort of custody case – which I'm assuming you won – otherwise why have we never seen sight or sound of our father? Not once. Not so much as a call, or a card, or a sudden dramatic appearance? His total silence for the past twenty-four years is deeply weird, by the way.' Had their mother fixed that as well? Had she blocked their father out of their lives, with solicitors and by lying low? Her concern about her privacy made sense now. His head hurt. 'And why – and this is the part I really don't get – why all that bullshit about our dad being the best dad ever? Why did you create a pack of lies and feed them to us, on a virtually daily basis? What the fuck was that all about?'

Sab now did go to speak, but Beth stopped her. 'No. He's every right – you both have,' she looked from Oli to Joe, 'to be confused and angry. I did lie to you.' She stopped abruptly, precisely at the point when they needed her to keep speaking.

'Well?' Oli pushed. He looked at Joe, whose expression was too guarded to read, but his body gave him away. Oli had never seen his brother so rigid.

Their mother gathered herself. 'I took you away from Ian, and from Newcastle – from the North-East – because I truly believed I had no choice. To this day I don't know whether he would ever have hurt you, but I couldn't be sure. There was a part of him he couldn't control, as much as he tried. And... and...' She swallowed. 'I didn't want you growing up around that sort of darkness. I didn't want it to infect your lives and affect the people you would become. I wanted you to grow up as far away from that sort of damage as possible. The courts agreed, eventually. They awarded me full custody when you were two. By then your father's mental health,' she paused again, 'had deteriorated. Quite markedly.' She looked down at her hands, then up again. 'It seemed safer and more straightforward for you to think he was dead. You didn't remember him, and he hadn't come looking for us. I had a choice to make: tell you a hard truth or a kind lie. I wanted you to have a father who loved you.'

Oli still wanted more. 'So you made one up?'

'Yes.' There was another pause, this one embarrassed as well as distraught. 'In hindsight, it was a stupid thing to do. Sab has always said it was madness.' They glanced at each other, tight as ever. 'I did it because I wanted you to grow up thinking your father was a decent man. I wanted you to have a role model to help guide you.' She stopped speaking again. Each new reflection seemed to hurt her. 'If it means anything, I've always felt guilty about it, but,' she straightened up slightly in her seat, 'I still believe it was the right thing to do.'

What could he possibly say to that? He was so confused and angry, but whether that was because of the collapse of his belief in his father, or in his mother, Oli couldn't work out.

Perhaps fearful of his conclusion, his mother shifted her attention to his brother. 'Joe. Are you all right? You're very quiet.'

Prodded into a response by her question, Joe blinked and finally moved. As he stretched out, a flash of pain rippled across his features. He'd been sitting immobile for too long. They all had. His reply, when it came, was hardly worth waiting for. All he said was, 'Yep.'

So Joe had nothing to contribute. How very like his brother.

Silence descended on the room. It was oppressive. Oli felt like he was suffocating.

Ever the person to move the agenda on, it was Sab who finally spoke. 'Well, now you know the truth, what are you going to do?'

'About Ella?' Oli asked.

There was another long, heavy pause. Then Joe said, 'Or about our long-lost, abusive, mentally unstable, not-dead father?'

Chapter 84

JOE USED THE EXCUSE that he wanted to stretch his legs to leave the house with Oli. He needed air and movement, and distance from the story his mother had just told them.

They walked in silence for the first few streets. At the main road, by unspoken agreement, the brothers crossed over and headed into the park. Old territory. When they reached the football pitches Joe slowed. Oli noticed. 'Are you all right?' He wasn't. 'You need a sit-down?' Joe nodded. They veered over to the benches under the trees, where Joe used to sit and watch Oli practise his Cruyff turns.

Oli launched into his take on everything, barely pausing for breath or, seemingly, much reflection. Joe listened without comment. Oli was so impatient, so quick to decide what he thought, and felt, and what he was going to do about it – which was, apparently, go up to Newcastle, meet Ella and their dad, have it all out in the open, as soon as possible. Basically, his plan was to shake the tree and see what fell out.

They were so different. Always had been. Always would be.

When Oli finally ran out of steam, he waited a single, solitary beat before demanding that Joe voice his opinion. 'For fuck's sake, say something.' He was relentless.

'Such as?'

'Whatever is going through your head. You've barely said two words.'

It depressed Joe that they always seemed to end up in the same old territory, trading the same old insults. He tipped his head back and looked at the sky. It was blank. 'I've been mainly thinking... it's that bastard's fault I have CP.'

It was obviously not what Oli was expecting. For once, he was speechless.

Joe looked down at his cramped hand, which he'd tried all his life to hide; he felt the knots buried deep inside the muscles in his legs that no amount of physio and exercises would ever smooth away; and he zoned in on the nagging pain in his left foot that made him walk like a fucking cripple. That word – the one his mum hated. An outdated, insensitive, deeply offensive word and yet it lived in his head, because he saw it in other people's eyes every day of his life. He set free his anger. 'She was seven months pregnant. He knocked her to the floor in a rage. Why? Because she didn't get up and make his breakfast! Then he left, as if nothing had happened. She went into labour. Prematurely. They had to yank us out of her nine weeks early. Way too soon.

He caused this.' Joe gestured at his body, at the cramped limbs he'd learnt to live with, and accept, because of the old, well-worn mantra – namely, that his CP was simply a cruel twist of fate, that his disability was no one's fault. Except it was. There could have been, should have been, a different outcome. 'I have CP because our father was violent.'

'Shit, Joe!' Oli exhaled.

There was a long pause.

Then, for the oddest of reasons – possibly it was the sound of the breeze in the trees, or perhaps it was the sight of a dog tripping over itself in pursuit of a squirrel, or it could have been Oli's oh-so-familiar lack of sensitivity, or maybe, just maybe, it was the release of his own outburst – Joe felt the tension drain out of him. He laughed. A short, hard bark of a laugh that frightened the dog and sent it skittering back to its owner. 'Thanks for that, Confucius.'

They looked at each other.

'Sorry,' Oli said.

'What are you apologising for?'

'That it was you who copped it, not me.'

They'd never done this before: faced head-on the profound difference between the two of them, their mockery of the essential sameness of twins. They were a joke that wasn't funny.

At last, after weeks – no months – of feeling that he and Oli were drifting further and further apart, Joe finally felt a connection with his brother. He was grateful for his apology. No one had ever said 'sorry' to him before. Sure, the apology was coming from the wrong person, but he'd take it. Being disabled sucked, surely he was allowed to say that. Because as much as Joe had always envied Oli's CP-free existence, he knew that his resentment was unreasonable.

'It isn't your fault.' It wasn't. In many ways Oli had as little control over his life as Joe.

'Nah, maybe not, but it has – as I so eloquently put it earlier – been shit for you.'

'Yeah. It has.' Joe listened to the trees. For a change, Oli lived with the quiet. 'I know you think Mum has always favoured me.' Again Oli looked thrown by the change of topic, but Joe was in confessional mode and it felt good, so there was no stopping him. What better day was there for truths? Weird and warped as things had been over the past few days, the revelations about their father had created an opportunity for them to reset their dynamic. And many things in their lives needed a reboot. Whatever happened next, Joe wanted his relationship with his mother and his brother to be more honest. He wanted all of his relationships to be truthful. 'And that she still does. Maybe that's true. She's always watched over me like some sort of guardian angel – ever-vigilant, ready to swoop in and rescue me. But that's only because of my CP. Have you ever thought about how humiliating that is? Let me tell you, most of the time it's a complete pain in the arse. And there's always this pressure on me: to do my best, to try my hardest, to never let my CP get me down. I have to smile and suck it up, crack on. Trust me, Ol, that much attention can be fucking exhausting.'

It was true, you could be loved too intensely. 'I've always envied you.' Now Oli looked puzzled. Joe helped him out. 'You got to… just be.'

It was Oli's turn to laugh and spill the beans. 'Snap! When we were kids I was so jealous of you. You were the twin who could do no wrong, even when you did. I always felt like a bit of an afterthought. It drove me fucking crazy.'

'I know.' Joe laughed again; this facing things and blurting them out was addictive. 'That was the one upside for me: how pissed off you were – all the time. I used to love watching you get riled up. I thought it balanced the scales a bit.'

They sat for a few seconds doing nothing, thinking their own thoughts, not communicating, but not competing, either. Something had shifted between them. Joe wasn't sure what, but he was glad.

Eventually Oli said, 'So, seriously, what are you going to do?'

Joe rubbed his hand across his stubble-free chin and thought about Carrie and the chink of hope she'd offered him, and he thought about the tenacity of his mother, which was as much a part of her as her over-protectiveness. And he knew, without a shadow of a doubt, that both of these women were far more important to him than a man who had done nothing but cause pain and damage. He wasn't prepared to waste time and energy on a past he couldn't change. Instead, he needed to put right his own wrongs against the people he loved in the here and now.

'Ironically, Oli... I'm going to do precisely what Mum has always expected of me. I'm going to get on with my life.' He stood up. 'And I'm going to have nothing whatsoever to do with our bastard father.'

Chapter 85

JOE WALKED OLI to the Tube. Oli didn't try to dissuade him, although he knew his brother's legs were bothering him. It was up to Joe how hard and how far he pushed himself.

The mood between them was, surprisingly, relaxed – which made a nice change. When they said their goodbyes, Joe went in for a hug. It was the first time in months they'd had any physical contact. The disparity in the strength of their grip was very noticeable. The consequences of Joe's CP were always there, and always would be. It reminded Oli of just how readily he chose to forget the challenges his brother faced every single day of his life.

They promised to speak again the following day, keep each other in the loop. Both of them confirming, in a low-key throwaway manner, that their relationship had been set back on its feet by their conversation in the park.

Oli walked down to the platform and parked himself on one of the metal benches. The next train was due in four minutes – enough time for some uncomfortable reflections, but not in relation to his mother's lying, or the frankly appalling new version of his real father, but more in regard to himself.

He was a rubbish brother. An even worse twin. He'd spent his life wanting what Joe had – namely, the unconditional love of their mother – without really thinking about what life had been like for him. He'd even, God forgive him, been jealous of Joe's CP. How fucking immature was that?

And... he prompted himself to face it.

Train due in three minutes.

He was sleeping with Carrie. Carrie – the love of Joe's life. Oli watched the rubbish between the rails lift and stir.

That was bad enough. But the bigger problem was that he wasn't messing. He was deadly serious. He loved Carrie, was in love with her. Even now – maybe especially now, given everything that was going down – all he wanted to do was be with her, talk to her. He wanted to fold himself into her body and have her make all the crap fade into the background. If she'd let him. He was in deep shit.

Two minutes.

People started standing up. He joined them.

Should he head home to his empty flat, process this on his own, like a responsible adult? Or should he go to her, press himself into her kindness, ask for her love? His indecision hurt. It was unfamiliar.

One minute.

Everyone moved closer to the platform edge.

Was he going to choose himself? Or his brother?

The air changed. The rush of the oncoming train. The rubbish danced higher.

Train approaching.

Chapter 86

OLI DISAPPEARED INTO the Tube station. Joe stayed where he was, watching people arrive and depart, getting on with their lives. He didn't want to go home. Didn't want to be with his mum. Didn't want to talk about the past. Absolutely did not want to discuss his father. Yet he had to go somewhere. He set off walking, back the way he'd come. Decision delayed.

What he wanted was to be with Carrie. But did she want that? *Did* she want him? He truly didn't know what was going on in her head and her heart anymore, which was fair enough, he'd forgone that right by the way he'd behaved.

She had let him in the previous night – but only because he'd been distressed.

He had talked for hours and she'd listened – but only because she pitied him.

She had offered him comfort and calmness – but only because she was kind.

She had made him feel a bit better, a little stronger,

slightly more hopeful – but only because that was the type of person she was.

But he didn't want to be that sort of person with her, for her. He didn't want to be needy and reliant. He didn't want to be Carrie's 'project', her responsibility. Not anymore.

He wanted to hold *her* up for a change, wanted to protect her, wanted love not sympathy, passion not compassion. And for that to be possible he needed her to forgive him. But why should she do that? Because he loved her? That wasn't enough.

He reached Jarmon Road. Decision time. Left led home. Right led to Carrie. One a short journey. The other far longer. The traffic flowed past. After a few minutes one of the drivers spotted him standing at the kerb. She slowed to let him cross. Joe waved her on.

Chapter 87

THE BOYS HAD LEFT the house with nothing agreed. Beth knew they needed time to process everything she'd told them, but it was hard to bear their withdrawal from her. Neither of them had kissed her goodbye. They were her world. But she had shattered theirs.

Sab stayed behind and Beth was grateful. For the thousandth time she wondered what would have happened to her, and the boys, if she and Sab hadn't met and become friends.

'Well, at least that's done now.' Sab said it as if something positive had been achieved.

Beth appreciated the sentiment, but she was too clear-sighted to be reassured by it. 'Hardly.' She had a pain in her stomach that she knew would only ease when they loved her again, without hesitation. Her fear was that she didn't know when that would be.

'You know what I mean. They know the truth about Ian now, and they didn't implode. They'll come to terms with it. And it'll be better in the long run. No more pretending. No more worrying. That's got to be a relief, hasn't it?'

'Yes.'

Sab waited, knowing there would be more.

'But Oli's right. It's all still up there, in Newcastle, waiting for me, and them. Ian. This girl Ella, their half-sister. I can't just ignore it.'

'You have for the past twenty-four years.'

Beth conceded that it might have looked as if that was what she was doing, but in truth the past quarter of a century had been a huge act of will on her behalf. She hadn't been ignoring her past, she'd been keeping it at bay. It had been a wearying battle of attrition.

Ian, and what he might or might not do, had stalked her. His spectre had lurked in the shadows at every landmark date in the boys' lives. Might he have tracked them down? Might he turn up, out of the blue, on their birthday, at Christmas, on Father's Day, or just randomly one day, to confront her and flatly contradict her carefully created fiction? And what would she do if he did? Ian had been inside her head every time she'd lied, in person and on forms – as she had, over and over again. *Marital status – widow. Title – Ms. Husband – deceased.* No, you're not! 'No, I'm not!' Ian had hissed. And, most powerfully of all, Ian haunted her every time she'd looked at Joe.

Joe's CP and his painful, frustrating journey through life all traced back to Ian. And that fact, awful as it was, was what had sustained Beth. It had strengthened her resolve to absorb her guilt and made her determined never, ever, to let him anywhere near either of her boys.

'Beth! What are you thinking?' Sab looked concerned.

'That I have to go to Newcastle.'

Beth knew that deciding to act, rather than trying to sit it out, wouldn't make the pain in her belly go away, but it would be a distraction. And she was also certain that if she didn't make the journey up north to face her past, either one or both her boys would. And soon.

'I'll meet this girl. See what she's like. And find out what I can about Ian.'

'On your own?'

'Yes.'

'Why?'

'Because I should. This way, I can work out what it is they – we – are facing.'

Sab folded her arms. 'You know they're fully grown men now, don't you?'

'I do.'

The old argument: when did your children stop being your responsibility? Sab knew Beth's answer was *never*.

'Let me come with you.'

Sab had always been her wingman. 'No. Not this time. This is a mess of my own making.'

Her friend shook her head and smiled her familiar, frustrated, disagreeing, but accepting smile. 'Of Ian's making.'

Chapter 88

BETH WENT the following day. No time like the present – after almost a quarter of a century.

The train was busy. The usual business travellers and students, with their inconvenient luggage, and lots of women, in pairs, having trips away, their cans of chilled gin and tonic open before the train had pulled out of King's Cross. Beth felt conspicuous, because she was alone, and because of the peculiar purpose of her journey.

As the train picked up speed through the grime and graffiti of north London, the covert nature of her trip chewed at Beth's conscience. More secrets. More excuses as to why they were necessary. History repeating itself.

But her lies had saved her in the past.

Beth had looked at the messages on Oli's phone when he'd gone to the loo after their long and difficult talk the day before. It was another flagrant breach of trust, but a necessary one – without it, she'd have been unable to contact Ian's daughter, which she'd done as soon as Sab had left.

She and the girl had kept their text exchanges to a cool minimum. Beth had introduced herself and explained that she'd spoken to Joe and Oli and that she'd known nothing of Ella's existence up until a few hours earlier, but now that she did, she was keen to meet – as soon as possible. Ian's daughter had acquiesced. They'd set a time and a location for their rendezvous. Train tickets had been booked. And now, thirteen hours later, she was on her way.

It would be her first time back in the North-East since she'd left Mags's house. The big question, and the reason for her racing heart, was that she had no idea who would be waiting for her on the station concourse. Beth had made it clear that she wanted their first (and secretly she hoped it would be their only) meeting to be just the two of them, but she knew Ella's agreement to come alone was no guarantee. If she told her father that Beth was coming to Newcastle at long last, what were the chances Ian would stay away? Low to nil. Bitterness and anger that fierce would surely burn for ever.

As the train passed through the miles of faceless countryside, and as the women with their gin got louder and merrier, Beth allowed herself to think about Ian.

Like a difficult jigsaw, she started with the easy pieces.

He would be fifty-seven now. In her mind she opted for grey hair rather than baldness. As a younger man he'd had nice hair – thick, wavy, always in need of a trim. She'd cut it herself in the early days, before she became too anxious about getting it 'just so'. Ian's face? For the first time in a very long period she let the memory of Ian's smile rise to the surface. When he'd been happy, which was often, his smile had been infectious, seductive, lovely to see. Quickly she flipped the image to a different expression, the one she'd grown to dread – not his anger-filled face, she rarely saw that because she used to look away when he lost it, but she'd spent years being watchful for the closed, tight blankness that always proceeded his outbursts. The memory of his pent-up anger brought back the familiar watery feeling in her bowels, but she made herself stay with it. If there was a chance of him confronting her when she stepped off the train, she wanted to be prepared. Or at least as prepared as she would ever be.

Would Ian still be as physically intimidating, after all these years? He had been tall, lean, strong. Now? She imagined him weaker – wanted it to be so. She added degradations wrought by age and anger; surely they would have dulled the clean edges, made him slower. Would the intervening years have added blurry weight or stripped flesh from his frame? The thought of Ian diminished was both reassuring and worrying. Beth had always been clear-sighted enough to know that, in escaping with the boys, she'd damned him to a very specific type of purgatory, a state of enforced limbo that she wouldn't have wished on anyone. Not even him.

After the courts finally sanctioned her flight, awarded her full custody and destroyed his hopes, Ian had gone into free-fall. His mental-health problems had escalated dramatically, exacerbated by a raging anger denied its real target, and by bouts of heavy drinking. He'd lost his job. Got into fights. Become known to the police. By that point Mick and Heather had had enough. Living on edge all the time, waiting for the abuse, having to call 999 in the early hours of the morning when he came to their house, raging and demanding the truth, had simply become unbearable. They sold up and moved away. The guilt that her actions had robbed Heather and Mick of their much-loved family home had never left Beth.

The other downside of their move was that, with Mick and Heather safely away from Ian, Beth's direct pipeline of information was cut off. She'd tried to keep track of him, of course. She followed local newsfeeds, googled his name, picked up snippets here and there – usually bad. She knew he'd spent three short stints in prison: one for non-payment of fines, another for a public-order offence, the third for assault. It was a clear catalogue of his worsening state, and a painful reminder of the price other people were paying for her escape.

Then, when the twins were four, he went dark. Nothing.

That was almost worse. When he'd been raising hell, at least she'd been reassured he was still in Newcastle and, she'd hoped – terrible as the thought was – too preoccupied with his own misery to cause any for her and the boys. Not knowing where he was and what he was doing was more troubling. During that period her mind had gone into overdrive. What if he got clean? Would the old Ian be resurrected? And if that happened, would his outrage find its proper focus and could it galvanise him to come looking for her? Might he start earning again, scrape together enough money to have another go at the legal route? He could appoint a different solicitor, make the case that he'd changed, cleaned up his act, and claim he had the right to see his sons?

But weeks passed. Then months. Then a full year, and still Ian didn't come banging on their door. Beth started to believe he'd given up. More time passed. Still nothing. And she had, she confessed to herself, started to think, even hope, that he might be dead. A fight that got out of hand, perhaps? She even allowed herself to think suicide. That was painful to dwell on, though dwell on it she did. The guilt wouldn't leave her alone. No matter how many times Sab counselled her to let it go, she couldn't. Perhaps that was why she clung to her ridiculous myth of Ian as the tragic, decent, but lost father. It was a comfort to her as much as the boys and, in a perverse way, a kinder epitaph for Ian himself.

The sensation of the train slowing brought Beth back to the present. They were pulling into York. She watched people rise and start gathering their things, clearing their rubbish, saying goodbye to their fellow travellers, where conversations and connections had been struck up. Once more she felt her isolation acutely. In just over an hour she would be in Newcastle.

The question was, would she be face-to-face with a young woman who could answer her questions? Or face-to-face with Ian himself?

Chapter 89

NEWCASTLE STATION had changed a lot since she'd last been there. It was a change for the better. The dirty, austere grandeur had been remodelled. A nice-looking wine bar and a couple of chain coffee shops now graced the entrance, and the addition of floor-to-ceiling glass doors stopped the biting North-East wind from whistling through the station concourse. Playing games with herself, Beth reasoned that if she didn't actually step through the automatic doors onto the street, then she could argue that she hadn't actually set foot in Newcastle. She was, after all, only visiting in order to lay old ghosts to rest.

She scanned the crowds, recognised no one. No one recognised her. All good, so far. She opted for Caffè Nero. There were a few customers sitting at the scatter of tables, but it wasn't rammed, most of their trade being takeaways. She reasoned that it would be easier to talk there rather than at the already-busy bar. Pints and Prosecco at 11 a.m. – Newcastle living up to its party-town reputation.

Beth ordered a tea and took it over to a table tucked in a corner near a clump of fake foliage. She sat with her back to the dusty plastic trees, facing the main set of doors. It was a good vantage point from which to watch everyone coming and going – although looking around the busy concourse, she realised that her spot actually afforded very little real security. There were multiple entry points to the station through which Ian's daughter, or Ian himself, could arrive.

Beth had lied to Ella about what time her train got in. She'd wanted to give herself some breathing space to get settled and compose herself before their meeting. In hindsight, it had been a bad idea. Beth felt anything but composed. Repressed panic – an emotion she'd not felt in years – expanded inside her. Her desire to simply stand up, walk back through the barriers and onto the next available train heading south grew. She could simply run away, as she had twenty-four years ago.

Instead she took a sip of her tea.

That wouldn't be fair. And it would solve nothing. She told herself to get a grip. To cement her intention to stay put, she sent Ian's daughter a message: Arrived. Sitting in the Caffè Nero on the station forecourt. See you soon. B

There was a burst of laughter from a group of girls drinking at the bar. They were a tribe, identifiable by their matching blonde hair, tight dresses, high heels and contoured faces. A fresh bottle of Prosecco was being ordered, before the previous one had been drained. Girl power, alive and thriving in Newcastle. Despite her nerves, Beth smiled, approving of their attitude, and their energy.

She looked at Ella's profile photo again. Even allowing for the poor quality and flat lighting, it was obvious that Ian's daughter would not cut it within such a group. Her natural, simple haircut and her everyday features lacked the shine and the self-investment. She was an exceptionally average-looking young woman – which was going to make spotting her amid the waves of people washing through the station difficult.

'Hi.'

Beth looked up from her phone. The real article was standing in front of her. 'Hello.'

The next train for Edinburgh Waverley, stopping at Cramlington, Morpeth, Widdrington, Alnmouth and Berwick-upon-Tweed was announced. Ella fled to the counter. When she returned, five minutes later, Beth's pulse had slowed a little. It appeared that Ella had kept her promise and come on her own.

Settled in the seat opposite, the girl said simply, 'So you came.'

'I said I would.'

'Yeah. You did.' But the implication was... she'd doubted it.

There was no momentum to their conversation yet. There were too many places to start, too many ladders to climb and snakes they could slide down. Off to their left a couple embraced, oblivious to the restless swirl of travellers flowing around them. Beth and Ella both glanced at them, then away. They met each other's eyes. It was Beth who looked down first. So Ella might be average-looking, but she was not average in nerve and determination. Beth made herself sit with the silence. This girl had started this drama, so it was for her to steer it.

At last she said, 'I was surprised when you got in touch.'

'Why?' Beth asked.

'Because I'd been messaging Joseph and Oliver... not you.'

'Joe and Oli.' Beth corrected. She immediately regretted it.

'Sorry.' Ella didn't look sorry. 'My mistake.' There was a slight pause. 'But an easy one to make, in the circumstances.'

Beth knew Ella was alluding to her efforts to hide her own and the boys' identities. This girl warranted her respect, if nothing else. She'd succeeded in tracking them down where Ian had failed, or never bothered. 'How *did* you find us?' Beth reasoned that if she could get her to talk about the practicalities of her search, the 'how' would lead to the 'why'.

Ella shrugged off her jacket. So at least she was intent on staying. 'The usual way. The Internet.' She left another pause. Beth held back on filling it. 'I started looking for you first under your married name.'

'But Ian and I were never married.'

'Yeah. So I discovered. The next step was to bung your maiden name into Google. This isn't the movies. I reckoned you wouldn't have created a whole new identity for yourself, but that didn't produce any hits, either. You really don't exist on social media or anywhere digitally, do you?' Her voice was low, but her tone was sharp.

'No.' Beth agreed. That, of course, had been deliberate. They'd used Sab's name, and face, for the business. Sabine had wanted to step into the light, to defy Leon, show him just how far she'd come without him. Beth had been happy to stay in the shadows, for obvious reasons. 'Is that why you switched to looking for the boys?'

'Boys?' She said it with heavy sarcasm.

Beth understood, but it was uncomfortable to face into. She corrected herself. 'The twins.'

'Yeah. I reckoned it would be easier to find them, given their age. And it was. But I was confused by what I found.'

'Why?'

'I found Oliver first – sorry, Oli.' There it was again, that spikiness. 'There was quite a lot of stuff from when he was playing football. He was the right age, had your surname. It looked likely I'd got the right person. So then it was a case of establishing whether he had a twin brother.' She sat back, took a sip of her drink. 'That's when it got odd.'

This time Beth couldn't resist filling the silence. 'What do you mean?'

'Well, the Oliver Truman I'd found did have a twin called Joe.' She left a pause. 'But the Joe Truman I found was disabled.'

Beth felt the immediate, hardwired urge to reframe Ella's comment. 'Joe has CP – cerebral palsy – but it's never been an issue for him.'

Ella's expression flickered. 'Yep. I gathered that. He's some sort of tech guru, isn't he? He was working over in the States for a while.'

'Yes.' Beth didn't want to get into that, proud as she'd been initially. 'But why did Joe having CP surprise you?'

'Because Dad never said anything about either of them having a disability.'

Beth sat silently for a moment. The train announcer filled in the gap. Thinking about it, it made sense. Ian never knew what Joe's life became because he never got to see him grow up. After years of denying it, suddenly here on this station concourse, with this slight, softly spoken, but steely young woman, it was important to Beth that she acknowledge the truth. Out loud. 'Joe and Oli are Ian's sons.'

Ella nodded, brushed her fringe out of her eyes. 'So they are my half-brothers?'

'Yes.'

The train for Leeds is departing in three minutes.

'If you really are Ian's daughter.'

That silenced her. They stared at each other, emotion flickering between them.

'Why else would I go to the trouble of finding them?'

Beth toughed it out. 'I don't know. Why have you?' She watched the girl stiffen. Pride and hurt. Defiance combined with a curious defencelessness. Ella lifted her chin and flicked away a tear. Anger or distress? The mother in Beth wanted to reach out and comfort her, but she held firm. This girl was a threat to the stability of her family – the thing that mattered most to Beth.

Ella swallowed, got herself back in control. 'Because for the whole of my life I've had to listen to him talk about his *other family*. About you, and Joe and Oli – his beautiful, lost boys.'

Did that surprise Beth? Not when she thought about it. Ian would have created his own fiction to make his life bearable, to render his role in what happened palatable. She'd simply never bothered trying to imagine what that version might be before, or who might have to listen to it. 'What did he say about us? About me?' She was genuinely curious.

Ella looked flatly at her. 'That you fucked off out of it with his kids, and you didn't – from what Dad said – so much as look behind you on your way out, so what do you care what he felt? At the time, or for years afterwards?'

There it was, Ian's anger passed on to his daughter. Because there was no doubt in Beth's mind now – this was his daughter.

Was Ella justified in her bitterness? What had Ian told her about why Beth had walked out on him? Not the truth, that was for certain. And Beth had been listening carefully to Ella's words as well as her indignation. She'd heard the *for years afterwards*. Her own and Ian's actions had had consequences, for many people, including this angry, tearful young woman. She softened her tone.

'Please. I want to know. I want to try and understand what it's been like for you.' *So I can work out what Ian is likely to do...* she did not add.

Ella sat back, obviously considering her options. She chose to open Pandora's box and let the contents fly up into Beth's face. 'He talked about the twins, a lot. It was confusing, especially when I was a kid.' She stopped, added, 'Confusing and really bloody hurtful. It was like I had these big brothers who were great, certainly better than me, but they only existed in my dad's past, where I couldn't ever reach them.'

'I'm sorry.' Beth was, but Ella was in no mood for apologies.

And she wasn't done. 'And it got worse, the older he got.'

'Worse?' Beth asked, dreading the answer.

She didn't hesitate. 'He was an alcoholic.' She stared at Beth. Blame placed firmly at her feet, where Ella obviously believed it belonged. 'He had patches when he was okay – when he was working, functioning – but he always went back to it.' She needed to hurt someone, because she'd been hurt. Beth got it. She let her talk. 'When he was drinking there was no filter. He'd go on and on about you. Some days it was all about how much he'd loved you, how perfect you were together. Other days he'd get hung up on you leaving him like you did, stealing his sons. Then he'd rage on and on about how you were a lying, deceitful monstrosity of a mother. But it always came back to Joe and Oli. How special his boys were. How the pain of losing them had changed him. It was his obsession. It ate him up.'

She paused and Beth had a painful image of Ella being forced to sit and listen to Ian's litany of grievances, and his grief.

'He had a huge wallet of photos of you and the boys as babies. He used go through them compulsively – cursing and crying.'

The ache in Beth's stomach deepened, not for herself, but for Ella; and for Ian.

'I knew, from being quite young, that me and Mum were just stand-ins, a pale imitation of what he thought he'd had with you and the twins.' She looked so sad, but she was astute as well. *Thought he had*. Ella had lost faith in what her own father was saying long ago. How hard must that have been? 'It hurt, being an also-ran – after his memories, and the booze.'

Beth gently tried to steer her onto less glass-strewn ground. 'Tell me about your mum?'

A new expression flitted across Ella's face. Frustration? Pity? Fatigue? Love? 'What's to tell? I assume she loved him when they first got together, that he was different, but what I mostly remember is them arguing. They'd fight, make up, fight again. And there were always money worries. It wasn't a happy environment. For any of us.'

'And now?'

Her expression tightened. 'What do you mean, now?'

'Sorry, I know it's not really my place to ask, but are they still together, Ian and your mum?'

'No.'

A flat, bald statement. How Ella felt about the split, Beth couldn't tell. She waited.

'She stuck it out until I was thirteen, then we packed up and left. Mum had no contact with him after that; well, not once he gave up bothering her.'

Beth took her next step gingerly. This was Ella's life, her story to tell, or not. 'You said "she", as in your mum. What about you?'

Ella studied Beth. She seemed to be weighing up what to say. 'Me?' She laughed, without humour. 'He was my dad. I stayed in touch. Helped him, as best I could. I didn't really have a choice, did I? He was on his own at the end. He'd burnt all his bridges, except the one to me.'

At the end? Beth waited.

'He died three months ago.'

Beth said nothing. She didn't trust herself to; showing even a glimmer of the grief, regret and sadness she was feeling would have been totally inappropriate.

Ella went on, in a monotone. 'I found him on the floor of his shitty little flat. A heart attack.'

So Ian was dead. Beth's tie to him was finally cut. It was over.

The tannoy announcements rumbled on, sending passengers on their way to York, London, Bristol, Penzance.

Beth and Ella stayed where they were.

Chapter 90

BETH KEPT AN EYE on Ella as she queued for their second round of drinks, fearful she might bolt, but she simply sat, shoulders sagging, staring at the girls laughing and chatting in the bar. It was even busier now. The lunchtime crowd in full swing. Two worlds, so close together and yet so far apart.

Armed with two coffees and, foolishly, a slice of cake – Beth felt the need to give Ella something – she made her way back to their table. Ella pulled the cup towards her and ran her fingers up and down the grooves. Self-soothing. She ignored the cake, but took a sip of her drink. Beth went for a simple statement of the truth. 'I'm sorry.'

Ella took another drink, then shrugged her shoulders.

'Is that why you contacted us?' Beth prompted.

'What?'

'Ian dying. Is that what made you decide to try and find the twins?'

'Yeah. It was something to do. I had time on my hands.

No more running around after him, doing his shopping and his washing; and I didn't have to keep going to A&E in the middle of the night to pick him up, after he'd had yet another fall and bashed his head again.'

Beth's sympathy had sharp, uncomfortable edges. She'd escaped Ian. Ella had not.

'Almost as soon as he died, the council wanted his flat back. I had to clear out all his crap. There was a lot. He never let anything go. Finding the photos set me off. It started bugging me that I knew nothing about what happened after you left.' She looked up, straight at Beth. 'Why did you leave like you did?'

More pain for another innocent – that was her and Ian's legacy. Beth felt shame, but also the compulsion to tell Ella the same truth she had told her brothers – finally. 'I left to protect Joe and Oli.'

Ella bristled. 'He wouldn't have hurt them. He loved children. He did his best, however rubbish his best was. And besides, he never got the chance to hurt them. You took them away from him the minute they were born.'

Beth wasn't going to quibble about timelines. 'I did.' She let that hang. 'Haven't you ever wondered why I'd do something so drastic, and so difficult?'

Ella looked confused. 'What are you talking about?'

'Are you sure you want to know?' Beneath the confusion, Beth saw ripples of suspicion and a dawning realisation. She dealt the blow quickly. 'Ian was violent.'

'He wasn't.' Ella paused. 'Not intentionally.'

Beth wondered about Ella's mother and what she'd

had to put up with before she left. But that was her story to tell or her secret to hold. Beth had only her own truth. 'He was towards me.'

Ella seemed unaware that she was shaking her head. 'He was too sad to be violent.'

'Not when I knew him.'

'So you're saying you left because you were frightened he'd hurt the boys.'

'He already had.'

'How?'

'There was a reason I went into labour so early.'

Ella was still shaking her head, but now more with distress than denial.

Beth kept going. 'He was always very up and down, even when we first got together. He'd have long patches of genuine happiness then, without explanation, sudden deep troughs of darkness. As my pregnancy progressed, he became more volatile. Excited one minute, then intensely jealous the next. On the day I went into labour he woke up in one of his dark moods. I did something that irritated him.'

'What?'

'It doesn't matter. It never did. He lost his temper. He pushed me. I fell. It bought on my labour. The boys were born nine weeks prematurely. It was touch-and-go. They nearly didn't survive.'

Ella raised her hand to her mouth, but no words came out.

'I nearly lost them.'

'Christ!'

Beth nodded. She watched Ella's face, sorry to be adding to her load. She was obviously struggling to process this new, bitter truth about her father. Love didn't switch off in an instant, at least not normally, no matter how heinous the transgression.

'So Joe's CP?' She was a bright girl.

Beth nodded. 'They couldn't be one hundred per cent certain, but yes, it seems likely that it was caused by the birth trauma.' The air went out of Ella and she sat back. 'That's why I left when I did, as I did; and that's why I fought to keep Ian away from them and keep us hidden, as best I could. Not that I did that very well. You found us, simply by looking.'

Ella managed to nod.

Beth reached out a tentative hand, but the girl flinched and moved away. Beth accepted it was too soon. 'I knew that me taking the boys and leaving' – be honest, she told herself – 'disappearing like we did would devastate him, but I couldn't stay with him. I'm sorry it had such profound consequences for Ian... and for your mum, and you.'

There was a burst of raucous laughter from the bar. It underscored the moment, harshly. Beth took the moment to reflect on her own feelings. The fear she'd lived with all of her life had lifted. The pain in her stomach was gone. Ian's death meant they were free.

But it wasn't the end of it. Especially not for Ella.

'Ella?'

The girl pulled her attention back to Beth from whatever point in the past it had been snagged on. She obviously had so many memories to return to and reassess.

'I can't do anything to make up for what you've been through, I know that. But...' Beth hesitated, not because she was unsure what she wanted to say, but because she was nervous about how Ian's daughter would respond. 'If, and when, you want to, you'd be welcome to come and visit us. Get to know Joe and Oli. They are keen to meet you.' She wasn't sure of that, but Ella had the right to meet the family that had been so pivotal in her life. It was a family she was part of. She was their sister, after all. 'Do you think you might? Like that? At some point? In the future? Or soon? Whatever is best for you.'

Ella rubbed her eyes and sighed.

Beth didn't blame her for feeling exhausted. She hurried clumsily on. 'If the cost is an issue, I'd be more than happy to pay the train fare. And you could stay with us.' She realised that would be too much, too soon. 'Or not. There are plenty of hotels nearby. Again – no cost to you. We can take it at whatever pace is right for you. I know it's all a bit overwhelming, but I think, now that we've met, it would be a tragedy...' Wrong word. She was gabbling. Ella let her. 'I mean, a waste if we didn't get to know each other, properly.'

At last Ella spoke. 'We'll see.' Then, with a defiant lift of her chin, she added, 'And I'm good, thanks. I don't need your money. I can stand on my own two feet. I always have.'

Chapter 91

THEY AGREED to stay in touch. Beth watched Ella walk away. She trod a lonely path through the crowds. Ian's daughter had got her answers, but the truth had not lightened her load, it had added to it. Beth was sorry. At the main exit Ella stopped and turned round. Beth waved. Ella paused – a still point in a sea of movement – then, hesitantly, she raised her hand. A second later she was gone.

Beth gathered up her things and headed to the concourse. She looked up at the display. There was a train to King's Cross leaving in fifteen minutes. Five hours and she would be home.

But instead of heading through the ticket barriers onto the platform, she followed in Ella's footsteps, through the sliding glass doors, out into the sunshine.

She had come all the way to Newcastle, it would be a shame not to pay her respects.

Chapter 92

IT WAS A SMALLER garden than the one they'd had in Fenham, but it was equally well tended, filled not with flowers this time, but with a ripple of softly shifting grasses. Beth stood, took it in, felt the tension in her shoulders ease a little. She knocked at the glossy green front door. No one answered. The sun was out. She thought she might simply sit on the step and wait, but then she heard the sound of a radio. There was a path running along the side of the house. She took it.

There was a back yard, with a few tubs, a washing line, a bench and a shed. The shed door was open. The radio was playing, the local news. The accents still sounded like home after all these years. There was the click-click of something mechanical, the creak of the shed floor.

'Mick?'

He had his back to her. Still broad, still tall – the stoop necessary only because of the slanted roof rather than as a result of his age. He turned round. He held something in his hands that looked as if it came out of a car engine. 'Beth!'

'I happened to be in the area, thought I'd call in and say "hello".'

He smiled at her blatant lie, laid aside his current work-in-progress and reached for a rag. He wiped his hands diligently, before stepping out of the shed. He straightened up and pulled her into his embrace.

Beth listened to the travel news as he hugged her. Her face was squashed against the breast pocket on his shirt, the button pressed painfully into her cheek. It would leave a mark. She didn't care. *There were temporary traffic lights in operation on Forth Street, in front of the Royal Mail building, and a wide load was causing delays on the A1 near the Metrocentre.*

Finally he let her go. 'A brew?'

'Always.'

They drank their tea sitting in the yard on the bench by the back door.

She asked him how things were going.

Mick sounded content as he told her funny anecdotes about his 'job', which involved ferrying 'old dears' to and from their many hospital and doctor's appointments. He was seventy-nine himself. She imagined he was popular with his 'clients' – reassuring, patient, charming in his own quiet way. Neither of them mentioned his very first dry run of such kindness. She imagined he rarely, if ever, thought of it. She did.

She asked after his family.

Claire still lived around the corner. Steve and his family in Cullercoats. He saw a lot of his grandkids

405

and his great-grandchildren. They were the reason for his move to Whitley Bay, five years earlier. Most of his now-extended family had settled close by, except Lacey. She'd recently taken a senior nurse's role in Watford. This prompted promises of a visit down south, soon. Beth reminded him that he would be welcome, any time. He chattered on about them all, updating her on their normally imperfect, but largely content lives. His pride and pleasure were as evident as ever.

'You obviously enjoy being the head of your ever-expanding brood,' she observed.

He smiled. 'Aye, family matters.' He finished his tea. 'Enough of me and my lot. How are Oli and Joe getting on?' It was an innocent enough question.

She could have glossed over it all, to protect him from the worry, but she had come to see him precisely because she wanted his advice. 'Not great at the moment.'

He put down his mug. 'Go on.'

Mick listened without interrupting or asking any questions, as if her tale was perfectly sensible and coherent. She got to the end and sat back. He clasped his hands together. The skin made a rasping sound. She'd always found his hands comforting. She waited for his judgement or, more accurately, his wisdom.

'So, she's a nice lass?'

It was not what she'd been expecting. 'Ella? Yes. I think she is. Troubled and angry, as she has every right to be, but I admired her. Liked her.'

'Impressive, if you think about what she's had to deal with.'

Beth flushed. The guilt making her face, and her heart, hot.

He saw and laid a heavy hand on her arm. 'Now don't start with that nonsense. I didn't mean anything by it. You've always been a devil for claiming credit for every bad thing under the sun. All I meant was… she must be something special, if she's had Ian for a dad and she's grown up to be a nice person.' He was right. 'So what's the problem?' he asked.

She turned and stared at him. He stared placidly back. 'Apart from the boys having lost any trust they ever had in me. And me having to go back and tell them that their dad really is dead, so any contact they might have wanted to have with him is never going to happen. And that he ended up an alcoholic.'

Mick tilted his head, considering her comments. 'I can't see they'd have wanted anything to do with him; not now they know what he was like. They may have lost a deadbeat dad – who they never knew existed until a few days ago – but it sounds like they've gained a halfway-decent sister. That's not too bad a trade.'

She studied him, checking he was being serious. He was seeing it in his usual black-and-white terms. Good or bad. Worthwhile or worthless. Decent or not.

'But it's come at the worst possible time. Joe is still in a huge slump after his break-up with Carrie. I just can't shake him out of it. Nothing I do makes any difference. I'm really worried about him, Mick. And Oli.' She sighed.

'Well, he *still* doesn't know what to do with his life. He's drifting. Has been for years. And...'

Mick held up his calloused paw of a hand. 'And. And. And. You need to draw breath, girl.' A smile started playing around the corner of his lips. 'You seem to have forgotten the basic rule of parenting.'

'Go on, remind me.' She found she was repressing a smile.

He straightened up and tugged his shirt down over the comforting paunch of his belly, readying himself to impart his wisdom. He was mocking himself and, very gently, her. Beth found she didn't mind; indeed, it was a relief after so much intense emotion. 'All you can do is... love 'em, trust 'em and leave 'em be.'

Now Beth did smile.

Mick seemed pleased to have got through to her. A problem fixed. It was, after all, his forte. 'They're good lads, Beth, and you're a good mum. I'm sure it'll all come out in the wash.' A Heather phrase – comforting, pragmatic and hopeful.

It felt good to have her with them, in spirit, as they sat together on Mick's bench, in the sun.

PART FIVE

Chapter 93

TWO YEARS LATER

'THINK OF A DESERT – nothing but mile upon mile of sand dunes and the occasional camel.' He mimicked a camel, all lolling tongue and grinding teeth. 'Or cream crackers. A whole, mouth-puckering gob full of them.' The required facial expressions were very similar and, thankfully, within his limited range.

'You're really not helping.' She dug her fingernail into the stitching on her rucksack, a displacement activity to stop herself staring longingly at the sign for the Ladies. It was illuminated. Way to go, on rubbing it in.

'Better than talking about dripping taps and cascading waterfalls.'

She punched his arm. Laughed. Looked horrified. 'Stop it!'

'Sorry. It can't be much longer.'

Surely it couldn't be. The other couple had come out of the examination room, all smiles, ten minutes earlier. It was definitely their turn next. It had to be.

Of course Carrie, being Carrie, had followed the

instructions to the letter: 960 millilitres of clear fluid, seventy-five minutes before their scheduled appointment. That was a lot of fluid to have sloshing around a bladder that was already being squashed by the weight of a twelve-week-old baby – *their* twelve-week-old baby. A living, growing, tiny human being who would, in six months' time, become their son or daughter.

He was acutely aware that Carrie was already living with the seismic changes that having a baby entailed – the waves of sickness, her changing body, the massively heightened compulsion to plan, but for him it was still a fact he couldn't quite believe. Not that he wasn't delighted, and giddy, and overwhelmed, and scared. He was all those things, and more. And yet this baby, their baby, still didn't seem real. He hoped the scan, and the brief glimpse it would allow him inside the hidden world of Carrie's womb, would change that. And reassure him.

'Carrie Truman!'

At last.

They followed the sonographer into the examination room.

There was a landing strip of blue paper laid out on the bed. The sonographer gestured to it. 'Okay. Hop on.' She turned and busied herself with the ultrasound machine – it looked like an old desktop computer.

Carrie made bunny ears. He laughed. The sonographer glanced at them, not smiling. They quit pratting around. It was the nerves. Carrie wobbled as she took off her Converse. Irrelevantly he wondered how far into her pregnancy she would insist on wearing them. They were so bloody awkward to get on and off. He had a mental image of her rocking up at the hospital, in labour, and of him struggling to unlace her high-tops in time.

The paper crackled as Carrie boosted herself up on the bed. She lay back and pulled up her top to reveal the pale dome of her belly.

'You can take a seat.' The sonographer obviously wanted him out of the way.

He did as told.

The sonographer tore off another strip of paper and tucked it into Carrie's knickers. She took a bottle from the side and shook it vigorously. 'Now this will feel a bit cold.' Carrie winced as the gloop was squirted on her belly. The sonographer pushed the head of the machine against Carrie's skin and started sweeping it around.

Silence.

The seconds ticked.

He'd imagined something more life-affirming, more personal. This felt very much like a medical procedure where they were looking for something wrong. He didn't like it. He liked it even less, the longer it went on.

'Is everything okay?' he asked. He saw Carrie wince. A reaction to his question or to the examination she was having to go through with a full-to-bursting bladder?

'Sorry,' the sonographer finally looked away from her screen. It was angled so that she could see it, but they couldn't. 'I should've said – I need a good few minutes to have a thorough look and take some measurements, then I promise I'll talk you through everything.' She went back to pushing and prodding Carrie's stomach and the baby inside it.

Carrie looked at him for reassurance. He took her hand.

More silence. More prodding. More studying the image and clicking.

After what felt like an age: 'Right.' The sonographer sat back. 'My suggestion, if you want to, is that you bob to the toilet, Carrie. I know how uncomfortable it is, having a full bladder. Then I'll show you what's on the screen.'

Carrie climbed down off the bed and dashed out of the room.

Then there were two.

Now the silence wasn't simply strained, it was brittle. The pulse in his neck ticked. He couldn't stand it any longer. 'Please. Just so I'm prepared. Is everything all right?'

'We should wait for your wife.'

'Please.'

Finally she met his eye. She understood his question well enough. 'From everything I can see, at this early stage, things are looking... normal.'

Never had a word meant so much to Joe.

Chapter 94

They didn't go straight back to the car; instead they found a small garden with a bench and some sad-looking clumps of dead lavender. It was empty. It was perfect. Both of them had stupid expressions. It was as if their features were too big for their faces. 'Who shall we call first?' Carrie asked.

Her cheeks were red, the end of her nose oddly white – like a reverse clown. She'd never looked more beautiful to Joe. 'I don't mind,' he lied. He wanted to call his mum.

'It's got to be your mum.'

He loved her. 'Are you sure?'

'Yes.'

'She's gonna cry.'

Carrie's smile stretched even broader. 'I'm counting on it. Go on. Put her out of her misery.'

Joe clicked on his call log – his mum was top of the list. She answered after two rings. 'How did it go?'

'Hi to you as well, Mum.' He had her on speaker, so

Carrie could hear. 'It went well.' He paused. Carrie poked his leg. 'All good. Everything as it should be.'

'That's great.'

Despite the years of pretending his CP didn't matter, Joe could hear the relief in her voice. He didn't blame her. How could he? He felt the same. He knew the chances of hereditary CP were low, but it was a worry that had ballooned in his brain as he lay sleepless next to Carrie, in the dark. Was it bad that the thought of passing on his condition terrified him? Was it a sign that even, after twenty-six years, he still hadn't accepted it?

Sod that! He did not want his kids to have CP. No parent would. And the scan said they didn't. As far as they could tell, everything was progressing as expected. A normal pregnancy.

'And did you ask the sex?'

'We did.'

Another pause. Another poke in the leg from Carrie.

'Is it something you and Carrie want to keep to yourselves?'

Carrie had had enough of the teasing. She stepped in. 'No, it isn't, Beth. We're having a little girl.'

There was an intake of breath. When Beth spoke again, it was obviously through tears. 'Oh, that's lovely. Congratulations. Lovely, either way. But a little girl. Oh, I'm so happy, for you both.'

Her delight set Joe off. He started laughing, pure joy bubbling through him. This was real. This was their future.

Carrie whispered, 'Tell her.'

'And a little boy.'

'What?' Down the line, the crying stopped.

'We're having twins, Mum. A little girl *and* a little boy.'

After that there wasn't much else to say.

Chapter 95

Freya Elizabeth Truman and James Michael Truman were born by elective Caesarean section, exactly as planned, on 16th May at 2.30 p.m. and 2.48 p.m.

Freya emerged first, weighing a healthy five pounds eleven ounces. James followed four minutes later, weighing exactly the same – which made them something of a cause célèbre at the hospital.

Equal-weight twins were rare.

The symbolism of their matching birth weights wasn't lost on Joe and Carrie, or Beth, but they didn't make a big thing of it. What mattered far more was that they were both healthy. There was no need for the NICU, no specialist nursing, no incubators and tubes, no panoply of machinery, no heart-stopping alarms, no holding your breath as they struggled for theirs – there was just three nights on a busy, noisy postnatal ward, then home

The twins' arrival turned Carrie and Joe's life upside down. They were sleep-deprived, shell-shocked, fascinated and confused by every tiny thing they did.

But, exhausted as they were, Beth had never seen them happier. Joe and Carrie were now the family they were destined to be.

Soon after the birth Carrie announced they had no intention of getting the twins christened. Her decision came as no surprise to Beth, but, she argued, the lack of a formal christening didn't mean they couldn't have a party.

What better excuse was there for getting everyone back together?

Chapter 96

IT WAS AN INVITATION he couldn't decline.

He was an uncle. That was a big deal. Anything else was just noise. The echo of an old love song. But the thought of having to witness, at such close quarters, Joe and Carrie's understandable delight at becoming parents made Oli feel sick. It was going to be difficult. More than difficult. It was going to be heart-breaking. Two years later and he was still not over her.

Oli hadn't realised it at the time, but his short, intense relationship with Carrie ended on his twenty-fourth birthday, the tipping point of so many things. From that day onwards, everything changed. It was not the best time for her to choose to withdraw from Oli, but that's exactly what happened. The first sign that he was on his way out was that she started making excuses about why she couldn't see him, then she took ages to respond to his messages; she even, on one deeply depressing occasion, pretended to be out when he called round – he caught a glimpse of her on the landing, fleeing from any contact with him. Her abrupt abandonment of him hurt. He felt like an orphan. His mother and father weren't the people he'd believed them to be. His childhood was a fiction. Even Sab was a liar. At *the* critical time in his life, when he most needed someone to put up the barriers around him and control the spinning, Carrie disappeared, leaving him ricocheting in the void.

He had his suspicions why. There was someone else hurting and in need. Someone she loved more. Joe.

She avoided him for six days straight. On the seventh she summoned him to her house: 9.30 a.m. on the Sunday morning. The precision of the instruction told him everything he needed to know.

He knocked. She let him in. Led him into the lounge, not up to her bedroom. Even then, knowing full well that she was going to end their relationship and insist it remain a secret – something to be ashamed of, for ever – he still yearned for her to pull him into her arms and hold him.

She spoke softly, gently, as she broke his heart. 'I'm sorry, Oli. I think you know what I'm going to say.' He didn't help her out. 'We can't see each other anymore.'

'*See?*'

'Sleep with.'

He lashed out. 'Is that all we've been doing... screwing?'

She flinched, but continued to meet his gaze. 'Yes.' She looked sorry for him. That didn't help.

'That's not true!' What words could he use to get through to her? He went for the truth. 'It isn't just sex. I love you.'

She bit her lip, folded her arms across her body, held herself away from him. 'Do you really?'

'Yes. I have done for years.'

'Oli!' She looked trapped, desperate, but still unreachable – at least by him. 'Please don't make this any harder than it needs to be.'

'I'm not – I'm making it as hard as it is. For me!' She shook her head. It was an involuntary gesture. He had to make her realise that what she was denying was real. 'I've been around you for years. I understand the way you think. What makes you happy. What makes you sad. I know the things and the people that make you mad, even though you pretend they don't. And I know you're special. That's why this is different. You're not some stranger. I love you because I know you. You are part of me.'

'I'm not, Oli. I'm part of your family, not part of you. That's why what we were doing was so wrong.' She had already moved them into the past tense. 'I should never have turned to you.'

'Yes, you should. I wanted you to. I've always wanted to be there for you.'

'I was a mess. Not thinking.'

'No. That wasn't it.' What they had – what they'd had – had be more than a painful, tacky rebound from his brother. Oli couldn't, yet again, be simply the other, less-wanted twin. 'You felt it. I know you did. It wasn't just fucking.'

Finally she nodded. 'I'm sorry. You're right. It wasn't just sex.' She was conceding that what he was saying was true, but not true enough, because she went on, 'I did it to make myself feel better.' She swallowed. 'And if I'm honest, I think – in some really pathetic way – I felt it balanced up the scales… after what Joe did. It gave me some of my power back.' She dropped her gaze. Went into her own world, where he couldn't follow. 'Me and Joe have always been so wrapped up in each other. I was struggling even before he cheated on me. I couldn't deal with him leaving, and coping without me so well on the other side of the world. Now I've had time to think about it, I can see that some part of me wanted him to rely on me and, when he didn't, it shocked me. It changed the dynamic between us. That threw me. But you did seem to need me, or at least want me.' She looked up. 'Oli. I'm so sorry. It was cruel of me to let anything happen between us. Cruel and deeply selfish. But I honestly thought that because you'd slept with loads of girls, it wouldn't mean much to you.'

He was horrified. 'Couldn't you tell that I had feelings for you? Real feelings.'

She paused, obviously having to think about what he'd said. It was awful. Was he really that sealed off? 'Yes. I realised. After a while. And I should have stopped it.'

'Why didn't you?'

'Because it felt good.' She was being brutal with herself. He'd always admired her honesty, in the past.

Now he wanted none of it. She was relentless. 'I do like you, Oli. Truly I do. But we're not right for each other. You do know that, don't you? And...' she drew a shallow breath and delivered the *coup de grâce*, 'I don't love you.'

The tension in the room collapsed. Both of them were too sad to continue speaking for a few seconds. He'd lost her. No, he'd never had her. 'So that's it.'

She nodded. 'It has to be. It's not fair on you.' A tear dripped off her cheek and fell onto her joggers, leaving a mark. Oli stared at it.

'What now?' He meant between her and Joe, but he couldn't bring himself to say his brother's name. He didn't want Joe to be present, through Carrie, for his final humiliation. But who was Oli kidding? Joe was always there, in the background of his life, in his thoughts and in everyone else's.

She gave her head one last shake, but whether it was a 'yes' or a 'no' was unclear. 'I don't know.'

But he did. He stood up, took one last look around the room, and at Carrie, and left.

Oli moved north a couple of months later. Watching Carrie go back to Joe had been unbearable.

That his break-up was the thing that finally spurred him on to apply for, and get, a job back in football was an irony not lost on Oli. Player development in an academy wasn't the same as playing, but the role suited him. He was, after all, well placed to advise the lads on the highs – and many lows – of the hard path they were embarking upon. And he was good at it. He was liked and respected, especially by the hotheads. Perhaps they were able to sense a kindred spirit.

Living with Mick had not been the long-term plan, but the arrangement had proved beneficial in a number of ways. For the first time in a long while, Oli had a real home instead of a faceless rental, and Mick had the only thing he claimed to need in order to be happy: namely, company. They undoubtedly made an odd couple, but it worked. They shared the bills, Oli helped with the maintenance of the house – under Mick's still eagle-eyed supervision – and, besides, they liked each other. Oli could have moved out once he got settled in his job. He could have afforded to rent somewhere on his own, might even have been able to buy somewhere, but every time he'd half-heartedly raised it, Mick had demurred, found some football on the TV, dug a tenner out of his battered wallet and sent Oli to the offie to buy the beers, and the conversation was parked.

Two years later, they were still happily drinking IPA and watching the match together.

Their living arrangement also had one other major upside – proximity to Ella.

Mick had been instrumental in them getting to know each other. The warm welcome that he extended to both of them in his little house in Whitley Bay had made a real difference. Having Mick pottering around in the background, asking gentle but illuminating questions and telling stories about Oli's childhood misdemeanours had smoothed the way to Oli and Ella making a connection. Indeed, it was Mick who had pointed out that they shared more than just a biological father; they shared similar personality traits: a certain brusqueness, a quickness of temper, humour, fierce loyalty and an even greater competitiveness. Mick wasn't wrong. It was strange, but no less true that Oli's half-sibling was much closer in temperament and outlook to him than his actual twin.

In the beginning their relationship had felt forced, both of them conscious of and inhibited by the weirdness of the situation. But as Ella had started to relax, her natural bluntness had emerged and that had been their salvation. Frustrated by his mother and Joe's concerted efforts to keep everything 'nice', Ella had turned to – or maybe it was more accurate to say turned 'on' – Oli. She was a force of nature, asking question after question about Beth, Joe's CP, his failed football career, what it was like having a sibling, especially a twin, and about Carrie. She'd become increasingly persistent on that subject, but he'd held her at bay. So far.

In truth, Oli had found many of Ella's questions difficult to answer, but his struggle to come up with adequate responses had made him think and reflect. And although this was an alien activity to him, it had been helpful in a way he couldn't quite put his finger on. His burgeoning, at times combative and at other times joyous relationship with Ella had been a major influence on his decision to stay in Newcastle.

All ways round, Oli's flight north had been a good decision. For the first time in his life he felt able to be himself and he didn't feel alone.

Chapter 97

IT WAS A TYPICAL early July Sunday in Whitley Bay, in that it was slashing down. Not the sort of day you'd plan to go for a walk, but that was exactly what Ella was proposing. Oli looked at the rain squalling against the windows and pulled a face that provoked a barrage of 'Soft Southerner' comments. Five minutes later he found himself shrugging on his Rab jacket and lacing up his boots. His wardrobe had changed since moving north. They headed for the beach, on foot – Ella was opposed to the comfort of car travel when a howling gale was readily available.

Unsurprisingly, the beach was empty except for what looked like an old guy, but could equally have been a young woman, or a Hobbit, bundled up in bulky waterproofs, down by the shoreline. Whoever it was, they appeared to be collecting seaweed, for reasons Oli couldn't fathom. They leant into the wind and set off walking.

It was cathartic in a harsh, wet, cold kind of way. As Ella strode ahead, Oli followed in her wake, amused and mildly resentful; he was missing the build up to the

England-France match for this. Aware he was lagging behind, Ella slowed her pace, linked her arm through his and tugged him along. He was used to her direct approach now, liked it.

They reached a long spit of sand. The sea rolled in on either side of them. Oli watched the tide. It was coming in. He could tell now. You had to look at the line left by the retreating waves. The townie was learning.

But Ella was, unfortunately, not in the mood for watching the waves and having a nice moment. 'Is there a reason I'm having to field questions from your mother about this party for the twins?'

'No.'

'She says you haven't confirmed what time we'll be there. Whether you're sleeping at the house or "with friends". Whether we're staying through to Monday morning. You know – all the basics.'

'She fusses.'

'Yeah, she does. And you know that going dark on her will only whip her into even more of a frenzy. It's a big deal for her. They are her first grandchildren.'

Oli nodded. He knew.

She gave him a gentle shove, demanding more of a response from him. 'You're dreading it, aren't you?'

'No.'

She huffed. 'Liar.'

'Well, okay – a bit. It's going to be wall-to-wall baby talk, isn't it?'

'Well, yes. Of course it is.'

Oli liked the whispering sound of the waves on the sand, as it filled the gaps in their conversation, but evidently not enough.

'Oli!'

'What?'

'Quit it!'

'Quit what?'

'Your silent, brooding routine.'

'I'm not brooding.'

'Yes, you are.' Ella's nostrils flared, a sure sign she was in one of her persistent moods. 'You're worried about being around Carrie, aren't you?'

'No.'

'Again – and I say this because I care about you – liar!'

There it was, encapsulated in one sentence: the reason he cared about her too and why she so infuriated him. 'I don't want to talk about it.' There it was, the admission she'd been pushing for, for months: direct acknowledgement that there was an 'it'. But Ella knew that already. How? Because she'd seen them all together – at those first, deeply awkward family get-togethers, at Joe and Carrie's engagement party, at their lovely, typically alternative but interminable wedding, at the subsequent weekend gatherings that his mother insisted on. Ella had been at Oli's side – with the eye of an outsider – at most of them, observing and filing away all the tiny tells that he tried so hard to hide. So yes, she did know that he and Carrie had history, because she was astute, and she wasn't blind.

That didn't mean he was willing to talk about it. He stared at the waves, waiting for her to back off. His brief, intense, painful relationship with his brother's wife was a secret he was compelled to keep. Hence his memories and feelings had to remain buried, however much they still hurt. It was for everyone's sake.

Suddenly he was stumbling. His feet lost purchase on the wet sand and he fell. The next thing he knew, he was on his hands and knees, in freezing-cold water. 'What the fuck!' He scrambled to stand up. To his shock and disbelief, Ella leant down and pushed him again. He landed on his side. Salt water splashed in his face. Some of it got into his mouth. It tasted sour. His eyes stung. What the hell was she playing at? He scrambled awkwardly to his feet; as he did so, he felt fingers of cold water slide down between the layers of his clothes. 'What the hell was that for?'

'To wake you up.'

'Ella, what the fuck are you talking about?'

'You can't sleepwalk through life. You have to be awake to be alive.'

He was furious with her. 'You're talking total crap.'

She reached out and grabbed his arm; the urge to seize hold of her hand and yank her fingers off was powerful. But he didn't. She clung on. It made him look at her. Her expression wasn't mocking or angry, it was sad. 'Oli, I'm worried about you. You're holding so much in. So much anger and unhappiness. This thing, with Carrie, it's stopping you from getting on with your life. It's fucking up your relationship with Joe, with your mum and, the way you're behaving, it's going to screw up your relationship with the twins. That's not allowed.' She softened her tone. 'Come on, Oli, you and I both know that with two saints for parents, those kids are going to need a badass uncle.'

He couldn't raise a smile. He was kneeling in freezing-cold sea water, being lectured by his little sister. And she wasn't finished.

Her expression darkened again. 'I've seen it before, remember. And look how that worked out. I don't want you to end up like our dad, hanging onto something that is over and done and is never coming back.' She paused, checking she was getting through.

He nodded, he agreed, but that didn't mean he could do what she was saying. He was trapped in the past, but it wasn't his choice.

'You're my brother and I love you. Trust me... you have to let it out and let it go, or it will stop you living.'

'I don't know how.'

Ella tilted her head, looked at him intently, then she smiled. 'Scream!'

'What?'

'Run and scream it out. Tell it to the seagulls and the sea. They don't give a shit what you and Carrie did.'

She was mad.

But the next thing he knew, she was tugging him along with her. The wind at his back helped, it pushed him along. He pumped his legs, worked hard, his body warmed and grew hot, the icy sea water replaced by sweat. He was vaguely aware he was outpacing her. As he left her behind, he heard her shouting, 'Scream her out, Oli. Scream!'

So he did.

He ran and he yelled. He ran and he roared. He ran until he had no more beach, or breath, or anger left.

Chapter 98

ELLA LEFT IT TO Oli to organise the logistics of their trip south for the twins' non-christening party. She said it was his job; being only the half-sister gave her a frequently used pass to only half-commit to anything family-related. Besides, as she pointed out – while they got dry after their *interesting* beach experience – her role was more on the emotional-support side of things rather than the practical. He let her have that one.

They met in the bar on the station concourse. Just enough time for a swift half before they set off, or so Mick insisted. Oli wondered what the other customers made of the three of them. A grandad travelling with his grandson and granddaughter? How sweet! It wasn't so wide of the mark.

As Mick went off to buy their drinks – his insistence on standing his round was something not to be argued with – Oli and Ella sat and watched the crowds. It was a comfortable silence, but he noticed that she looked pensive.

'Are you okay?' Oli ventured.

'Yep. You?'

'Yeah.' She was looking over in the direction of Caffè Nero, her expression still thoughtful.

'You sure?'

'Sorry.' She zoned back in. 'That was where I met your mum for the first time. Hard to believe it was over two years ago.'

He was about to make some facetious comment about water under the bridge, but he stopped himself. The new him had to create space for other people's emotions as well as his own. Just so long as Ella didn't start screaming. They watched Mick mingling with the crowd at the bar. He'd obviously got into conversation with a group of girls on a hen-do. It was typical Mick; the older he got, the more gregarious he became.

'You don't regret it? Do you?' Oli asked.

'Regret what?' She shifted her gaze back to him.

'Getting to know us. Getting sucked into the madness of our family.'

She tilted her head. It was endearingly child-like. He was tempted to tell her she looked like an owl when she was thinking, but he wanted her to answer him, not smash her fist into his bicep.

'No. I don't regret it. Not most of the time, anyway. I was intimidated, to start with. You look like the perfect middle-class family. The surface gloss was so shiny it was blinding. But I know, now, you're as fucked up as everyone else, underneath.' He couldn't argue with that. 'I suppose that messiness made feel I could fit in.'

He laughed. 'You fit right in. You're as mad as the rest of us.' At that, she did smile. 'Well, I, for one, am very glad you did hunt us down.'

'Hardly... hunted.'

'You know what I mean.'

'I do.' There was a beat. It felt warm and good. With Ella by his side, Oli knew he would be okay. Maybe, in the long run, more than okay. He hoped they both would.

Mick finally appeared, carrying a tray on which their drinks balanced precariously. They both knew better than to stand up and offer to help. Miraculously he made it to their table with minimal spillage. Once settled, he raised his beer. 'To Freya and James Truman.'

'To family,' Oli added.

They clinked glasses.

Chapter 99

THE NON-CHRISTENING PARTY went well. Everyone said so.

The weather was kind.

The babies didn't cry – well, no more than your average two-month-old tended to.

People mingled and chatted and cooed over the twins.

Most of the guests brought gifts, many of which Beth knew would end up being donated to the local baby bank. Carrie was not a fan of pink for girls and blue for boys, although you'd never have known it, judging by how wholeheartedly she smiled and thanked everyone who handed her a pastel-wrapped parcel while she breastfed one or the other, or both of the twins, at the same time. She was getting the hang of motherhood.

The majority of the buffet got eaten and not all the booze got drunk.

But it wasn't until Beth closed the door on the last of the guests, some of whom seemed impervious to hints that it was time to leave, that everyone breathed out properly.

Carrie spread a blanket on the lounge floor and put the twins down, before disappearing off to change into her PJs, while Joe ripped off his tie, declaring it had been strangling him all afternoon. Sab, who had been barefoot since mid-afternoon, threatened to take off her bra, which raised a laugh – until they realised she was serious. Even Oli, who'd said he might not stay the night, but would probably go and see some friends in Hitchen, seemed inclined to linger. He sat between Ella and Mick on the sofa, the Geordie cohort, drinking a beer.

As Beth watched them all get comfortable she reflected on how unpredictable life was. Oli's decision to take the job up in the North-East – a job he'd applied for without saying anything to her, so soon after the revelation of Ella's existence and Ian's death – had shocked her. It seemed typically rash. Typical Oli. She knew he'd been communicating with his half-sister and had been up to visit her, but that was hardly grounds for uprooting your whole life and moving so far away, especially to a city with such conflicting associations. When she'd asked him why he was going, she'd been left strangely dissatisfied by his response.

He'd shrugged and said, 'There's nothing holding me here anymore. Apart from you,' he'd added quickly. 'And it's a good opportunity.' It was obviously not the truth, but he'd refused to explain further.

And yet despite her grave reservations about his motivations for going and her sadness at losing him, even more than she already had, his move north had worked out. Mick had played a major role in that, of course, as had Oli's step back into football. Going back to his first love had, undeniably, been good for him. It was less well paid than recruitment, far less glamorous than his playing days, but for the first time in years Oli seemed happy in his job. The other upside of his relocation to Newcastle was that it had drawn Ella into their lives far more naturally than Beth had had any right to hope. She still felt a tension between the two of them – there was too much history on that slate for it to be wiped clean – but Ella's relationship with the twins, especially Oli, was lovely to see.

Yes, all ways round, Oli's decision had drawn them closer – at least emotionally, if not geographically. Without it, she doubted they would all be together now.

Carrie was back: PJs on, her hair pulled into a messy ponytail. She flopped down on the sofa next to Joe. They were complete. Beth realised they were sitting in a circle around the twins. A ring-fence of love.

Freya and James were lucky.

They had a family, which although far from perfect, worked.

They had their parents. Two grandmas. Uncle Oli and Auntie Ella. Sab and Aleah.

And, at least for a little while longer, they had Mick.

Decent people – who would love them, trust them and, when the time came, let them be.

Acknowledgements

BOOKS DON'T SPRING OUT of the ether; the ideas and emotions that drive them often come from real-world people, events and issues. *The Day We Left* grew out of three issues that I have an interest in and experience of.

The first is the inclusion of people living with disabilities in society.

Disability, in all its varied realities, is far more prevalent in life than in books or onscreen. In my small way, I want to contribute to the broader and better representation of the glorious diversity of human beings. In this context I must mention Geena, my middle daughter, whose disabilities have shaped her and our life in so many ways – some challenging and others joyous. Geena will never read any of my books, but she has played an important role in me becoming a writer. My contact with the 'disabled experience', through her, continues to influence what and who I write about.

The second issue is domestic abuse – the reality of living with it, escaping from it and surviving it.

I volunteered for a number of years with Victim Support. During my time with the organisation I learnt a huge amount about the resilience of women, especially mothers. Many of the individuals I spoke to were dealing with the dilemmas that Beth and Sab confront in this book. Their day-to-day bravery was inspiring, whether they stayed or left. The number for the National Domestic Abuse Helpline, mentioned in *The Day We Left*, is 0808 2000 247.

Third, and conversely, this book explores what makes a decent man and how boys become one. That's obviously a huge topic, but as the mother of a son – and as someone who has worked with many young men throughout my different careers, in settings as diverse as universities and prisons – it's a question that interests me.

In this context I want to take this opportunity to recognise the many eminently sound young men I know.

First, much love to Alex, my lovely, kind, very tall son. He is a good brother and partner, though not, to my despair, a big reader – which just goes to show that the theory that books are essential for developing empathy is rubbish! Also respect and love to my nephews, Joe B and Joseph T. Yep, a name so good we used it twice – or three times, if you count the Joe in the book. Both my nephews, along with David, are thoroughly decent young men, although Lauren and Lorna and Hannah might add that they could all up their game when it comes to the laundry. And hello to Issac, the newest member of the clan, who is currently too preoccupied with tractors to care about much else. I also want to mention my dad, Peter Brian Bond, who was the inspiration for Mick, the most decent of all men, and whose hands appear in all my books. And finally, as ever, a huge thank you to Chris, my husband, for his belief, his support and, above all, his patience.